Fireworks on the Fourth

Fireworks on the Fourth

A Musical Murder Mystery

B.J. Bowen

Kenmore, WA

A Camel Press book published by Epicenter Press

Epicenter Press
6524 NE 181st St.
Suite 2
Kenmore, WA 98028

For more information go to:
www.Camelpress.com
www.Coffeetownpress.com
www.Epicenterpress.com
www.barbarabowenauthor.com

This is a work of fiction. Names, characters, places, brands, media, and incidents are either the product of the author's imagination or are used fictitiously.

Cover design by Scott Book
Design by Melissa Vail Coffman

Fireworks on the Fourth
Copyright © 2023 by B.J. Bowen

Library of Congress Control Number: 2022947617

ISBN: 978-1-68492-111-9 (Trade Paper)
ISBN: 978-1-68492-112-6 (eBook)

Printed in the United States of America

*To Annette, who involved me in her writing group
and believed in me. I miss your joyful, gentle presence.
Enjoy eternity!*

ACKNOWLEDGMENTS

IT TAKES MANY PEOPLE TO COMPLETE a manuscript and turn it into a book. I would like to acknowledge a few here. In no particular order they are:

Jennifer McCord, my editor and publisher, who, as always, helped me fine tune my concept, found and corrected hiccups in my writing technique, and expressed and shared her love of music with me.

Rusty, for insight into the wonder of golden retrievers and their capacity for healing.

The artists at Camel Press, whose covers attract attention and readers.

Peter Nichols, for explanation of water rights. Any errors are the result of my slip-ups, not his expertise.

Jim Cara, for advice on computers, cell phones, and other electronic gizmos. If I have made mistakes, I apologize. Your patience was legendary!

The La Dolce Vita Writers Group, which started me on the first book of this series.

Leisel Hufford, for her internet know-how, the elegant simplicity of her changes, positivity, interest, enthusiasm, and, most especially, for rescuing me from hideous blunders.

Sarah E. Burr, who helped this old fogie with social media, putting together beautiful artwork for advertising the book, always making me feel like I "CAN DO" and more: that the book and I are worth it.

Nancy Andrew, my flute expert who patiently and quickly answered all my questions.

Joshua Long, who advised me on guns, which I know nothing about, and prevented glaring errors. Any further mistakes are a result of my ignorance, not his tutelage.

Molly Lord, for her inspiration and faith that "the Camino provides."

Mary Zalmanek, for her extravagant creativity, unshakeable logic, positivity, and native grasp of compassion and consideration.

Marylin Warner, for forming and maintaining the writer's group for so long, and for her help filling in the details.

The Writers of the Roundtable, who gave me excellent advice, provided encouragement, read the fledgling versions, found the incongruities, and, most of all, were my friends throughout.

ONE

THURSDAY, JULY 4, 2013, 9:00 P.M.

City Park, Monroe, Colorado

I COULDN'T HEAR THE SOUND OF MY FLUTE over the massive, suspended carillon bells ringing madly, and the eight cannon from the nearby military base firing continuous volleys. The climactic moment of this year's annual outdoor Fourth of July performance of Tchaikovsky's *1812* Overture had come again, and synchronized fireworks exploded high in the Colorado sky behind me.

In the flute section of the orchestra, covered by the shell around and above me, the fireworks weren't visible but, even with musicians' ear plugs that cut volume but not clarity, I could hear the "ooh's" and "aah's" from a rapt audience. Somewhere among them here in Monroe, Colorado's City Park were my friends and family munching fried chicken and potato salad and listening to Tchaikovsky's festival of sound with 100,000 other people.

AFTER THE CONCERT I WATCHED the crowd disperse, becoming first impatient, then worried. I had agreed to meet the rest of our little group in front of the orchestra shell after the show. Where were they? I had time for a conversation with a couple of stagehands and our Assistant Conductor before my friend KC and her fiancé Steve Palmer, my sister Kathleen and her fiancé Police Lt. Paul Gordon, and my lawyer and long-time friend, most recently with benefits, Barry Reitman, showed up. The only members of my family missing were Mom, who traveled with a friend this holiday, and Kathleen's son Charlie and his girlfriend Ana. They had moved to Oklahoma City, where Charlie, a percussionist, would start work with the symphony in the fall.

Winded, KC gasped, "Sorry we took a long time, Em."

She was one of only two people who called me Em, rather than my full name, Emily.

"It's my fault. I got lost finding the Porta-Potty. I delayed the whole group."

Steve put his arm around her. "Stop apologizing. You're worth the wait."

She blushed and leaned against him. Turning to me she said apologetically, "We saved you some potato salad."

As we headed for the van, Paul's cell phone rang. "Gordon here . . . Uh-huh . . . Uh-huh . . . okay, I'll be right there. I'm close, at the park, but I'm on foot. It may take me a couple minutes to get there."

Closing the phone, he turned to us. "Gotta go. Police business. Don't bother to wait. I may be awhile."

Kathleen tugged at his sleeve. "Oh, Paul. Not tonight!"

Each of us had reason to be angry with her fiancé, Lieutenant Gordon, not least of all Kathleen herself. After all, he had arrested her son for murder. But when Charlie's innocence was proved, the lieutenant had earned her understanding and her love with his humor, tenderness, and desire to serve his community, and now, a year later, they had become engaged. Following her example, in a testament to second chances, the family had forgiven him and started fresh. Paul's abrupt departures had become familiar.

He touched her hand gently. "Sorry, I have to go."

"How will you get home?"

"One of the guys'll take me." He gave her a peck on the cheek and headed toward the blue and red flashing lights across the park.

I knew the request for his presence promised bad news for somebody. He directed the homicide squad.

WE HAD RENDEZVOUSED AT STEVE AND KC's place, and I'd left my car there. Barry already knew he'd have to be at the courthouse early for a client's arraignment in the morning. He had come separately and went directly home.

I said a warm goodbye to everyone and headed for my place alone, tired, and looking forward to my retriever's welcome. Golden, always glad to see me, showed it by wiggling, licking, and bringing toys.

Tonight was different, though.

Golden wasn't at the door to meet me. When I called, I heard her whine from a distance, and went searching. I'd strapped her into her calming shirt before I left, but I found her in the bathtub, tail between her legs, paws over her ears, cowering with each new explosion of neighborhood fireworks or firecrackers.

She lifted her head and made a pathetic effort to wag her tail when I appeared, but ducked and covered her head with her paws almost immediately as new noises assailed her. I knew from experience she responded best if I brought her a treat and acted as if nothing was wrong, trying to convey my confidence. She was such a blessing, I wanted to be there when she needed me, and encouraged her with an upbeat voice while praying the fireworks would stop soon.

Gradually they died down, and by midnight I coaxed Golden out of the tub, although I had to go outside with her while she did her business. Inside, I got ready for bed and settled down for the night. Golden snuggled close to me and flinched at the occasional firecracker until we both finally fell asleep around three or four in the morning.

TWO

Meeting of the Symphony Board Planning Committee

CURTIS STRANGE WAS LATE.
A land developer and member of the Symphony Board, he had once been a client of my friend KC in her days as a paid escort. I had gotten to know him when I joined the Symphony's Planning Committee.

The committee included three members of the Symphony Board and three members of the Orchestra Player's Organization (OPO). The three OPO members were me, Susie Melendez (violin), and Tyler Washington (string bass). Beside Curtis, the Board members were Mel Harmon, president of both the Symphony Board and the bank where we were meeting, and Jane Rice, the small but assertive and socially-prominent wife of a local granting agency's CEO.

I was trapped. On a beautiful July day, instead of walking Golden in the fresh air and sunshine or reading an entertaining whodunit, I ostensibly helped plan the future path of the Symphony at a long, cherrywood table in a stuffy bank conference room with no windows . . . and waited for Curtis.

Good thing the symphony schedule was light in the summer, because these meetings held more tension than any major solo.

Curtis was the source of the strain. He spent much of the Symphony Planning Committee's time feuding with Mel and Tyler. The two men worked together, arguing with Curtis politely and not so politely—okay, venomously—trying to persuade him to their way of thinking.

A died-in-the-wool tree hugger, Mel opposed almost every project of Curtis's on general principles, since C.H. Strange Development Corp. wouldn't spend a penny for environmental care, tearing down trees, polluting water, and building energy guzzling edifices. The enmity between the two men leaked over into symphony projects.

Tyler struggled to make ends meet. As the single parent of two boys, he felt the musicians needed, and deserved, more money to live on. That was the position of most of the musicians including Susie and me, and the reason all three of us had been elected to the Player's Organization and then the Symphony's Planning Committee.

Mel agreed the Symphony needed to grow to support an expanding community, and acknowledged that meant additional work and a higher salary for the musicians. Development would pay for itself through additional revenues and donations, he believed. "Build it and they will come" summed up his position.

But Curtis stubbornly opposed any type of Symphony expansion. He had argued vociferously against adding a conservative two services next year, because that would increase musician salaries by a tiny amount, although he enthusiastically supported community growth. He maintained Symphony finances would not support even a small increase.

Curtis, Mel, and Tyler spent so much time attacking each other that their disagreements hamstrung the Planning Committee. The rest of us were used to listening to the three of them feud until someone, usually Jane, managed to get a word in edgewise and return order to the Committee's proceedings. Even then, though Curtis held the minority opinion, the small committee was able to make only incremental progress over his continual objections.

Showing every sign that Mel had exhausted his limited patience, he drummed his fingers on the table and said, "He's ten minutes late! We can't wait forever, but we can't go on without him." He turned to Jane. "Did Curtis say he wouldn't be here?"

Following a negative response from Jane, Mel massaged his temples. "This is unconscionable. I'll call and see where he is."

He disappeared from the room.

While he was gone, the rest of us made small talk. Everyone had been to last night's concert, the musicians as part of the orchestra, and Jane as part of the audience.

"Such a wonderful evening!" Jane smiled. "It must be terrific to be a part of something like that."

Since the orchestra shell prevented us from seeing the whole show and we'd done this for years, allowing boredom to creep in, we didn't necessarily agree. But Tyler knew he shouldn't express cynicism to a Board member. He nodded and managed to resist rolling his eyes. Susie and I smiled. "And we get to do it every year," she said.

A short silence followed.

Ever the social adept, Jane recognized a need and filled the awkward pause with a new topic. "There's a new wrinkle in my kitchen remodel. It's been a challenge from the very beginning." Jane sighed. "Nothing's gone as planned, everything takes longer than expected, and the workers have been quite rude, but the robbery takes the cake."

That startled me. "Robbery?"

"Can you believe it? I discovered it the day before the concert. The jewelry in my bedroom had been taken, some cash was gone, and my gun was missing."

"How awful! You must have felt so violated!" Susie sounded understanding and concerned. "When burglars hit my apartment, it took weeks before I felt safe in my own house again."

Mel had been gone a long time. I wondered about it as Jane and Susie continued talking in shocked tones. Tyler commented occasionally.

Finally, Mel finally reappeared, looking pale. "Curtis is . . ." He hesitated. "Curtis is . . ." He seated himself, hesitated again, and took a deep breath. "I guess there's no good way to say this. Curtis is dead."

I sucked in a quick breath. "What? How do you know that?"

"I thought Curtis might have left a message on my home phone. I called there first. No message. Then I called the Symphony office. The intern told me Curtis hadn't called, but that the police had." He glanced at a piece of paper in his hand. "A Lieutenant Gordon wanted to speak to me. I knew the police wouldn't call on an unimportant matter. I decided to return the call right away. When I did, the lieutenant told me Curtis was the victim of a homicide last night at the concert. Gunshot. He arranged an appointment to discuss it."

I remembered the red and blue flashing lights after the concert, and Paul's cell phone summons to business. The murder explained police activity.

"I think under the circumstances we'll adjourn the meeting for today. I'll let you know when the next will be. Thank you all for coming."

Mel might have adjourned the meeting, but none of us left immediately. I knew neither I nor my colleagues particularly liked Curtis, but that he should be snuffed out . . . it seemed inconceivable. We had all argued vociferously with him in the past, but in this moment we were shocked, or at least I was.

"I should have gotten to know him better, maybe invited him to the Christmas party we had . . ." Jane sounded remorseful.

By this time, Mel had fully recovered. "No sense beating yourself up. Curtis probably wouldn't have come even if you'd asked him. He kept to himself."

"But I should have tried. I shouldn't have let our differences—"

Mel shook his head. "I don't think it would have done any good." Mel stood. "Since we're not meeting, I'd better get back to work."

That signaled the rest of us to leave.

On the way home I remembered Curtis's interactions with my friend, KC. At the time, she had described him to me as a jerk. But I was sure her tender heart would be distressed by his murder.

I called her from the car.

KC rang true to pitch. "He couldn't be described as anything but a disgraceful human being, but to die such a terrible death! How sad."

I had mixed feelings. It seemed a dreadful way to die, but I couldn't summon much of a feeling of loss. Mentally, I shrugged my shoulders and wondered about his Planning Committee replacement. I certainly wouldn't miss him. I didn't think anyone else would, either.

His business would be leaderless now. Who would replace him? I hoped it would be someone more environmentally conscious. It wouldn't be a great loss if all of Curtis's projects died with him.

The demands of everyday living soon put Curtis's murder on a back burner in my mind. My trio had been hired to play a birthday party. The hostess surprised her husband, a serious Symphony supporter and a friend of Mel's, with a celebration for his fiftieth.

The trio consisted of me, the Symphony's third flutist Jen Feifer, and Alice Smithson from the cello section. Alice mysteriously knew everything that happened in the Symphony almost as soon as it took place. As we were setting up chairs and stands she asked, "Lots of news. Have you heard?"

Jen looked blank. "Heard what?"

Alice broke the news of Curtis's death to Jen—for once I knew about it before Alice, though I didn't say so—then moved on. "And there's more."

I hoped this wouldn't take too much longer, since we were due to start playing soon.

"You know Tyler Washington, the string bass player? Well, he *left the stage* at last night's concert during *1812*." She paused dramatically, hanging over the chair she had unfolded. "Can you believe it? He left the stage. During a concert!"

For a musician, deserting your post during a concert constituted the ultimate emergency or sin, depending on the circumstances. "What happened?"

"Nobody knows." Alice looked satisfied and pleased, like Golden after a good meal and a nice pet. Next to a scandal, a mystery couldn't be beat, and when you combined the two, well, Alice couldn't help but, figuratively, rub her hands in glee. "The basses are at the back of the stage, right next to the stage door. Tyler played the exposed section at the beginning of *1812*, then laid down his bass and left like a shot without telling anybody anything. Only his stand partner, Conner, saw him go, and he returned with no explanation to finish up 'Stars and Stripes Forever.'"

I shook my head in disbelief. As far as I knew, Tyler personified reliability. "How do you know all this?"

"I got it straight from Conner." She sounded proud. "The best source you could have."

"Has anybody asked Tyler about it? Maybe he needs help." But I wondered. If he did, why didn't he mention something at the Committee meeting? Had he only had to go to the rest room urgently? Surely not. Everyone in the orchestra is professional enough to plan ahead. Only diarrhea could be serious enough that he would abandon his post and leave the stage during a concert. And in that case, he would have called in sick.

"Well, if he did need help, the crisis must have passed because he hasn't said anything. People are thinking maybe he killed Curtis." Alice shrugged. "I don't know about that, but I do know they hated each other." She'd dropped a bombshell, but she didn't wait for a reaction, and started her warm-up without another word, ending the conversation.

Now that Alice had rung that particular bell, it reverberated through my head as I picked up my flute. Could Tyler be Curtis's murderer? He could have easily hidden a gun in his concert clothes, then left during *1812*, killed Curtis, and returned. I knew personally that Tyler didn't get along with Curtis and I knew that Tyler's reasons were personal. He saw Curtis as withholding money he, Tyler, needed to support his boys. But I couldn't believe it. Surely not Tyler. He was my friend. I *wouldn't* believe it. I'd been the victim of symphony gossip a few years ago, an unreliable and vicious source. I cleared my head of Alice's poison and returned to the business at hand.

As the party warmed up, there was lots of drinking, lots of hilarity, and no one paid attention to the music. That wasn't unusual for a party gig, and it released the pressure to perform perfectly. We were squeezed into a corner with Alice farthest away from the crowd to minimize the risk of a drink spilling on her cello. Jen and I were more mobile, and our instruments were silver. We found ourselves constantly moving in our chairs, avoiding bumps and other minor contacts with partygoers.

As more people arrived and drinks flowed, the noise level rose until we could have gone home and no one would have noticed. Mel and a friend of his, a tall, beautiful black woman, were shouting to be heard, standing right beside us.

"At least the bastard won't be standing in our way anymore. We couldn't get anything accomplished, thanks to him. This city and this symphony deserve a better chance at success than that." To me, Mel sounded angry.

"I imagine the earth'll breathe a sigh of relief, too. I can't think of a single project of Curtis's that has ever been kind to it. He always pinched pennies without concern for anything else. That way he could pay for caviar, cigars, and fancy cars. The three Cs."

The two laughed and held their drinks out of the way to prevent spilling them on a giggling group of women making their way to the patio. The women ducked and weaved, while Mel and his friend sidestepped. These maneuvers took the conversation out of earshot, but I had to wonder. Who was the woman Mel talked to so frankly? They had seemed awfully callous. Only a day since Curtis's death, you'd think they'd be kinder. I didn't particularly like him, either, but didn't they have any respect for the dead?

THREE

MONDAY, JULY 8, 2013, 9:30 A.M.

KC AND I TOOK OUR TIME enjoying a comfy breakfast at my house. She lived with her fiancé, Steve Palmer now, and I didn't see her much. But today the Articulate Artichoke, the vegetarian restaurant where she worked as head chef, closed, and she had the day off.

I had time on my hands, too. Responsibilities tapered off in the summer. The Symphony had a few more Concerts in the Parks in the coming month, but there'd been only one rehearsal, and it had been earlier in the summer season. Outdoor music tended toward the loud and bombastic. Second flute would be unheard and I wasn't worried about practicing the music. We were scheduled to play warhorses we'd done before—"Stars and Stripes Forever," "Dueling Banjos," "The Comedians," etc.—an eclectic mix, none of which had exposed second flute parts. Contributing to the sense of leisure, many of my private flute students were on vacation.

Both the freedom and the opportunity to get together with KC were a treat.

Golden, too, reveled in her attention. My girl hadn't had one of KC's patented neck rubs for many a moon, and closed her eyes in ecstasy while KC attended to her. We lingered over our tea, occasionally throwing a ball for Golden between ear rubs, content to enjoy the day and each other's company.

With the relaxed schedule, we planned to shop. KC had asked me to help her find a wedding dress. Her mother wasn't in town and she'd never mentioned the woman, although she had talked about a sister long ago. As far as I knew, neither the mother nor the sister had been invited to the wedding. I wanted to know why, but hadn't asked questions. "Where do you want to go first?"

If KC had her druthers she'd have a small wedding in my backyard. But Steve was on the Symphony Board and owned Media Masters, a media consulting firm well known in the community. He couldn't limit the guest list without offending someone. KC had no choice. They'd have a big wedding (250 guests) in the large stone Lutheran church downtown, a gothic building complete with spires, huge stained-glass windows, echoing sanctuary, and an aisle a mile long. The reception would be in the Articulate Artichoke, which would close in order to celebrate the wedding.

KC had to have *a dress*. Steve took care of the guest list, the invitations, the reception; everything but *the dress*. This was our third day of shopping. In my opinion, KC, with her graceful figure, high cheekbones, twinkling blue eyes, and long auburn curls, looked good in everything she tried on. She hadn't liked any of the dresses we'd found, though, and her nerves were beginning to show. She'd been hesitant about commitment anyway, but Steve had persuaded her. Despite her best intentions, the wedding preparations were dredging up her not-so-well-hidden fears. I determined to make the process as easy for her as possible.

"I don't know, Em. We've tried the big wedding shops and the main department stores. Maybe I should look on the internet."

She was twenty-four, of the generation that goes online first for everything. I was forty-four, and didn't like cyber shopping. "That's no fun! Besides, don't you want to try your choices on?"

She sighed. "I suppose so. But let's try unusual places. Places no one else would think of. Hole-in-the-wall boutiques. Or consignment stores, maybe."

"Aren't you concerned that a used dress might have bad karma?"

KC laughed. "I don't believe in that stuff. If it fits me and fits my budget, I'm in."

"Well, then . . ." I thought for a moment. "There's a vintage clothing store on Ute that might have something."

She smiled. "A vintage clothing store. I like the sound of that. Let's go."

We piled into my Subaru and arrived about ten thirty.

I glanced around the small store. "Not many wedding dresses here." I had hoped for more choices.

"Let's see what they have." She browsed through their limited selection. "Look, Em." She held one dress against her. "What do you think? Would it look good on me?"

"Only one way to find out. Try it on."

She returned in the dress a short time later.

"Em, I love it! And it's colorful enough that I won't look like a ghost." Champagne satin covered in antique lace highlighted her flawless features, with a V-neck and half sleeves of sheer lace. Full skirted and gathered at the waist, a modest train completed the picture. She glowed.

Tears sprang to my eyes. "It's gorgeous!" When I first met KC in the police station bathroom several years ago and watched her wipe smeared mascara from her bruised face, I never imagined someday I'd feel she was the daughter I'd never had and be shopping for a wedding dress with her.

"I think this is the one. It'll have to be altered, though." She pulled the extra material at the waist, showing me.

"That's no problem. I know a seamstress who can make anything fit. We'll stop at her shop on the way home."

She hugged me. "Thanks for suggesting this place. The dress is perfect."

She turned to go back to the dressing room.

I stopped her, my hand on her arm. "Please let me get this. As a wedding present?"

"Oh, Em. You're already doing a lot, with your trio providing the music and all. And it's awfully expensive, you know? You don't have to."

"I know I don't have to. I want to."

KC's eyes filled and she gave me another hug. "I can't thank you enough. For everything."

I paid for the dress while KC changed.

We went to lunch at a patisserie and deli I knew, St. Pierre's. After placing our orders at the counter, we got our food, then found a table.

"Your mother won't be offended, will she, that I bought your wedding dress? Sometimes I feel like you're my daughter."

"Don't worry about her. I haven't talked to her in four, no five, years."

I raised my eyebrows in a question I hoped she'd answer.

She seemed about to say something, then didn't.

"Won't she be coming to the wedding?"

"No." She spoke in a small but determined voice. "It's a special day for Steve and me. I'm not going to let her spoil it. She's like a dark cloud. She'd ruin everything."

"Are you sure? It'll be your only wedding, hopefully. Isn't there a chance you can work out whatever issues you have with her?" I tried to tread carefully. "I don't want you to regret not inviting her."

Though they didn't spill over, tears returned to KC's eyes. "She doesn't approve of me. She's never approved of me. Let's change the subject. Please?"

I cleared my throat. "What about your sister?"

"I'm debating. She would have disapproved of my job as an escort, but now that I'm in a socially acceptable career, and marrying a man who's wonderful and a community leader, maybe I could invite her."

"Would she tell your mom?"

KC frowned. "I thought we'd changed the subject."

I'm nothing if not stupidly persistent. "And your dad?"

KC glowered at me but didn't answer.

I gazed at my plate and decided to get totally away from the subject of KC's family. "You're breathtaking in that dress."

KC wasn't one to hold a grudge. Her smile dazzled. "You think? Steve won't believe it's me."

"Sure he will. He'll think you're beautiful, like always, and be proud of you."

She blushed. "Let's get to the seamstress'. I want to nail down everything. Then I can relax."

I smiled. "Okay, let's go."

KC tried on the dress again for the seamstress, and again the impact touched me. The woman pinned it, and we left it for alterations.

Lt. Gordon, I mean Paul, my sister's fiancé, waited at my house.

As we got out of the car, he approached KC. "We need to go to the station and have a little talk."

KC's mouth hung open and she seemed unable to speak. I stepped in. "What about?"

"C'mon, Emily. This is police business."

It took KC an instant to regain her ability to speak. She echoed my question. "What about?"

"I'd like to ask you about the Fourth of July, KC. Specifically, your whereabouts and observations."

"But you were with me." KC sounded confused.

"Not all the time. I'm particularly interested in your lengthy absence."

KC looked at me, then back at the lieutenant. "Will I be home for dinner?"

"I hope so. It depends on your answers."

I'd had personal experience with police questioning. I addressed Paul. "Is this routine?"

"We're in the initial stages of the investigation. We're just gathering information."

But KC definitely looked scared. "It's okay, KC. I'll call Barry. Don't say anything 'til he gets there."

Paul tsked. "Don't make a big deal of this. She's not being arrested."

But KC seemed relieved at the mention of Barry. "Thanks, Em." She hesitated. "And can you call Steve, too?"

"Will do."

Lt. Gordon escorted her to the squad car and helped her in.

Haunted by KC's look of fear and concerned, I autodialed Barry, who answered before I even got inside.

FOUR

I DIDN'T HEAR FROM KC the rest of the day. Barry had promised he'd call as soon as he got home from helping her. No word from him, either. I worried, and wished someone would clue me in.

Around nine Barry finally showed up at my door.

I hugged him and said, "I've been waiting for word on pins and needles. What happened? Where's KC?"

He cleared his throat. "I've been with KC all afternoon and evening. I just dropped her off at Steve's." He produced a bag from Valenti's, an Italian restaurant whose food was to die for. "I brought sustenance for us both."

I laughed. "You know me well, but I ate hours ago."

"Well, I'm starved. Let's go dish this up, and then I'll tell you all about it."

He headed for the kitchen and pulled down a plate from the cupboard, then sat at the table, spooning out lasagna.

The serious look on his face told me this discussion required tea. I put the kettle on to boil, then got down two mugs and placed a bag of cinnamon tea in each as I listened to Barry.

"You're not going to like what I have to tell you." He paused while he took a bite of lasagna and swallowed it. "I don't need to remind you not to repeat what I'm about to share. It's confidential. I wouldn't be able to repeat it except that KC signed a release. I can talk to either you or Steve about her case."

"I understand. I won't say a word." I sat down across from Barry at the table.

"Paul had questions for KC in the murder of Curtis Strange."

"He suspects her?"

"Not officially. Yet."

"That sounds ominous."

Barry sighed. "Paul started off the session by acknowledging that he'd been at the concert with KC and a few other friends. His questions centered on the details of what she had done when she was absent. Where did she go? Who did she see? When?"

"What did she say?" The kettle whistled. I rose and poured the hot water into the waiting mugs.

"She claimed that she left near the end of the show to use the Porta-Potty, before the *1812* Overture and the fireworks. Picking through the crowd, she'd seen Tommy Molina who she works with, and Curtis Strange, who manned a Symphony donation booth collecting funds for the fireworks."

"Paul knew where she'd gone." I carried the mugs to the table and stirred honey into my tea from the always-ready honeypot on the table. "Only the details are new."

Barry attended the concert on the Fourth. He had heard KC's account of her Porta-Potty trip. It was news to me that she had run into Tommy and Curtis, though.

He nodded. "Paul asked KC if she'd heard any gunshots. She said 'No.' Then he asked why she'd been gone so long, reappearing only after the concert ended." Barry rubbed his eyes. "She explained that the Porta-Pottys were a long way off and that she'd gotten lost on the way back. She couldn't find us in the crowd until after *1812*, 'Stars and Stripes Forever,' and the fireworks were all over."

"That's what she said when you all met me after the concert. Paul heard that. It shouldn't have surprised him."

"No." Barry took another bite of lasagna. He took a moment

to swallow and sip his tea before he continued. "Paul probably just wanted to get it all on the record. The surprises came later. He wanted to know about KC's experience with guns. She said she didn't have any. Then he started asking about her relationship with Curtis."

In mid-sip, I sputtered. "She didn't have a 'relationship' with Curtis." The term caught in my throat and I brought it out reluctantly.

"I know, but Paul asked about that. Then he wanted to know if KC knew that she was listed in Curtis's 'little black book,' and that his rating system listed her as 'very hot.' At that point I refused to let her answer any more questions."

My feelings as a female were outraged. "That slimeball!"

"I know. Paul asked about three specific occasions from three years ago—"

"Those must be the symphony picnic and the other two times she saw him."

"You knew about those?" Barry sounded surprised.

"Yeah. We talked." He didn't need to know that on the last two of those occasions KC had been helping me find my friend's killer by discreetly investigating Curtis.

"Apparently the dates were recorded on an old calendar." Barry shrugged. "Then the lieutenant asked whether KC knew that Curtis's walls were covered with photos of her. Forensics had taken pictures, which the lieutenant showed her. Curtis had a veritable shrine to her. He had pictures of KC shopping, leaving the Articulate Artichoke, getting into a car, even shots that looked like they were taken through the curtains at your place and at Steve's . . ."

I had no idea!

". . . and they were all arranged around a giant blown-up picture of you, KC, and Golden taking a walk, with KC looking happy and wind tossed and sparkling."

"He stalked us!"

"Not you, Em. KC."

"What'd she say?"

"You should have seen her face. Her mouth went slack and she seemed absolutely dumbfounded. In shock. To his credit, Paul was very gentle, and tried to persuade her to talk by saying he'd understand if the murder had been self-defense." Barry paused to take another bite of his lasagna and wolf it down. "She insisted she didn't know about the stalking and certainly hadn't killed Curtis. Paul asked if she knew Mr. Strange had used his phone to take more pictures of her at the concert. At that point I ended the interrogation. Paul didn't arrest her, didn't have grounds, but I think it's pretty clear that he's suspicious."

I was speechless. It's a good thing KC had admitted to Lieutenant Gordon that she saw Curtis. If she had denied it or not mentioned it and then the lieutenant had found the photos Curtis took at the concert, her role would have looked even more suspicious than it did now.

Barry paused as he sipped his tea. "Then I talked to my friend at the PD. Apparently nobody noticed the murder. The theory is nobody heard the gunshot because all the cannons and fireworks drowned out the shot. To a bystander it would have been just another 'pop.' Another flash and noise. The body was discovered after the performance by one of the Boy Scouts whose troop sat nearby."

"Nobody saw anything?" *Hard for me to believe.*

"Not that the cops have found. It's early days yet, but it was probably dark when the murder happened, and the fireworks display would have been making people look up. If somebody did see a flash, they would've put it down to people in the audience setting off firecrackers. That's supposed to be illegal, but it happens. And if the murderer used a suppressor, well . . ."

Barry took a breather to sip his tea and finish off his lasagna. "What's really odd is that, according to my source, other members of the Board said Curtis always took his gun when he volunteered to collect donations for the fireworks. He knew he'd be handling a lot of cash and felt safer with it there. But he never drew his weapon. It was found on his body, yet the cash he'd collected was missing."

"The motive could have been robbery, then."

"Except there were no signs of a struggle. Cops figure the murderer must have been somebody he knew and that the money must have been taken to disguise and confuse the facts."

"How do they know that? The murderer could have taken Curtis by surprise. Or maybe Curtis didn't think the donation basket worth fighting about. It seems early to discount the robbery possibility."

Barry shrugged. "I'll run it by my source. That's the working theory right now, though."

I didn't have the faintest clue how to investigate the possibility of robbery. I had to trust the cops there, although it made me feel uneasy. I knew sometimes they needed a fresh viewpoint.

By this time it was ten-fifteen, and Barry looked worn out.

"I appreciate all you did for KC. Why don't you stay here with me and Golden tonight? It would give us some time together. We haven't had much of that given the way our schedules conflict. I've missed you."

"Good idea, Em. My court date tomorrow isn't 'til ten-thirty. I'll have some time in the morning to sleep in and go get fresh clothes from my house. And I'd love your company tonight."

The phone rang at eleven, after Barry and I had gone to bed. We had been snuggling when the phone rang and I wasn't going to answer, but the caller ID showed it was KC. I picked up.

"Emily, I know it's late, but Steve and I were wondering if you and Barry could come to a breakfast meeting. We wanted to discuss what to do from here about the case. Please?" She sounded scared and overwhelmed, and Barry and I were glad to come, even though it meant we'd have to start the day early.

FIVE

TUESDAY, JULY 9, 2013, 8:00 A.M.

KC AND STEVE LIVED IN A RANCHER with multicolored bricks in shades of red and white. The kitchen was a huge room featuring a fireplace in the same brick as the outside, and a potbellied stove with a table and chairs next to it. The chairs sported blue seat cushions, and the table was covered with a blue and white plaid cloth that picked up the blue of the counters. Plants hung in every corner. The business end of the kitchen stood off to the left.

KC welcomed us, moving and talking faster than her usual pace, and Barry and I seated ourselves at the table. Fruit already waited on a platter there, and the table was set with silverware and plates for four.

Steve made tea, Morning Thunder, to wake us and keep us alert, I assume.

KC, at the stove, scrambled eggs, in hyperdrive. "Em, did Barry update you on what went on yesterday?"

At my affirmative response KC continued, "Good. We're all on the same page. I wanted to talk about what comes next. I got the definite feeling I wasn't off the hook, even if Paul, that is the lieutenant, didn't arrest me."

"First, is there anything you want us to know that you didn't tell Lieutenant Gordon? Maybe something you forgot? I know it's hard to remember everything under pressure." I'd learned from experience.

Steve brought Barry and I our tea, then returned for his and KC's mugs.

KC carried the skillet over and gave each of us a serving of eggs, then returned the pan to the stove. She didn't immediately answer. After she sat down, she concentrated hard on stirring honey into her tea.

We all watched her.

Finally, she responded. "I told them everything—except for one detail."

"Give."

She stirred her tea some more.

This had to be the best-stirred cup of tea ever.

She sipped from her cup and at last responded, "I didn't tell the lieutenant *why* I got lost."

"Tell us." I could see she needed some encouragement. "Why did you lose your way?"

KC put her tea down and looked at each of us, in a silent appeal. "I had run into Curtis on the way. I was polite, I said hello and asked how he was, but he made me uncomfortable. He stared at me with this expression . . . I don't know . . . it made me feel . . ." She searched for a word, then repeated, "uncomfortable." She gazed pleadingly at Steve. "We went on three dates. I didn't do anything to be remotely ashamed of, but he gaped at me like I had." She glanced down at her eggs, which she hadn't touched. "I have a new life. I have a man I love, a home I love, a job I love . . ."

Steve captured and held one of her wildly gesturing hands in his.

". . . and I don't need that kind of presence. I decided to go back a different way. I didn't see him again, but in the dark I couldn't spot you." She met each of our eyes with her own. "I couldn't go the straight route back for fear of running into Curtis. I got confused, winding around people, and it took a long time to find you." KC dropped her gaze.

"It's okay, Love. Don't stress. I believe you." Steve circled the hand he held with his thumb.

KC raised her head and stared intently at Steve. "That means a lot. You're important."

I, for one, was embarrassed to intrude on their moment.

Barry took a banana off the fruit platter and peeled it as he spoke. "It might make a difference to Paul. Might speak to motive, or lack thereof."

KC's expression changed quickly enough that it startled me. "I can't . . . that is . . . I don't want to . . ."

"I'll explain it to him. If it becomes important he might call you in and get it on the record, but until then, don't worry about it. I'll do my best to see you won't ever have to be bothered."

KC started to cry. "This is such a mess. I didn't do anything wrong!"

Steve patted the hand he held. "We know, Love."

I gave her a tissue and concentrated on getting every last bit of information. "You're the one who talked to Curtis. What about the people around?" I still found it difficult to believe no one saw anything.

"There were lots of people close by. After all, a crowd of thousands was packed together." KC spoke slowly. "But the only people that I knew were Tommy from work, and his girlfriend. They were sitting maybe a quarter of a football field from Curtis's booth. They weren't that close to Curtis, but they might have seen something. I don't know . . . in the dark . . ." KC slumped in her chair. "Other than that, just a Boy Scout Troop. Number 31, I think the banner said. They were older kids, maybe fourteen years old."

She didn't speak for a moment. "It's just occurred to me. Maybe the murder was an accident. Maybe Curtis wasn't the intended victim at all. You saw the crowd. Maybe the killer meant to murder someone else." To me, she sounded desperate, like she clutched at straws.

I didn't say anything. Neither did the others.

She said defensively, "Well, it's more logical than thinking I'd kill anyone."

I owed KC a lot, and I didn't want to discount her ideas. "True."

We were all quiet.

"I'll talk to Tommy at work tomorrow." KC's voice was small and despairing.

The air, or maybe hope, seemed to have gone out of the room.

I tried to outline a positive action. "I'll follow up on the Boy Scouts. I think one of them discovered the body."

"We intended to discuss further actions, but I don't think anything is necessary at this point." Barry didn't feel comfortable with his clients nosing around. He had tried to talk me out of it when he was my lawyer. "After all, there were a hundred thousand people at the park listening to the performance that night, including Paul, and they all had an opportunity to kill Curtis. The lieutenant's gotta do better than find a few pictures of you that the victim took without your permission or awareness."

KC sniffled and quit crying.

I wasn't fooled, though. Barry is in the business of calming his clients down. He'd done the same with me. I selected an orange. "I don't think it would hurt to poke around a little. Make sure KC's protected."

Steve nodded vigorously. "I have friends on the Board. I can talk to them, draw them out. See if I can find out any facts about Curtis or the murder."

"Do you know specifics about Curtis to start?" Holding my tea in both hands, I sipped.

"Not a whole lot." Steve tilted his head thoughtfully. "I know his company designs and builds new developments like shopping centers, subdivisions, and office parks. They have a reputation for being environmentally reckless. Beyond that, the biggest criticism I've heard is that Curtis has defaulted on paying contractors and subcontractors."

"Do you know who? I bet they'd be up in arms." I looked around the table and saw my friends agreed.

"No details. I try to stay out of these things. I've heard enough that I always say my firm is too busy to take new clients. That way, Curtis has to take his business elsewhere. There's no friction." Steve looked at his watch. "I'll try to find out more information."

"That would be great. I can talk to the members of the Planning Committee." I hadn't heard when Mel would reschedule the meeting, but its members would know more about Curtis. "Maybe I can find out new facts about him, too. I can already tell you he wasn't popular." *An understatement if I ever heard one.*

Barry selected a bunch of grapes. "I'll stay in contact with the PD." He began pulling them off the stem and eating them.

KC cried again. "You all are great. I never thought I'd have such good friends."

"It takes one to know one." I rose and put my arm around her. "You deserve the best."

Barry looked embarrassed and nodded at me. "I hate to eat and run, but I do have to be in court later this morning, and I've gotta catch a shower and change my clothes at home first. If there's nothing else you can think of, I'll be off. Do you want to ride with me, Em? If so, we've gotta scoot."

KC needed me. I turned to Steve and KC. "Can you guys take me home?"

She nodded. "Of course, Em."

"Then I think I'll stay awhile, Barry."

Barry gave a thumb up and left.

KC continued the conversation. "What did you mean when you said Curtis wasn't popular?"

I explained how many meetings I'd sat through with Mel, Tyler, and Curtis bickering, and what I'd overheard at the birthday party.

"I'm not surprised." KC reminded me. "When I questioned him for you a couple years ago he made it clear that, although he believed in music and its positive effects, he didn't think musicians deserved to be paid more. I'll never forget what he said. 'I *work* for a living. They *play*.'"

"Can you believe there are Board Members who feel that way?"

"Fortunately, not many." Steve sounded disgusted.

I'd pondered the question when I'd had the misfortune of dealing with one of them. My button pushed, I started on a rant. "As if we didn't deserve to be paid for our craft like any other trained, educated, responsible professional who keeps his skills current."

Steve interrupted before I really got going. "I hate to break up the party, but I've gotta be at work shortly, and I need a shower."

KC glanced at her watch. "I didn't realize. I need to get to the restaurant, too. C'mon, Em. I'll take you home."

Steve went off to shower while KC and I left for my house.

When the police had suspected me I'd felt afraid, outraged, vulnerable, and violated. I felt almost as bad about their doubts about KC. I didn't know how to help her, though. From my experience, only being fully exonerated would heal her life, inside and out.

"Don't worry, KC," I said as we pulled into my driveway. "Everybody's working on it. We'll figure it out."

"I know. I couldn't ask for a better group of friends."

I hugged her goodbye, and she clung to me long and anxiously.

Watching her drive away, I saw her take a tissue and wipe at her eyes. Damn Paul! KC didn't deserve this kind of aggravation. I'd do what I could to help her.

AS A NEXT STEP, I DECIDED to consult the internet. I'm not very good with a computer, but I'm getting better. Curtis's company, C.H. Strange Development Corp., must have a web page.

Sure enough, there it was. At first glance, there wasn't much information, just pictures of happy people in front of picturesque homes, tall buildings with beautiful landscaping, and shopping centers with crowded parking lots and smiling shoppers carrying full bags.

Then I read the list of C.H. Strange Development's properties. Some were the subject of articles I had seen in the paper. I read between the lines, combined what appeared on the computer with facts remembered from local news reports, and looked up other details.

One of the office buildings Curtis's company had designed was in litigation. Lessees claimed the lower offices flooded during heavy rainstorms or snow melt. After repeated requests, C.H. Strange Development hadn't solved the problems. A shopping center was sixty-four percent vacant because no one filled tenant requests for repairs to leaky roofs and dim or non-existent lighting.

Contractors and subcontractors for several projects claimed they had not been paid, and Norton Plumbing and Heating sued for damages.

But the kicker was Antelope Run. The website pictured happy people in front of well landscaped attached homes, and listed a planned clubhouse, tennis courts, walking paths, and close-in shopping. It solicited reservations and a "small" down payment. However, in reality the development was deeply mired in legal battles.

Environmentalists claimed a wild area close enough to the city to be a refuge but far enough away to be uncrowded would become a wasteland if Strange Co. completed construction. They were most upset about the plan to drain the existing stream and replace it with a concrete drainage ditch. Trees would be cut down. A whole habitat would be eliminated leaving beaver, fish, squirrels, deer, rabbits, ducks, bears, birds, butterflies, bees, crickets, woodchucks, and dragonflies homeless. Wildflowers would be replaced by pavement. The ditch would create water management problems downstream; in peak seasons water flow speeds would increase, creating flooding and requiring taxpayer disaster relief.

The Colorado Water Conservation Board had recently taken C.H. Strange Development to court, seeking an injunction. It claimed the company's destruction of an existing stream to build the concrete conduit would cause injury to their instream water rights.

In response, the company claimed building the development itself would create 500 construction jobs and, long-term, provide reasonably priced housing for 1500 tax-paying citizens. The use of the water would benefit those residents and would not diminish the amount of flow to which the Colorado Water Conservation Board was entitled. The court hearing over the site would be in two months.

In the meantime, construction on Antelope Run had been halted. To me, it seemed dishonest to accept deposits from hapless wanna-be owners.

A company with these kinds of business practices and mores had to have made nearly everybody who came in contact with it angry. And Curtis *was* the company.

I glanced at my watch. Only noon. I decided to see for myself the spot Curtis had picked for Antelope Run. It couldn't be as scenic as the environmentalists claimed, or I would have heard of it, wouldn't I? I packed a sandwich and some veggies and fruit, sunscreen, and water for Golden and me, put on my hiking boots and drove out of town.

SIX

TUESDAY, JULY 9, 2013, NOON

ACCORDING TO THE INTERNET, Antelope Run would be located an hour southeast of town. I followed the directions and met with a surprise.

The surrounding country had been flat prairie land with nothing visible for miles but scrub oak and grass. The road unexpectedly descended into a valley undetectable from ten miles away. I followed the signs to:

> *Butterfly Hollow*
> *Future Home of Antelope Run*
> *Luxury Townhomes for the Future*
> *from C.H. Strange Development Corporation*

A short, winding dirt road led to the bottom of the valley and a stream. And, as the ecologists said, it was a different world. There were trees and many different kinds of shrubs. A rabbit hopped away as I drove up. Cutting the engine, I heard birds singing, and a kaleidoscope of butterflies fluttered above.

I parked in the dirt parking lot, big enough for about six cars, although mine was the only one there. A barbed wire fence blocked the trailhead, with *No Trespassing* signs posted on either side. I moved the gate aside and, not letting her off the lead, led Golden through. I didn't want her to chase the rabbit I'd seen. Besides that, the trail was unfamiliar.

A footpath ran parallel to the stream. Down the trail a way, I came to two beaver ponds. Deer peeked from cool grass under the trees eyeing me warily, and ducks swam on the pond. Dragonflies flew above the water.

Though Golden pulled to get loose, I continued past the ponds. About half an hour later we came to a perfect spot for a picnic. In the shade of several towering pine trees a large, flat rock about the size of a king size bedspread lay next to the brook. A squirrel chittered at me from the safety of a low hanging branch.

I hadn't seen a person the whole time I'd been here and decided to free Golden. She deserved her slice of paradise. There were obviously no cars nearby, we were well past the ducks and, I rationalized, though she'd chased many a rabbit, she'd never been fast enough to catch one. I dropped her lead. She circled the rock, sniffing and exploring, then rejoined me, found a patch of sun, and lay down. Her eyes closed and her head dropped lower and lower, until at last she fell asleep, head resting on her paws.

From my perch on the rock I nibbled my sandwich and watched the stream. Near me it calmed before it found its way around the rock, and several fingerling trout took advantage of the shelter it provided. Farther down the stream, larger fish lay in wait for insects and jumped from the water for their lunch. A black and yellow swallowtail butterfly mistook me for a flower and lit on my shirt. I waited motionless, and it stayed for quite a while before flying off. I lay back on the rock with my backpack as a pillow and let the sound of buzzing bees milking the wildflowers for nectar lull me to sleep.

When I woke I didn't see Golden. She must have wandered off while I dozed. I called her, but she didn't come immediately. *Unusual.* I called again, beginning to worry, until I heard her collar.

Following the sound, I found her digging furiously beneath a tree invisible from the path.

"Golden! Come!" She ignored me. For my completely obedient therapy dog, *that* was unprecedented.

I had started toward her when, from the other direction, a man descended a small knoll. As he approached, I could see he was in his late twenties, dressed in jeans and a t-shirt, and wearing hiking boots. He seemed to be following the sound of Golden's collar, too. "Excuse me. Can I help you?"

Uh-oh. The signs were clear, but I had ignored them and trespassed. "I was trying to get my dog to come. It's unusual that she ran off."

"This is private land."

I feigned complete innocence, which he would realize was faked if he knew how plainly the trailhead was marked. "Really? I'm sorry, but we've hiked here for years."

"It's recently been sold."

"Oh, I didn't realize. It's been such a refuge for us. Are you the new owner?"

He seemed uncomfortable and shifted his weight from foot to foot. "My uncle bought the property."

So he was Curtis's nephew. I'd never heard of any relatives, but then I didn't know Curtis very well. Nobody did. "I didn't mean to trespass. We'll get off your property as soon as we can."

While we talked, Golden continued digging. The ground was damp and loose, and she had dug a deep hole by the time I approached. To my horror, I saw she had unearthed a withered human hand. Mercifully, the rest of the body was covered beneath a layer of earth.

Desperately, I called "Golden, leave it! Come!" then picked up her lead and pulled her away from the hole, the hand . . . and the stench. I turned to the young man. "Uh, I think you'd better see this."

He moved toward us. When he was close enough to see the hand and smell the body, he blanched and backed away, patting his pockets. "This is awful! I need to call the Sheriff, but I left my phone in the car."

The property lay outside the city limits and would be in county jurisdiction.

I pulled out my phone. "I'll call 911."

The dispatcher knew where Butterfly Hollow was. I answered her questions, which took a while.

When I gave directions to the spot, Curtis's nephew interrupted. "You can reach it more easily from the south side parking lot. It's just over the hill."

I conveyed this information to the dispatcher. She instructed me to touch nothing and wait for the Sheriff.

Uncomfortable, I considered what to do next. Small talk for the discovery of a body wasn't covered in any etiquette books that I knew. I reached out my hand. "I'm Emily Wilson."

He returned my grasp. "Roland Strange."

I figured Curtis's death had occurred long enough ago that Roland could expect everyone had heard the news. "Any relation to Curtis Strange? Owner of C.H. Strange Development?

"I'm his nephew. My father was Stan Strange, Curtis's brother."

"I heard about Curtis's death. Murder, wasn't it? At the Fourth of July concert?" I knew the answer, but it seemed natural to ask.

"Yes." He sounded resigned.

"My condolences."

"It's okay. My father and Uncle Curtis weren't close. Never met the man, but it seems I'm the sole living relative. The lawyer called me in Montana last week. First I'd heard of the murder."

"Do you have any idea who the body is?"

"You got me." He shivered. "Uncle Curtis wasn't a nice man, according to my father, but I hope he didn't do . . . this." He gestured at the hole.

"It's an out-of-the-way spot, off the footpath. Anybody could have disposed of a body here."

Roland nodded and seemed encouraged by this theory.

I volunteered to go back to the path and wait for the officer. "He'll need directions to the . . . spot." I figured this would relieve us both of the need to make small talk, and might be helpful to the Sheriff.

"That sounds like a good idea." As I left, he sat down to wait.

Back at the path I found a shady spot and amused Golden by throwing a ball I'd brought.

The Sheriff's officer arrived some time later from the same

direction Roland had come. "Are you the one who called in the body?"

"Yes. I'll show you. Follow me." I led him back to the hole. Both Roland, who had hurriedly risen, and I gestured at it.

The officer, whose name badge read "Serna" approached the hole, then tsked. "I'll have to call the coroner, then hike back and get a shovel." He took his cell phone out of a pocket in his uniform and made the call.

I spoke up. "My dog uncovered the body while we were hiking. I don't know anything beyond that. Can I just leave you my contact information? Roland, here, owns the property."

Putting his cell phone back in his pocket, Sergeant Serna whipped out a notebook and penned all my information. "Thanks for your help, Ma'am. Here's my card if you think of anything else."

I waved as I left, beginning the trek back to the footpath and my car.

A pall had been cast over Butterfly Hollow, but I could see it was a refuge from the heat, the city, and human interaction—all the environmentalists had claimed, and more.

Urgency propelled me to the car. Strange Development must *not* be allowed to ruin this place. Were the Hollow and Curtis's murder tied together? I could imagine a bitter battle over Butterfly Hollow. There were too few wild refuges left. Surely Strange Development could find another place to build its houses, closer to the city, in less attractive areas.

There were questions, too. What effect would Curtis's death have? Had future plans for Butterfly Hollow died with Curtis? Or would Roland continue to build Antelope Run? Did Curtis have anything to do with the unidentified body Golden had dug up? Would the discovery of a body make any difference to the future of the Hollow? Roland seemed nice enough and claimed to know nothing of the murder, but the inheritance might have provided a motive for Curtis's death. What if Roland had lied? That would clear KC. There were a lot of complex questions, including the big one. Who was buried in the hole? The answers could greatly affect Butterfly Hollow . . . and KC.

SEVEN

WEDNESDAY, JULY 10, 2013, 8:00 A.M.

After Golden got me out of bed with her joyful and persistent nudging, licking, and whining, we went for our morning walk. My thoughts seemed especially clear, and I mulled over the facts I knew about Curtis's murder. Curtis had been a Board Member and volunteer collecting donations for the fireworks from the concert attendees. He had been killed out in the open, but none of the 100,000 people present had noticed the murder due to darkness and the loud cannons and fireworks. A nearby Boy Scout had discovered the body after the concert. Presumably Curtis had collected a lot of money—all missing. Though he had a gun, he had not drawn it and there were no signs of a struggle. Because of these circumstances, police had concluded the killing was carried out by someone he knew. No murder weapon had been recovered. By KC's admission, Curtis had talked to her at the performance, and photographic evidence proved he had been stalking her for years.

Those were the facts as I knew them. The police had been drawn in KC's direction by the photographs Curtis had taken. But there were other possibilities. What if the police were wrong in their interpretation? What if the motive for the murder had been robbery? But in that case, why didn't Curtis draw his gun? Was he taken by surprise?

And what about Curtis's business? I'd guess that the people angry with Curtis because of his shoddy building practices would fill a good-sized auditorium. Had he infuriated someone to the point of murder?

Or was his obstructionist attitude at Planning Committee to blame? Mel and Tyler were at odds with Curtis on almost everything. Mel fervently believed in the importance of sustainable building. Both Mel and Tyler were rabid about the need to increase of the size of the symphony and provide pay raises for musicians. But did Mel attend the concert the night of the murder? He'd been out of the room when the rest of the committee discussed the concert. And what about Tyler? Where had he disappeared to the night of the murder during *1812*?

I couldn't ignore KC's ideas. She had always been a sensible light to me, at least when she wasn't panicking. In my opinion the Boy Scout who found the body couldn't possibly have any helpful ideas—surely the police had thoroughly questioned him?—but I'd see what he had to say, anyway. At least KC would know we were looking into everything.

I found a phone number for Troop 31 on the internet and called.

"Scooter Bayfield, Scoutmaster. May I help you?"

"Hello." I used my maiden name in case Scooter listened to the symphony regularly and might recognize my name. "This is Emily Rizzuto. I'm following up on the murder of Curtis Strange and I wanted to talk to the scout who discovered the body."

Scooter responded with suspicion. "All parties gave contact information to the police the night of the concert."

How much should I tell him? "I'm not with the police." I briefly considered a lie to explain my nosy questions, but decided the truth was a lot less complicated. "A friend of mine is under suspicion, and I know she couldn't have committed murder."

This seemed to make Scooter even more suspicious. "I'm sure the police have good reasons for their thinking."

"Please. I know she's innocent."

Scooter heaved a sigh. "Fine. If you'll give me your phone number, I'll pass it on to the family of the Scout in question. It's really the family's decision if they want to talk to you or not."

"That would be great." I gave him my number and an email address, in case they wanted to make contact that way. "Thanks for your help."

I made myself an early lunch and pondered the situation further. What constituted a motive for Curtis's murder? Nothing, it seemed to me. Obviously, someone disagreed.

I'd have to wait for the Scout to contact me. Curtis's nephew claimed he hadn't known about the murder until afterwards when the lawyer notified him. The most logical next step seemed to be identifying people with grudges against Curtis. Given his business malpractice and general unlikability, there should be plenty of them. I decided to head to the offices of C.H. Strange Development.

CURTIS'S ASSISTANT WAS IN. I judged her to be in her late twenties or early thirties, dark-haired, with frown lines in her forehead and pictures of two children, both younger than six, on her desk. A placard identified her as "Lila Richford."

"Hi. I'm interested in talking about Antelope Run. Can you help me?"

"Appointments to view sites at Antelope Run are unavailable right now." Her voice was cold and distant. She seemed to assume I wanted a home there. I didn't correct her impression.

I parked myself in a chair on the other side of her desk, put my purse on the floor, and sat back, doing my best to look disappointed. "Can I ask why?"

Lila emotionlessly rattled off the answer, as if reciting a familiar statement. "The owner of C.H. Strange Development died suddenly."

"I saw that on the news. I wondered if it would impact the business, or if I could still buy a home in Antelope Run."

"The rights to the business are being processed. New business is on hold for the moment." Again, she said it like a memorized statement.

"That must be hard for the employees. Are you being paid?"

Apparently my concern touched a nerve because the robotic aspect of her speech disappeared. She sounded irritated. "I assume so. The next paycheck isn't due 'til the end of the month. In the meantime, nobody's closed up the office or told me to."

"What about the company? How can it stay in business? It must be rough under the circumstances." I did my best to break down her reticence with friendly curiosity.

"I'm not suffering. At least it's quiet. Mr. Strange used to . . . well, anyway, it's calm."

"How do you keep busy? I mean if the office isn't doing business, what's left?"

She glared at me. "Why do you care?"

I leaned forward confidentially. "I'm curious. It's a terrible trait of mine."

She apparently decided talking to me would pass the time and she had nothing better to do. "Whatever I have to. Sometimes when I'm *really* bored, I talk to nosy people." She arched an eyebrow at me.

I didn't take her statement personally, though I'm sure she wanted me to.

She continued. "There's always filing. And I deal with lawyers."

"Lawyers?" That captured my attention.

"Not everything can stop. Things that are already in the works need to be attended to." She crossed her arms and leaned on the desk.

"But lawyers?"

She narrowed her eyes. "I get questions sometimes."

"About what?"

"You really don't know how to mind your own business, do you?" She sounded more than annoyed.

"Don't you think I should research C.H. Strange Development before I deal with them? Isn't that being a smart consumer?"

She sounded resigned. "I suppose." Resting her chin on her hand she suggested, "Maybe you should look into the lawsuits first."

"Lawsuits?"

"Listen, I've already said too much." Lila began rearranging the pens in the holder on her desk.

"It'd be good to get Strange Development's side of the story. I really do want to deal with you folks, and it's important to hear you out."

Lila responded slowly. "The newest court case is with the Colorado Water Conservation Board over Antelope Run."

"Newest?"

She grimaced. "Since you're persistent, you'll find out about the other cases. Construction won't begin for a while on Antelope Run, if it ever does. Are you in a hurry?"

"No. I know building takes a long time and there may be delays. I want my dream home. Lots of natural surroundings and peace, but with amenities."

Lila shifted in her chair, looking uncomfortable. "We're claiming that Antelope Run will create construction jobs and, later, homes for tax-paying citizens, increasing the tax basis. The environmentalists claim Antelope Run will ruin the natural surroundings. Personally, I think they have a convincing argument, though I'll deny I said it if you quote me. Take away the stream, and everything else goes with it."

"Oh! I guess I'd better rethink this a bit. And you said Antelope Run was only the newest of the lawsuits. Is it common for developers to be sued more than once?"

Lila shrugged. "I haven't worked for any other developers. I don't really know."

She seemed to be relaxing. I pushed for more information. "What would you do if you were me?"

It took a moment before Lila responded. "I don't think I'd buy a place built by Strange Development. It seems there's no follow-up once the tenant has paid his money. That's what the suits are about."

"Really? Are they all small?"

Lila wet her lips. "A couple of them are. But there's one that's a coalition of all the residents of Homes at Skyridge led by one determined old man, Noah Wattle. They have complaints, some big and some small, but all the homeowners seem pretty irate."

"What do you have to do?"

"I get facts for the lawyers, send copies and faxes. That sort of thing."

"Well, it would worry me."

"Why would I worry?" She sounded smugly satisfied. "It's not my money. Or my reputation."

"Reputation?"

"I think the word is getting out. Don't buy from C.H. Strange Development." She started, seeming to remember herself. "I shouldn't have said that. Please don't repeat it. I need this job."

"It's okay, Lila." I stood to go. "I appreciate the heads up."

It was only one o'clock and nothing showed on my calendar 'til my trio gig. I decided to go to Homes at Skyridge and see what I could find out.

First, I went to the office.

"Can I help you?" The sales agent was a tall man, maybe in his thirties, with thinning reddish-blond hair and an eager expression.

"I wanted to move to this area and thought I'd see what was available."

"Great! This is a beautiful community. Let me show you a model home. First, could you fill out this form?"

Again using my maiden name and incomplete information I complied, then went to see the model home with him.

As expected, it was beautifully decorated. Creams and browns predominated, with bright yellow and orange accents, plenty of closet space, an island in the kitchen, and large rooms with beautiful views. In short, a stunning luxury townhome. "And all the three-bedroom homes are like this, with this floor plan?"

"Yes. Of course, there are some upgrades here. Clients want to see them before they buy."

"Upgrades?"

"Yes." He shifted his weight from foot to foot.

"What upgrades?"

"Just a few things."

"Like?' My dentist had pulled teeth faster than this.

"The ceiling fans in the bedrooms, the loft, the work island in the kitchen, the granite countertops, the cathedral ceilings, and the hardwood floors."

"What would this home sell for?"

He shuffled his feet. "It's not for sale, but if it were . . ." He named a figure $100,000 more than the price advertised.

"I see. Do you have any models that are more baseline?"

"No." He seemed put out that I wasn't a big spender. "Not right now."

"Well, thank you for your time." In reality, I wanted to shake the dust off my feet. I already felt sympathy for the concerns of the residents, without ever having met any of them.

LILA HAD SAID NOAH WATTLE LED THE RESIDENTS of Homes at Skyridge. Mailbox number 404 listed its owner as "Wattle." I drove around winding streets lined with sapling trees, some of them dead, before I found a building in which two units shared a dividing wall, one of them 404.

I rang the bell.

A tall gray-haired man, probably in his early seventies, answered the door.

"Mr. Wattle?"

"Yes?"

"I'm investigating the death of Curtis Strange. May I come in?" I hoped he would accept that. But, no.

"Are you with the police?"

"No. I have a private interest."

"Private interest?"

"Curtis Strange knew a friend of mine and treated her very badly. I'm trying to find out who killed him and why, since it looks like she may be a suspect. What *I* know is that she couldn't have done it." He impressed me. He had pried almost the whole story out of me, but hadn't let me cross the threshold.

"Any adversary of Curtis Strange's is a friend of mine." He opened the door wider and stepped aside. I entered, then followed Mr. Wattle to a large living room with cathedral ceilings and hardwood floors. I wondered if he had the other upgrades, too, and how he felt about paying the extra costs.

Mr. Wattle waved me to the sofa and chose a well-padded recliner for himself.

"How can I help you?" He leaned back and put up the footrest.

I sat on the sofa, with its low, sloping seat, and soft, yielding cushions, trying to keep my back straight. "I'm not really sure. The police seem determined to pin Curtis's murder on my friend, but there's no way she did it. I'm flailing around, trying to find the real killer."

He looked puzzled.

"I understand you and several other residents have a lawsuit against Curtis. Could you tell me about that, and about Mr. Strange?"

"I'd be glad to tell you all I know, but I'm not sure if it'll help."

"Let me worry about that." I settled farther back into the cushions.

"Have you toured the development?"

"I toured the model and saw the grounds between there and here."

"My wife and I thought we'd be very happy here. No yard to mow, no roof or fence to maintain. Natural surroundings. But it didn't work out as well as I'd hoped."

"How so?"

"It looks beautiful, doesn't it?"

I murmured in agreement. "Well, except for the dead trees."

"That's one of our beefs. A minor one, relatively speaking. Strange Development cut down the big old trees. Said the builders couldn't do their work, otherwise. My wife and I were one of the first families to move in, and the place alternated between mud and dust for months. When the company finally landscaped, they planted those skinny little saplings."

Mr. Wattle shifted in the recliner and adjusted the setting, sitting up straighter. "Personally, what most upset me was that the locks didn't work. It scared my wife. We couldn't secure the doors, and the world being what it is today, well, she worried. The first night we pushed the furniture against the doors, then I hired my own locksmith to come out and fix things. I sent the receipt to Strange for reimbursement."

"And?"

"That was three years ago. I've pretty much resigned myself to never getting repaid." He shifted in his chair. "I know construction on a new building has its glitches, but having locks that work is pretty basic. I wanted my money, and I wanted to be treated right. After six months or so, I threatened to turn my lawyer loose on the company."

Again, he adjusted the recliner. "Sorry, bad back."

"No worries. Please, make yourself comfortable."

He took a sip of water from the glass by the chair. "I started talking to people. Within a year of moving in almost everybody had problems: cracking walls, tiles and stucco; uneven floors; leaky windows; roofs with leaks or poor drainage; lights and appliances that quit working. Lots of those problems could be caused by a settling foundation. I used to work as a contractor, you know. I seemed to be the only one who had any ideas on how to resolve some of the troubles. When we had a meeting, the other residents elected me president of the Homeowner's Association."

"And how's it going?"

He thought a moment. "First, we hired a private inspector who verified that the homes weren't up to code even when they were first built. That implies that Strange Development bribed an inspector, because otherwise the homes wouldn't have been passed."

Mr. Wattle leaned left and right and forward and back, stretching. "As for the rest of it, I'm in pretty good shape compared to everybody else. They got problems that should never have happened. The corporation hasn't fixed most of those, and it's led to major problems. When the foundation settles, water gets in and then you got mold. Or it causes any number of other problems. Strange Development didn't always put insulation where it should be. That led to condensation between the outside walls and the drywall. Eventually, mold formed there, too. Needs to be taken care of by a professional. But the most common problem is damp basements. Again, settling foundations. It's reached the point some folks are having health problems. We've gotten some minor repairs done, but for the most part, nothing serious has been fixed."

He leaned forward and rubbed his back with both hands, then continued. "That's why we decided to hire a lawyer. Since then there's been a roofer out to smear some tar on some of the leaking roofs. I could've done that. Won't help with the serious problems, but it's somethin'. The major beefs, though, have to do with other causes of mold, especially, as I said, settling foundations, and there's been no progress there. Couple people are getting mighty impatient."

"Impatient?"

"Matlow in 302 badgers me at least once a week, maybe more. Travers in 603 goes off on a tirade every time I see him. I tell you, it's getting' me down. I wanted to come here for a nice, quiet retirement. Instead, I'm dealing with lawyers and lawsuits. The bright side is, after three years, if I could sell this place I could afford to move again. Bottom line, though, is that you can't sell these places, and you can't live in 'em either, or at least you can't live in 'em without aggravating your ulcers."

"I take it Curtis hasn't been very helpful."

Wattle snorted. "I've only seen him once. About a year and a half after we moved in, he came out and gave a bright, optimistic talk to the Association about how experts were working on it, and all the problems would soon be solved. Huh. That was the last I saw of him. Since then there's been managers and lawyers and engineers, but not any results."

"How's the suit going?"

"We were making a little progress. At least we had hope. But since Mr. Strange's death, everything's on hold again." He tsked.

"I can hear your frustration. I'd be frustrated, too. Do you have any ideas about who may have murdered Curtis?"

"I'd say the list is long and everybody here was livid enough to be on it. Except me. I stay home all the time, and Fourth of July was no exception. My concept of hell is to have to go to City Park and sit on either the ground or a bad chair and try to hear music over kids screaming." He grinned. "I'm too old and cranky and tired for that stuff, and too poor to hire somebody to kill Mr. Strange."

I chuckled. "Don't worry. Things'll work out. Maybe Curtis's death will actually help, in the long run." I stood and headed for the door.

"I hope so. And I hope you have better luck than we've had."

WHEN I GOT HOME I LOGGED ON to my computer. Now that I knew about the lawsuits Curtis faced, I went to the county court website and Googled his name. I quickly discovered that I didn't have enough information to make any progress. I called Barry's cell phone, hoping he could help me out.

He wanted more information. "Do you have case numbers or attorney names?"

"That's the problem, Barry. I don't know any of that stuff. C.H. Strange Development Corp. is the name of his company. Homes at Skyridge is one of the plaintiffs, and Norton Plumbing and Heating is another. An injunction was recently filed by the Colorado Water Conservation Board against C.H. Strange Development Corp., but that's all the information I have."

"I'll put Oneida on it. She's more or less a wizard at digging up data. If it's to be found, she'll find it. At the very least, she'll be the one banging her head on the desk instead of you."

Oneida was his paralegal.

"Thanks, Barry. I knew I could count on you." In more ways than one. He had shown dependability I wasn't used to, and almost overcome my skepticism about men. Almost.

By the time I finished talking to Barry, I didn't have time to pursue the two new leads Mr. Wattle had given me. I'd just have time to make myself presentable for my trio gig.

OUR TRIO HAD BEEN HIRED TO PLAY the opening of a new art show at the Creative Commonwealth Gallery. We started with the usual trio sonatas, keeping to upbeat selections. At the first break Harvey and Jane Rice talked to us.

"It's such a treat to hear you all play!" Harvey was the CEO of Environmental Responsibility, a local granting agency. I knew him through his wife, Jane, my fellow Planning Committee member and a prominent society matron.

It surprised me to see them here. "I didn't know you liked contemporary art."

Jane enthused. "Oh, yes. We're quite interested in a number of sculptures. Aren't we, Harvey?"

He didn't look as excited as he might have. "Absolutely." The way he said it, I suspected that he belonged to the "if-mama-ain't-happy-ain't-nobody-happy" school.

At that moment our liaison arrived to point out the food table and the location of the rest rooms. After a few minutes of introductions and chit-chat we trio members excused ourselves and followed her.

I noticed Mel's mystery friend, tall and elegant, alone in the moment. "Who's the graceful woman of color in the peach dress?" I hoped our liaison would know.

"That's Darlene Taylor. She's the new president of the Tourist Bureau. Why?"

"I'd seen her before at another function and wanted to attach a name to the face." Why would Ms. Taylor be hostile when Mel mentioned Curtis? I made a mental note to find out what I could.

The gig lasted three hours. After the first break, we continued with the virtually limitless trio sonata repertoire. In the days before radio, TV, social media, and video games, for entertainment folks played music with whoever happened to be available. Duets and trio sonatas were especially popular, since players didn't need to find more than one or two people to make up a group. All the famous composers, as well as the not-so-famous composers, had written those types of pieces. We had plenty of music.

Jen, Alice, and I took one more break between the second and third hours, and I noticed Harvey carrying a large, wrapped package as he and Jane left. It appeared they had bought at least one sculpture.

"GUESS WHAT!"

I had just gotten home and accepted Golden's wiggling welcome when Kathleen called. The mental concentration and energy of performance had made me tired even though it wasn't late, but Kathleen's enthusiasm made me smile.

"I found a house that's perfect!"

Kathleen and Paul weren't in a hurry to get married. She didn't want to give up her deceased husband's social security, and Paul's divorce had been a nasty affair. But they had been looking for a house they could move into together. The place Kathleen rented used to be a carriage house, and had barely room enough for one. Paul shared a house with two other policemen. They'd been looking for a while, but Kathleen was picky. It had to have a gorgeous view, be new, or at least recently updated, and "feel like home."

"Really? Tell me."

"It's in the west part of town, above downtown, but not quite to the mountains. It's an older home, but it's been completely updated. It has French doors that open onto a balcony which over-looks a waterfall across the neighboring canyon. The backyard has been left natural. And not only that, Paul loves it._We can move in immediately, because the owners have already moved."

"Awesome! It does sound perfect."

"We put in the offer today, and we're hoping for a quick turn-around. We just have to get an inspection. It will be wonderful when Paul and I can be together!"

She enthused a while longer—apparently the house had two floors, a large master bedroom, and an *en suite* bath. I listened, encouraging her when I could get a word in edgewise, until she wound down and changed the subject. "What about you?"

"Same old, same old. I'm concerned about KC, but I haven't discovered anything that could help, yet."

"Oh, me too. I'll talk to Paul and see if I can get any inside info."

That didn't sound like a good plan to me—too invasive—but I didn't say anything. Details of Kathleen's relationship with Paul were up to her.

We talked about incidental things for a few minutes. "How's Charlie?"

"He and Ana are getting settled in Oklahoma. She's at the same job she had here, but working remotely, and he's looking forward to getting started with the symphony. He won't have to work two jobs, and he'll get more time at home than he had in Monroe."

"That sounds serious. Is he planning to propose to Ana?"

"He hasn't said so, but why else would he be wanting more time at home?"

"Makes sense to me."

We speculated a little longer.

No sooner had we rung off than Steve called. "KC talked to Tommy at work today. He and his girlfriend not only didn't see anything, but they didn't know about the murder 'til they saw it on the news. I'm worried. KC's not her cheerful self. She seems distracted. I don't think she's slept since Paul questioned her. I wish she'd talk to me about it."

"If I know KC, she doesn't want to worry you. Have you found out any more about Curtis?"

Steve sighed. "I can't be too obviously seeking information, but I called Strange Corp. as if I didn't know anything about the death and inquired as to whether they wanted to pursue the PR promotion. I talked to Curtis's assistant, Lila. She told me about the murder. Said she didn't know anything about the PR campaign, which wasn't surprising because I made it up. She wanted to see if I could hold off until things settled a bit and said all the company's projects were on hold for now." I heard papers shuffling. Then he continued. "I asked if that included the Antelope Run subdivision, since it had gotten push-back from environmentalists. Lila said that yes, that included Antelope Run. I couldn't think of anything else to say. I offered my condolences and hung up. I didn't accomplish much, I guess, except to establish that we won't be getting much help from that quarter."

I paused to process. "I think you did accomplish something. You formed a connection, and you'll be among the first to know when things get moving again."

"You really think so?" Steve sounded pleased. "I'll keep my ears open at the Board meeting, too. That'll be in two weeks. Let me know if you think of anything specific I need to find out." Believe it or not, Steve sounded a little shy.

"For sure. We'll help Paul see options other than a case against KC."

I decided not to talk to KC right away. She'd be exhausted this late. Instead, we could touch base at her flute lesson on Monday. Maybe I'd have some definite news by then. Steve and I ended our call without involving KC.

Distracted, I let Golden into the back yard, then undressed and brushed my teeth. When she scratched to come in, we went to bed and I fell asleep wondering, what next?

EIGHT

THURSDAY, JULY 11, 2013, 9:00 A.M.

I WANTED TO FIND OUT ABOUT THE BODY Golden had unearthed. Who was it? Did it have anything to do with Curtis, his company, or his death? I didn't have any students, and I got the day off to a pleasant start walking Golden. I distractedly discharged my duty with a short practice session, just the basics, during which I thought more about the murder victims than the business at hand, and then eagerly followed up on the mystery.

Sgt. Serna had given me his card, and I called his cell.

"Hi. This is Emily Wilson. Remember me? I'm the one whose dog dug up a body."

"I remember. Pretty unusual. Your dog's a great detective."

We both laughed.

"I'm curious and wanted to check and see if you've had any luck identifying the body."

"I guess there's no harm in telling you. It'll be on the news tonight anyway. The victim's family has been notified. The body was Joe Connally's. Wealthy accountant. Retired."

Now I knew Mr. Connally's name and occupation. It meant nothing to me. Since he couldn't bury himself, I felt safe in assuming the death wasn't a suicide. Other than that, I knew nothing. Maybe Sgt. Serna could be persuaded to give me more information. I suspected the Monroe Police Department and Paul wouldn't have talked to me, but I hoped smaller, more rural Lincoln County was different.

"Have you found anything else out?"

"Coroner said Connally'd been in the ground about six months."

Six months ago Curtis had been alive and obnoxious. Maybe Curtis had killed Joe. That would give his family a revenge motive. "Curtis Strange owned the property until his death. Any connection to him?"

"How'd you know about that?" Sgt. Serna instantly sounded suspicious.

"He was an acquaintance of mine."

"You know an awful lot." He fell silent, and I feared he might not say more, but after a moment he continued. "I can tell you certain things. Maybe you can help. I talked to Connally's daughter. She didn't know of any links. She told me her dad liked the outdoors and lived on the land, especially in the summer. Sometimes he disappeared for months at a time. The family didn't worry when they couldn't get in touch with him. They figured he'd call when he got back in cell phone range. You know of any connection?"

"Sorry. Even though Curtis was an acquaintance, I didn't know him very well. Not well enough to know his friends." I thought for a moment. "Even though Curtis owned the Hollow you can't link Mr. Connally's death to him?"

"We're investigating."

Uh-oh. The tone of his voice told me to back off. "Well, thanks Sergeant. You've set my mind at rest."

"No problem. Thanks for your help."

I had been dismissed.

As we ended the call, I looked at my watch. I'd have time for a leisurely lunch and some processing before the Planning Committee meeting.

THE PLANNING COMMITTEE HADN'T MET since Curtis's death, and

I didn't know what to expect. Would there be a replacement for him? Would we be able to get anything done?

I should have known Mel was too efficient to waste any time. He had appointed a substitute for Curtis, Diane Gelbart. She had served as past president of Friends of the Symphony, a fund-raising arm, was on the Board, and supported the Symphony and its musicians with enthusiasm and a willingness to work that astonished me. At fifty plus, she was well-groomed in a motherly sort of way, and given to hugging hello. In short, a sweetheart. I felt a lightening in the atmosphere already.

Mel introduced Diane, then dove right in. There wasn't a chance to ask questions about Curtis or the murder. We discussed the possibility of increasing work, and therefore salaries, for musicians; scheduling conflicts; and possible solutions. Curtis might never have existed. Although the new Committee wasn't necessarily in agreement all the time, we worked well together on the same side. The Board members realized there would be no symphony without the musicians. The musicians knew the health of the symphony depended on its finances and therefore its Board members.

We'd been behind due to the stumbling block Curtis had become. Without him, we made heaps of progress, voting on the added services issue, and discussing possible future programs.

Mel summed it up. "I don't need to tell you we need to get moving on this. Even though we're working two years out, that's not a lot of time to get everything moving. The conductor has approved a list of potential soloists. Can you contact them, Jane?" At her affirmative nod, he continued. "The office staff should be able to provide whatever help you need."

Next, he turned to me. "Emily, can you, Tyler, and Susie find out if the proposed addition of one additional rehearsal and three concerts is okay?"

My enthusiasm knew no bounds. "Sure thing, Mel." Even though the suggested increase wouldn't buy anybody a yacht, this step took us in the right direction. Growth had to begin somewhere.

"Then let's get going."

The meeting broke up with lots of smiling and enthusiasm. The OPO members stayed, chatting with Board members.

I hugged Diane and told her what a breath of fresh air she was, then turned to Jane, who had been sitting next to me. "We did good work today. I'm sure the players will agree to the plan the committee put forward."

"It's amazing how much we could get done when we weren't being waylaid by Curtis." She pushed back her chair.

"It's a whole different committee without him," Mel agreed.

I folded the papers from the meeting, put them into my purse, and took the opportunity to discuss Curtis. "I hate to speak ill of the dead, but I bet there are other projects that will go more smoothly without him there to contend with." I addressed Jane. "No doubt your husband's non-profit will find that life is easier."

Jane laughed. "It's true that the two of them routinely butted heads. Can you believe Curtis expected the Foundation to fund Antelope Run? With the damage to the environment it would cause?"

"I don't think the environment mattered to him. He was pro-profit and pro-Curtis and didn't care about anything else."

"Sounds about right." She took her keys out of her purse and stood.

Mel stayed in the building. The rest of us walked together to the warm sun of the parking lot.

I felt a sense of camaraderie with all of them and waved. "Bye, Diane. Bye, Jane. See you next Thursday."

"See you then." Jane unlocked her SUV.

Diane waved and pulled open the door to a sporty little red button of a car.

This meeting had been friendly. I hoped the hostile atmosphere created by Mel, Tyler, and Curtis's disagreements would fade to a mere memory.

Had Mel or Tyler snapped and killed Curtis? That would be hard to believe. But where could Tyler have gone during *1812*? Was Mel even at the July Fourth concert? Were his, or Tyler's, disagreements with Curtis sufficient motive for a murder? Their arguments had been long-standing and wide-ranging, and all three men were increasingly angry and insulting, getting louder and more personal the longer they argued in support of their opposing positions. As a cringing witness, I had to concede that their loss of perspective made homicide a possibility. I'd have to look into both Mel and Tyler and their activities the night of the murder more closely.

Susie, Tyler, and I had a post-meeting snack at the Articulate Artichoke, which was nearby. KC worked there, and while the others waited to be seated, I went to the kitchen window and waved.

Dough on her hands, KC came to the door, pushed it open with her fanny, and hugged me with only one arm, no hands.

I expressed my concern. "How are you doing?"

"As well as can be expected, I guess. Work helps me. I lose track of time and everything else when I cook."

"They say that's the way to tell when you're really enjoying something. I'm glad you've found such a delicious escape."

We both laughed.

"Any particular recommendations from the chef?"

"Try the eclairs. It's one of my favorite recipes."

"Ummm. Yum."

KC looked over her shoulder. "I'll be right there." Turning back to me she said, "Sorry I can't talk longer. I've got to get back to work."

"Sure, KC. I understand."

Discussion had already begun when I got to the table.

"My concern is that we have to get moving on this but, other than the last three concerts in the parks, we don't meet again until September. Not even any rehearsals. We need to have everything decided by then." Susie Melendez was a very organized, petite, single mom, fortyish.

Tyler frowned and his tall, lanky form slouched in the chair. "Yeah, we're real far behind, thanks to that jackass."

"I thought maybe we could send out a questionnaire." I felt brimming with enthusiasm, and didn't think this would be a hard sell to other orchestra members.

"Great idea, Emily!" Susie's enthusiasm caught fire.

Tyler pumped his fist. "I'll put something together. We'll need to run it past the full Player's Organization before we send it out."

Seeing his gusto, I had trouble believing that he might be a killer. "Can you have it ready for the meeting Monday?" I didn't want anything else on my plate. I planned on being busy proving KC's innocence.

"No prob." Tyler leaned forward in his chair and smiled.

Susie excused herself to go to the restroom.

Left alone with Tyler, I took the opportunity to talk to him. "I heard you had to leave the stage during *1812*. Are you okay?"

Tyler frowned. "Sure."

I expected more of an answer, but he offered none. "What happened?"

"It's private." Tyler crossed his arms and leaned back in his chair.

"You should know the grapevine thinks you're guilty of Curtis's murder." Surely that would get more information.

Tyler tsked. "Figures."

"I know from experience that the grapevine can be really wrong."

"That's for sure." His nostrils flared.

"I'd be glad to spread the truth, if I knew what it was." I hoped my hint would lead him to confide in me.

"Thanks." Tyler had nothing more to say, but his face told me I should mind my own business.

We sat in awkward silence until Susie returned.

She bubbled. "It's about time the Committee made some progress."

With effort, at least on my part, Tyler and I tabled the heavy atmosphere, and we smiled. "Yeah. I think we can pat ourselves on the back and have an éclair to celebrate."

Tyler and Susie laughed. I treated. We clinked éclairs, and as KC had said, they were delicious.

I went home with mixed feelings.

We were making long-needed progress on the Committee. I was encouraged. But I had questions about Tyler's role, or lack thereof, in Curtis's murder. He had snubbed my every effort to offer help, and been downright evasive when asked a direct question. Why? If he had a legitimate problem, shouldn't he ask for aid from his friends? My doubts had gone from *pianissimo* to *fortissimo* in one short conversation. Hoping I was wrong, I added Tyler to my mental list of suspects.

ABOUT FOUR O'CLOCK THAT AFTERNOON the phone rang.

"Hey, Em."

"Hi, Barry."

"I've been thinking how much I'd like your company tonight."

I had my evening planned. I'd almost finished a whodunit, and the characters were at a crucial place. I had to read them out of a tight fix. This last-minute plan left me cold. I hesitated.

Barry didn't seem to notice. "I have an early court case and I've got to get up at o-dark-thirty, but it would be nice to wake with you beside me."

When I was twenty I would have dropped everything for a lovers' tryst, but I had my heart and mind set on a quiet evening. Barry's warmth touched my heart, though. I decided to be flexible. "I'd love to see you, but I warn you. I'm tired and I won't be very good company."

"That's okay. I just want to hold you. Remind myself that the world is a good place."

Who could resist being the good in the world? My book would wait.

NINE

BARRY HAD GONE EARLY. After he left, I fell back to sleep but woke worried about KC and anxious to do something to help. Tyler's evasiveness bothered me, but I didn't know any way to investigate his part in the murder for now. While I walked Golden and fixed breakfast, I considered. Noah Wattle had told me that Mr. Matlow in 302 and Mr. Travers in 603 were among the most disgruntled residents of Homes at Skyridge, Strange Development's residential community. I looked up both their numbers and called Matlow first. *No answer.* When I tried Travers he said I could come out if I came out right away, because he had to leave at ten-thirty.

I agreed and scurried to the development as fast as I could. The Travers home was one of the smaller units. Around the basement windows the earth crumbled and showed signs of erosion, with little tracks where water had begun to carve a path downhill. Weeds covered the area.

"Hi. You must be Emily Wilson. Come on in."

The townhome was one of the base models. There were no cathedral ceilings or other special features.

"You said you wanted to discuss the residents' court case and take a look at some of the problems." He seemed a pleasant man, short, dark-haired, and eager to please.

"Yes. That's right."

"I'll be glad to show you around my place." He closed the door and led the way to the living room, where he sat in a straight-backed chair. "Does that mean Strange is going to be doing repairs soon?"

"I'm afraid not. I'm involved in investigating the death of Mr. Strange."

Mr. Travers face reddened and I feared for his blood pressure. "You mean to say the company *still* isn't living up to its commitments?"

Wanting to get his viewpoint I emphasized my lack of knowledge. "I don't have the complete story. Can you fill me in?"

"I have three kids and a wife. I spent every penny I had to get us into what I figured would be a nice place, a place we could finally make a home. And instead, there's been nothing but problems."

"Like what?"

"Upstairs, the tub is separating from the wall and slowly sinking. Every time you take a bath or a shower you pray you don't end up downstairs in the kitchen. And o'course the crack lets in the steam and water. God knows what's breeding inside that wall, but my wife has constant colds and headaches."

"That's a little scary."

"No kidding. Then too, we keep having trouble with the appliances. They should last longer than the two and a half years we've been here. This development was built three years ago. Strange should have fixed at least some of the problems." Mr. Travers's red face turned a blotchy purple as I watched.

I made a sympathetic noise.

He rose and began pacing. "Did you see the marks the bulldozer left outside?"

Without waiting for an answer he continued, his steps keeping rhythm with his breathing. "That's actually one of our few successes. I had problems with flooding in the basement. Noah Wattle got involved and Strange Corp. sent a bulldozer out. It took about ten minutes. They rearranged the drainage. When the water flows downhill, it goes away from the house now, instead of toward the basement windows."

"That must have been a relief."

"Yeah, except they haven't reseeded or sodded. Now the freshly turned earth is full of weeds. It's been three months and they haven't been back. I can't get a real person on the phone, and they don't respond to messages. My wife goes out there and pulls weeds in her spare time. I'll reseed when she's done. Better to do it myself than have a heart attack."

I almost said something when he continued.

"It's the principle of the thing. I've certainly paid Strange Corp. enough money to live in a maintenance-free community. They should follow up."

"I'm sorry you've been frustrated. As I understand, all of the residents are upset. Do you think anyone could have anything to do with Mr. Strange's death?"

"If they did, I'd like to kick their ass. Things have come to a complete halt since the murder, if they ever moved. Now there's a recording on. 'Please understand our growing pains. The Strange Company is undergoing a reorganization. Leave a message. We'll get back to you as soon as we can.'" Mr. Travers tsked. "The message started playing a couple days after Strange's death. I've heard it often enough that I have it memorized. Nobody gets back in touch. It's been two weeks now. I've been talking to Wattle, seeing if he can get any results, but he says he can't get through, either."

I felt totally sympathetic. "I certainly understand why you might be frustrated. I wish I could help." If vexation and anger were motives, Mr. Travers certainly qualified. "If you don't mind my asking, did you go to the symphony concert on July Fourth?"

He shrugged. "I don't mind telling you. Me and my whole family visited my sister. I took a couple extra days off and we spent a long weekend at her place. We can't celebrate much of anything here. She's been real good about hosting Fourth of July, Christmas, Easter. All the big holidays. If this ever gets worked out, I'll owe her big-time."

I stood. "I hope everything is solved, and soon. Thank you for your help."

As I unlocked the car to begin the drive back, my mind focused on Lila, Curtis's assistant. She hadn't seemed to like Curtis or Strange Development much, and hadn't mentioned the recording. Maybe I should talk to her again. I glanced at my watch: ten-fifteen. Just time to visit her before I started teaching.

Lila looked up as I entered the office of C.H. Strange Development.

I'd checked the office hours as I came in and thought of a reason to be there. "I'm sorry to bother you again but I think I must've left my phone here. I realized it after business hours yesterday. When I called on the landline this morning a recording answered, and I figured it'd be easiest to come in. I really have to get my phone back, and since I had to come pick it up anyway . . ."

Lila looked confused, as well she might, since the whole thing was fiction. "I didn't find any phone, but I haven't really looked."

I sat down with a thump in the chair beside her desk. "It's not here? Then where could it be?"

"I'm sorry. Losing a phone is upsetting. Your whole life's in there. I haven't seen it, though." She did sound concerned.

"It would be right here if I left it. I didn't go anywhere. Did anyone else come in?"

"No. There hasn't been any business done here since Mr. Strange died, except that the court cases go on, like I told you yesterday. I put on a recording to discourage questions, since there's nobody to transfer calls to or give directions. The lawyers call my cell directly."

One question answered.

"What's your phone number?" Lila picked up the receiver of her desk phone.

I froze. My phone was in my purse. If it rang, she'd realize the whole thing was a fib. Instead, I gave her my home land line. Needless to say, her effort brought no response.

I did my best to look disappointed. "You're right. It's not here." I leaned back in the chair and settled in. "How are you doing?"

"I'm okay. Why wouldn't I be?"

Brightening, I played the voyeur and leaned closer. "You and I both know someone murdered Curtis. It's been in all the news media. You saw him every day. You knew every detail of his business. Administrative assistants always do. Who do you think did it?"

Lila looked uncomfortable. "I'm sure I don't have even a teeny guess."

"But you must have all the details."

"No."

Well, *that* was uninformative. I changed my attack. "The paper said Curtis Strange served on the Symphony Board. They're city royalty. Did you ever meet any of the other Board members? "

"Once. A lady brought some papers for him to sign."

I channeled my sister Kathleen's enthusiasm. "Ooooo. Who was it? Maybe she killed him."

"I think she called herself Jane, but she didn't seem like a killer. Small and mousy. Lots of jewelry."

"Just think. You've might have done business with a *murderer*. He may have sat right in this chair. You must have a guess. You're in a position to know."

She seemed put off by this onslaught of words. "I really couldn't say."

"The papers said the murder happened during the big Fourth of July concert in City Park, in the open in front of God and everybody. Incredible. I was there. Were you?"

"My family and I never miss the fireworks."

"You *were* there, then. Isn't it frightening? That something like that could happen?" I wondered if there were Academy Awards in the category musicians-investigating-the-murder-of-a-Board-member. If so, I'd be a shoo-in.

"I really haven't thought about it that much." She had withdrawn somewhere far within.

"Oh, come on. Your boss is killed at a function where you are, where your family is, by somebody you probably knew, and you haven't thought about it?"

She sighed. "Was there anything else?"

I had no intention of leaving, despite her unmistakable hint. "If there were many court cases going, I'll bet Mr. Strange had lots of enemies."

"Prominent men do. He was prominent." She seemed a lot less forthcoming than the last time I'd talked to her. Why?

I remembered she'd told me she needed the job. She must be acting under orders to keep quiet. Or maybe she didn't want to reveal anything important. I didn't think I'd learn anything else, but I tried again. "How did you like working for Mr. Strange?"

"He had his flaws, like everybody." She seemed increasingly desperate, and her gaze darted over my shoulder and around the room.

"Who's taking over the business?" I knew the answer, but I hoped she'd tell me her thoughts.

"His nephew will inherit."

"You didn't tell me that last time. Maybe he'll be a better boss."

"I didn't find out about it 'til this morning, not that it's any of your business." Her politeness had reached its limits. "I had plans for lunch. I hope you find your phone." She stood.

I had no choice but to stand, too. "Oh, of course. Thank you. I must have done something stupid with it. Thank you for your patience."

As I drove home to teach, I reflected that Lila was a good possibility. She had been at the concert and, from what she hinted before, hadn't liked Curtis much. She'd implied that she wouldn't be sad to see him gone.

I had eliminated Travers but found Lila an interesting possibility. It was as important to eliminate suspects as to find them. I assured myself I was making progress.

At home Golden greeted me and turned belly up for a tummy scratch. After that, I just had time to fix and eat a quick salad before my first student. That afternoon I only had three since I planned to play trios at Steve and KC's tonight. I would donate my fee, since KC was a friend. I wanted to give myself time to rest a little before the gig, then go early and help her set up if I could before my trio started playing.

The gathering had been booked months ago, intended as a get-to-know-the-new-fiancée bash with Steve's clients. He couldn't cancel at the last minute without awkward explanations. So, unable to back out, and drawing on her restaurant experience, KC had cooked and arranged everything herself, from the selection of hors d'oeuvres and sandwich trays to pastries and candies, seemingly effortlessly, intending to show off her cooking skills, charm the guests, and provide much appreciated support for Steve. Although I offered, KC turned down my last-minute help, saying everything had been done. I noticed Tommy, from the restaurant, helping in the kitchen.

Knowing her private hell, I had to think that KC wasn't feeling very social. But as her guests arrived, I watched her tend to them, and she seemed happy and eager to meet them.

I said something to her at the trio's first break about how well the party was going. "You've done a fantastic job, KC. If I hadn't known what you're going through, I never would have guessed. Thank goodness the media hasn't connected you with Curtis' murder."

"There'll be no publicity unless something concrete turns up. Steve has seen to that. And to this point, everything's been circumstantial. The cops won't ever find any facts implicating me. They can't. I didn't do it."

That should be true, but I knew misunderstandings happened, and I worried.

KC smiled. "It's a relief to do something that's fun for me, and that I do well. I can forget my troubles for a few hours and concentrate on my guests. Besides, Steve's happy, and that's better than the best. He has almost unlimited faith in me. His confidence convinced me I could chat to anybody about anything. Otherwise, I'd run at the sight of all these dignitaries."

The guests appeared to be a roll call of local VIPs. I recognized Phil Hall, Regional Manager of the several Goodwill stores, and his wife Donna, who were hanging out with local restaurateurs Jackson and Beverly Johnson, owners of three comfort food restaurants. George and Liu Springer from the Art Museum were talking to Harvey Rice, representing the Environmental Responsibility

Foundation. Mel Harmon, bank president, my fellow Planning Committee member and a major donor and president of the Symphony Board, was deep in conversation with Darlene Taylor, president of the Tourist Bureau. Whew! No wonder KC wanted this get-together to go well.

Which it was.

At the second break I watched as KC laughed and chatted, moving from group to group, the perfect hostess, Steve proudly beaming at her elbow. She impressed me, even though I knew her potential. She must have everything running like a metronome in the kitchen. If I had been the hostess, I would have been stuck there. As her substitute mom, I allowed myself a moment of pure pleasure.

Mel took advantage of the musician's break to say hello.

Hoping to discover his whereabouts on the evening of the Fourth, I brought up the subject of the murder. "Do you believe the police haven't found Curtis's killer? They haven't even found the gun. I thought sure everything would be solved before now."

Mel laughed. "Give them some time. Eight days isn't long."

"You'd think they'd at least be questioning people. Nobody's asked me who I saw at the concert. How 'bout you?"

"Oh, I wouldn't be much help. I didn't go to the concert. I've seen the performance many times. I wanted some peace and quiet. I went to the mountains with a friend."

There went Mel as a suspect. Unless he was lying? "Really? Where'd you go?"

Mel avoided the question. "If everybody knew about it, it wouldn't be peaceful for long."

We laughed and I figured he had just politely told me to keep my nose out of his business. Was he lying? His answer didn't put that question to rest.

I glanced at my watch. "Time to get back to business. Nice talking to you, Mel."

After the party, I offered to help clean up, but KC refused. "Everything's disposable. All I need is a trash can. I'll take the leftovers to the shelter tomorrow. Go home and get some rest. I'll talk to you later."

TEN

SATURDAY, JULY 13, 2013, 9:00 A.M.

D OMESTIC VIOLENCE HAD MORE OF A ROLE in my life than I wanted. Both a student and her mother had been victims, and my ex-husband had been abusive, too. I wanted to help solve what I saw as a pervasive problem, so Saturdays I volunteered at the Supervised Visitation Center.

In my role, I observed court-ordered supervised visits between parents and their children, usually either because of domestic violence or substance abuse. First, I aimed to make sure the children were safe and not used as pawns in a legal battle. Secondly, I wanted to encourage caring relationships between non-custodial parents and their child(ren). I worked the morning shift from nine to one.

Barry had been fully supportive when I told him I would be volunteering. I'd told him about my relationship with my ex, and he understood that I felt strongly about eliminating domestic violence. At the Center, my all-time favorite client had been a burly ex-marine with tattoos, a swagger, and a muscle shirt, whose five-year-old daughter wanted to play dress-up week after week. So, week after week, to his daughter's great delight, he donned a glittery crown and draped a too-small ballet tutu over his clothes. It made my day.

Whatever experiences I had, I usually went home smiling, either because the clients were funny and heartwarming, or because I had an opportunity to help a child.

In the afternoon I taught flute students. In the evening I usually had a symphony concert, so Saturdays could be busy. Tonight I would play an outdoor Concert in the Parks. Old, familiar favorites were on the program. None of them had important flute parts since most were loud and showy.

As usual, this morning I volunteered at the Center. Sadly for me, the marine and his daughter had graduated, and new clients had replaced them. Golden, my retriever, volunteered with me. She had passed her Canine Good Citizen test and also graduated as a trained therapy dog. On top of that, she seemed to have a natural sense of who needed her and how to help. I first discovered her talents a little over a year ago when she comforted one of my flute students during a lesson. At the Center the kids loved her, and she could often help bridge awkward moments with their visiting parent.

First today, Mr. Briggs visited with his ten-year-old daughter, Melissa. They gossiped about school, played hopscotch, and drew houses and butterflies. An uneventful visit that didn't require either Golden or me until Mr. Briggs started asking Melissa about her home life.

"How's your mom?"

Asking about the other parent was strictly forbidden, since it often led to inquiries about the ex's dating life, schedule, etc. I stood behind Melissa, where she couldn't see, and drew my index finger across my throat, signaling Mr. Briggs to discontinue the conversation.

Fortunately, Melissa answered with only, "Fine, I guess."

Her dad looked annoyed, didn't respond for a moment, then asked a question about his daughter's drawing.

Crisis averted. I made notes on both his conversation and compliance.

Next, a young mom visited with her four-month-old baby. The infant slept at first, and Mom held the sleeping child, rocking peacefully. When the baby woke, Mom gave her a bottle, pacing and humming softly. After the infant finished, Mom stood and swayed gently while she draped the baby over her shoulder and burped it. Though the Center never told us why clients were there, I guessed this to be a substance abuse case, since the mom seemed not stoned but a little spacey, very concerned, and involved with the baby.

My third family was the Martins. Today would be Dan Martin's last supervised visitation with his daughter, Sarah, age seven. He and his wife had completed counseling and their divorce case, and he had been cleared for solo visits with Sarah every weekend. I always hated to see my regulars go, but joy at their progress toward a healed family overcame the sadness.

I smiled when I saw him. "I hear congratulations are in order."

His arms were full of daisies and toys, and he beamed. "It's true. This is our last visit. No offense, but I hope never to see you again. At least not here."

I laughed. "No offense taken."

The rules required Dan to arrive fifteen minutes before Sarah's mom brought her. He sat and waited quietly. Sarah took him by surprise when, several minutes later, she ran to him and jumped into his arms.

"Hi, Pumpkin." He nuzzled her cheek with his own.

She laughed and rubbed her cheek. "You're scratchy." She bounced on his lap. "Daddy, Mommy said this is our last visit here. You and I can go to the zoo next time!"

"That's right, Pumpkin."

"I can't wait."

Sarah adored Golden. She loved dogs and even though she didn't need Golden anymore, she always greeted her and talked to her. Now she hugged the dog. "Golden, I'll miss you. You're my bestest friend."

She turned to me. "Can we come back and visit?"

I didn't know what to say. Only clients were allowed in the Center. Saying goodbye was one of the sad parts of the job. But if I told Sarah that, she could take her disappointment out on her dad. I didn't want that. I couldn't lie to her, though. "It's against the rules to have visitors. If you want to be free to go places and do things, you'll have to say goodbye to Golden. But you and your dad will have lots of fun together. Golden will miss you, but she'll make other friends and you will, too."

Sarah started to cry.

Well done, Emily.

Her dad hugged Sarah and gave her the flowers he carried. "These are for you."

Sarah wiped her tears. "For me? Like a real grown-up?"

"Like a real grown-up."

She laughed and Golden and I quietly backed away. Thanks to her dad, Sarah didn't notice we had distanced ourselves. *Thank heavens.*

I made notes on both Sarah's outburst, and also on how Mr. Martin successfully distracted her.

Mr. Clearwater and his son Travis, thirteen, and daughter, Constance, nine, visited last. They seated themselves at one of the tables and began coloring, or at least Mr. Clearwater and Constance did.

Travis wasn't having it. He sat leaning back in the chair with his arms folded. "No way. The last time I colored I was five. I don't like coming here. There's nothing to do, and they won't let me play video games."

Uh-oh.

Mr. Clearwater glowered. "It's your mom's fault we have to meet like this. If—"

I interrupted. "Constance, those are beautiful colors you're using." I stood behind Constance, but Travis and Mr. Clearwater could see me. I signaled to break off this conversation.

"I just told Travis the truth. Somebody has to. If his mother hadn't lied to the judge—"

I crooked my finger at Mr. Clearwater and led him into the next room, where I told him, "I can't let you continue this conversation. The kids are not to be brought into disagreements between adults."

"But he should know—"

"If you can't disengage, I'll have to end the visit." This kind of situation stretched my comfort zone. It wasn't easy for me to lay down the law like this, but the kids deserved a comfortable and safe environment.

"But his mom lied. She said I'd threatened her and the kids—"

"This isn't a courtroom, Mr. Clearwater. You can stay and play with your kids, or I can send them back to their mother. It's your choice, but decide now. It'll be your last chance. I can't give you another."

Mr. Clearwater turned stop sign red and pointed his finger at me. "You . . . you . . ."

The security guard approached.

Mr. Clearwater seemed to realize the stakes and took a deep breath. "Alright, alright." After a long, awkward pause, during which he alternately held his breath and then sputtered, he began to breathe normally. Finally he returned to the kids' table.

Feeling the tension abate, the security guard returned to his position by the door.

"Since Travis doesn't want to color, why don't we find something else to do?" Mr. Clearwater's spoke loudly and he gave me a furious look. "How 'bout Clue?"

Constance picked up on her dad's hostility. Her voice small and wavery, she said, "Whatever you want, Daddy." She sounded afraid.

Golden placed herself protectively between Constance and Mr. Clearwater, leaning against the little girl's legs.

Constance used both hands to scratch Golden's ears.

"Travis?" Mr. Clearwater didn't sound like he expected a refusal.

"Fine." Travis rolled his eyes.

Mr. Clearwater got the game from the closet. He came back and slammed it onto the table.

Constance hugged Golden, who turned and licked her cheek.

Without a word Mr. Clearwater took out the weapons tokens and placed them on the game board, catching and holding my eyes when he positioned the revolver.

I took it as a threat, and I crossed my arms and made eye contact with the security guard.

The guard had been unobtrusively pressed against the wall, but when I caught his eye, he came closer.

Mr. Clearwater watched him approach and looked down at his fingers.

I wasn't worried. Using a metal detector, security had thoroughly checked all participants for weapons on the way in. An armed guard watched over us. What could Mr. Clearwater do to me? Instead of stressing, I made notes on Constance's apparent fear, Travis' complaints, and Mr. Clearwater's hostility and veiled threats.

The family played a silent game, Golden standing close to Constance. The tension relaxed a little when she won. They went on to their next game, this time talking and even laughing occasionally.

Once more, crisis averted. I hoped they had a better visit next time, but I felt glad that I, and Golden, had been there, for Constance's sake.

THE CONCERT THAT NIGHT WAS OUTDOORS in the orchestra shell in a small neighborhood park, with an audience of about a thousand. As expected, there were no exposed second flute parts and the program consisted of music we had performed before. I played on automatic.

Barry had come to the performance, and we went to my house together afterwards. It had been a long day. Glad to return Golden's affectionate welcome, I saw to her needs, then headed companionably to bed with Barry. He seemed happy to be with me and held me close until we both fell asleep.

ELEVEN

SUNDAY, JULY 14, 2013, 9:30 A.M.

As often happened on Saturday night, Barry had left in the middle of the night to attend to a client who had been arrested. I couldn't go back to sleep right away and finally nodded off again around four-thirty or five, with the result that I slept in, okay on a slow Sunday morning.

As I fixed a leisurely brunch for myself and Golden, I turned my mind to KC's plight and realized that, ironically, Bastille Day, the day French rebels stormed the Bastille and released the prisoners, was today. Our local "bastille" was doing its best to capture KC. A kind of Bastille Day in reverse. I wouldn't let it happen. I summoned my inner rebel and considered my options.

Noah Wattle, president of the Homes at Skyridge Homeowners Association, had let slip that besides Travers, whom I had already interviewed, Matlow, in 302, was among the most disgruntled residents. I found his phone number and called. He answered, and we made plans to meet at eleven.

Since there were no commuters on Sunday, I relaxed and enjoyed the drive.

Number 302 was one of the smaller units.

Matlow answered the door. He was a modest-sized man, taller than my 5'6" but not by much, and heavily muscled, with an air of restrained power—think Popeye's forearms. "Yes?"

"I'm Emily Wilson. We spoke earlier on the phone. Thanks for agreeing to see me. May I come in?"

"Sure." As he led the way to the living room he continued. "I suppose you have to find Strange's killer . . ."

Sounded like he assumed I was with the police. I didn't correct him.

". . . but whoever got the bastard did the world a service."

"You sound like you didn't like him much." An understatement. I sat in a straight-backed chair.

The furniture showed no traces of color, all dark brown, faux-leather I assumed, since a faint smell of newish plastic filled the room. No pictures or feminine touches like flowers or pillows intruded, but plenty of newspapers littered the area.

"What's to like?" He swept the papers from the couch onto the floor and seated himself there. "The bastard supposedly built decent houses, but he sure slapped this one together as cheaply as possible, never resolved complaints, and spent his money on high-powered lawyers hired to stave off clients' grievances instead of fixing things."

"I do know that everybody here has been very frustrated." I tried to sound as sympathetic as I could. "Were any more upset than the others?"

"I'm as frustrated—no, irate —as anybody."

"What specific problems have you had?" I hoped I wasn't opening a shaken soda can.

"What problems haven't I had?" He paused a moment, rolled his eyes upward, gazed at me again, and continued. "After the first year, everything started breaking."

"Can you give me specifics?"

"Sure. I'm keeping a list, and finding more every day." He picked up the list from the coffee table and started reading. "Floors are warped, doors and windows don't close right, furnace doesn't keep the house warm, dryer broken and replaced, washer broken and replaced, fridge broken and replaced." His voice became more strident. "That's not everything, but it pisses me off to talk about all the stuff that's not right. Where things have been replaced, they've been replaced by me or on the manufacturer's warranty. Who can do without a fridge? Ditto with the washer and dryer. Strange hasn't done a thing to reimburse me. Not one thing. And nothing's been fixed, a year later. The whole thing's been a rip-off."

I didn't move for fear that he might explode if I interrupted.

Matlow held his breath for a moment, then continued, at a higher pitch. "The mold in the basement worried me most. The window leaked, and Strange didn't fix it. Mold started growing down the wall board where the water dripped. I didn't want to try and repair it myself because I didn't want to void the warranty, but I finally caulked the window. That stopped the leak. Then I put bleach on the water trail. That seems to have taken care of it, but I want someone to come out and make sure it's been done right."

He halted briefly, his face getting redder.

"Not long after that, I discovered the roof leaked. I didn't want a repeat of the window fiasco, so I got up there and smeared some tar around. Took me four tries, but I finally got the leak stopped. It's risky for me to get on the roof—I get dizzy a lot—but I did it anyway. Gotta take care of my stuff."

Throughout this recitation his voice had been getting louder and more shrill. "What kills me is all this stuff is dangerous, healthwise. The company doesn't care. If I finally get hold of an actual person, I know what they're going to say. They're going to say I voided the warranty by doing some of the work myself. Cripes!"

I used my most sympathetic voice. "I'd say you have a right to be angry."

"That's why we formed the residents group. Almost everybody has at least one complaint."

"Seems like lots of people here would've had reason to murder Curtis."

"I'd have done it myself if I thought I could get away with it."

We were both silent a moment.

I searched his face for a hint of guilt, but saw only rage. I pressed on. "Were you at the concert at City Park on July Fourth?"

"That's where the bastard was killed, isn't it?"

I nodded.

He tsked and continued. "I was there by myself. I'm a bachelor. No one can vouch for me. I suppose that makes me a suspect. Since I'm being honest, I have to say if I'd known someone was murdering the weasel I would have gone and cheered."

"There were quite a few people at the concert who had motives and could have murdered Mr. Strange. Did you see anyone who might have committed the crime?"

"Nah. I felt like I was in a bubble. Didn't see anyone I knew, didn't make friends with anybody."

"Do you have a gun?"

"Sure. More than one. Gotta protect myself. All my guns are legal."

After a moment's silence he continued. "Just 'cuz I have them doesn't mean I killed anyone."

"No, it doesn't. I'm only trying to get complete information. Thanks for your cooperation. You can call the police department if you think of anything else."

"Do you have a card?"

I went through my purse as if looking. "I'm afraid I left them in my other bag. Ask for Lieutenant Gordon's office. Someone there will be able to help you." I left hurriedly, before he could ask any more questions.

As I returned to my Subaru, I reflected that Mr. Matlow made a strong suspect: motive up the wazoo, opportunity, knowledge of guns, and no alibi—and anger, *lots* of anger—maybe *too* much. He openly detested Curtis. Would he speak with such rancor if he were guilty? Maybe not: not if he were smart. But he could have figured openly hostile talk would *deflect* suspicion by making him sound too obvious. Or maybe Matlow couldn't help but give vent to his fury. I felt cautiously excited. When the police found the murder weapon, I'd bet it belonged to him.

WHEN I GOT HOME I CALLED BARRY. "I talked to a couple people that might be good suspects. I want to see what else I can find."

"Yeah?"

I described Matlow's rabid rage at Curtis, his presence at the Fourth of July concert, his knowledge of guns, and his lack of an alibi, then Lila's presence at the Fourth of July concert and her possible dislike of Curtis.

"Otherwise Matlow sounds like a good bet, but he's awfully open about his presence at the concert and his familiarity with guns. Bothers me a little. Seems like those are things he would have hidden if he were guilty." Barry's voice sounded thoughtful.

"Maybe." That comment played into my own worries. "Or maybe not."

Barry's lack of enthusiasm had squelched my excitement. I felt like my two good possibilities weren't any good after all. "Well, I guess I'll let you go."

"Okay, Em. Didn't mean to spoil your mood. Love you."

Normally the "L" word is a treat from Barry, and reflexively I responded, "Love you, too," but I felt distracted by the conflicting theories I had about Curtis's murderer. Barry might be right about Matlow.

I wasn't concentrating on my afternoon students like I would have liked. Finally, I realized my students deserved better, put the questions out of my mind, and refocused on the job, and the joys, at hand.

TWELVE

MONDAY, JULY 15, 2013, 9:00 A.M.

OPO President Rex Minoa had scheduled our meeting for first thing in the morning at his house. Beforehand, I got up early and squeezed in my usual walk with Golden and a short practice session. I'd have to put my investigation on hold until after the meeting, but I felt enthusiastic about our contributions. For once Susie, Tyler, and I had good news.

After OPO approved the minutes of the last meeting, we reviewed the Planning Committee's suggested higher salaries and increased work for musicians. Tyler had a questionnaire ready to go and presented it as well.

Rex said, "In my opinion, a questionnaire isn't necessary. You said speed is important." He eyed each of us. "The players elected us to represent them, and I can't imagine there would be any objections to the proposed increase. Four paid musical services aren't many. It won't be a shock to the symphony budget. I haven't heard from anybody who's against increasing work. A few people might think it isn't a big enough increase, but we have to represent everyone. What do you all think?"

We discussed the issue and the rest of the committee agreed

with Rex. We took a vote on the proposed increase, which passed unanimously.

A few more items needed attention. One of the string players had filed a complaint after being put on notice, and a player who fell on the ice during our annual ice show claimed management had provided inadequate scaffolding. She'd filed for worker's comp. Luckily, there'd been no hint of a lawsuit since all parties were cooperating. The Board had requested a medical report, and the player had sent us a copy. We dealt with those items, then adjourned. I felt a subtle sense of satisfaction. We were helping our colleagues.

I HAD ARRANGED A MEETING WITH JOHN REEVES, head of the environmental coalition fighting Antelope Run, scheduled for one. I grabbed a quick lunch at a fast-food restaurant, then went to meet him.

His office was in a not-so-good section of town a few blocks south of the courthouse. I hunted for it for at least ten minutes. My GPS said I had arrived, but I couldn't find the address. When I stopped a passerby to ask directions, it turned out the office sat *behind* the buildings fronting the street in what must have been a garage at one time.

The inside wasn't any more impressive than the outside. I walked up three hollow-sounding wooden steps to enter a room about the size of my living room. With no reception area and only two small windows, located high on the wall, I could clearly see Reeves. His desk had been pushed into a corner and almost hidden by messy stacks of paperwork. They were the only things in the room besides filing cabinets lined side-by-side against a wall, and two barely padded chairs, one blue, one green, placed close to Reeves's desk.

"Hi. You must be Ms. Wilson."

His smile welcomed me.

"That's right. I called earlier."

From behind the desk he half-stood and stretched out his hand. "Good to meet you."

I clasped his hand, then sat in the green chair.

He reseated himself. "I understand you have questions about Antelope Run. It's been known as Butterfly Hollow for years. Only in the last few months has Strange Development started calling it 'Antelope Run.' I prefer Butterfly Hollow. It's as much an affirmation as anything else. If I have my way Antelope Run will never be developed. The area will remain Butterfly Hollow."

"From your lips to God's ears. I saw it for the first-time last week. It's a paradise."

Sgt. Serna had asked me not to discuss the body until the family had been notified. Now that they knew about it, I could have mentioned the discovery, but I wouldn't unless it had some bearing on our discussion.

Mr. Reeves smiled. "It seems like I remember a song. 'They paved paradise and put up a parking lot.'"

We both laughed.

I sobered. "Really, it's not funny. I understand the area is threatened by development."

A frown creased Reeves's forehead. "I'm afraid so. Strange Development Corp. wants to pave the stream and make it an irrigation ditch. It'll play havoc with the wildlife there."

"That can't happen. I'd like to help. Can you tell me what I can do?"

The smile returned to his face. "Right now, things are looking up. The Colorado Water Conservation Board has filed for an injunction to stop development. They're concerned about their instream water rights, since the planned drainage ditch will eradicate the stream. And frankly, the death of the developer, Curtis Strange, has given us a reprieve. All progress on their end has been halted while details of inheritance and succession are worked out."

"Do you know anything about what will happen?" Feeling relieved by his positive confidence, I settled back in the chair.

Reeves hesitated. "We'll have to wait to see who's in charge."

My chance meeting with Roland had provided the answer, but I wanted to find out what Reeves knew. "Who actually owns the land?"

"Unfortunately, C.H. Strange Development Corporation owns

the property. I couldn't tell you who will call the shots at the company at this point, but they can do what they will with both the company and Butterfly Hollow. Again, though, this water rights snafu may work in our favor."

I paused to put my thoughts together. "There's something that's been puzzling me." I paused again, unsure how to proceed. Land deals weren't my thing. "Butterfly Hollow is located an hour from the city. It's not far for a moderately determined outdoorsman, but it's certainly not close to city amenities. That's probably why it's untouched. Why would Strange Development be interested?"

"It may be far from amenities now, but the city is projected to grow rapidly in that direction as population increases. Strange Development snapped up the land while it was cheap. In a decade or so it'll be prime property if projections are right." He shrugged. "The company stands to profit from both the land and the homes it develops. For the developer, it's a no-lose deal. Even if they don't build, they can sell the land at an appreciated price."

"I understand you're the leader of an environmental coalition to save Butterfly Hollow. Can you tell me who's in the coalition?"

"Sure." Reeves leaned back in his chair, laced his fingers behind his head, and crossed his legs at the knee. "There's Coloradans to Save Our Open Spaces; Fresh Air and Clean Water; and Coloradans for a Sustainable Future. Citizens for Lincoln County can't contribute any money, but they've been helping out with volunteers. Our coalition recently received a grant from the Environmental Responsibility Foundation to help preserve Butterfly Hollow."

"Isn't the Foundation Harvey Rice's group?"

"That's right. Do you know him?"

"Slightly. And his wife, too. I'm in the symphony and she's on the Symphony Board."

"The symphony! I used to play clarinet. Only thing I play now, though, is CDs."

We both laughed. I'd heard the joke a million times, but I appreciated the light-hearted approach of an aficionado and music lover.

"You might speak to Harvey." He shifted forward and leaned his forearms on the desk. "He's personally interested in Butterfly

Hollow. Used to go there on Boy Scout campouts. Later, he took his sons there. The whole family slept under the stars. Learned about nature and ecosystems. He's an old park ranger, you know. Camps there when he has time."

"He sounds like a good person to have on your side."

"Yeah. We're lucky he's a friend. Wouldn't want him to be otherwise."

"Why not?" Was Reeves afraid of Harvey?

He shrugged. "Harvey's a celebrity. A real VIP on the local scene. Everybody knows him and he's got friends everywhere."

I relaxed.

"Can't afford for him to use his connections against us." Reeves unlaced his fingers and put his feet back on the floor.

"Well, then I'm glad he's with Butterfly Hollow, too."

"What's your interest in this?" John sat back in the chair.

"Curtis Strange served on the Symphony Board."

"Yeah. I heard that."

I continued. "I gathered there were environmental concerns with his planned development. Last week I went to see the Hollow for myself." I leaned forward. "It's an incredible place."

Again, I didn't mention the body.

I continued. "I decided I couldn't let Butterfly Hollow fall to developers. I came to see what I could do to help."

"You seem pretty well connected." He sounded thoughtful.

"I don't know about being connected, but music does bring people together."

"You can get involved in several ways." Reeves enumerated them, holding up a finger. "You can donate money."

I didn't have much money to give.

He saw my face and held up two fingers. "You can contact Citizens for Lincoln County. They're coordinating the volunteer front. I'm sure they can use you."

That would fit into my budget better, and might be just as helpful.

"And . . ." He held up three fingers. ". . . you can put in a good word for us with the Rice's, Harvey and Jane. You never know when the right word in the right ear will help."

"I don't think of myself as having much influence, but I *will* certainly put in a good word for Butterfly Hollow whenever I can, and with whomever I can." I smiled as I thought of it. "You've been very good to give me your time. I'll let you get back to work."

"Don't think twice about it. You've brightened my day."

I JUST HAD TIME TO CHANGE MY CLOTHES before my first student arrived at four. I taught her and then another student. KC's lesson was last, at five.

She seemed quiet and subdued. I could see why Steve worried.

"KC, before we start your lesson, I wanted to talk about a few things."

"Thank goodness! I've been worried, and I haven't been able to concentrate on practicing at all. It seems overwhelming to think about trading in the wonderful life I have now for a jail cell."

"I wouldn't worry about that. Simple robbery looks like a good possibility. Sometimes the simplest explanation is the best one."

KC didn't respond at all.

"And I haven't heard a flattering comment yet about Curtis. He had lots of enemies, many of whom were at the Fourth of July performance, I'm sure. My latest discovery is that one of the residents of Homes at Skyridge, who expressed intense anger at Curtis, attended the concert."

"Oh?"

"Curtis, in his usual uncaring way, hadn't done necessary repairs. The homeowner knows about guns and has a few."

KC didn't seem cheered.

I continued, trying to bring her natural optimism out. "Besides that, according to the internet and Curtis's assistant, the company was under fire from all sides. There were lawsuits from tenants about non-performance of contract obligations, lawsuits about poor drainage on finished projects, and pressure from environmentalists."

"You've been busy." KC had opened her flute case, but it remained in her lap, the pieces unassembled. "Tell me."

I summed up what I had learned.

"You found all that out from the internet?"

"And Curtis's administrative assistant. Plus, John Reeves, head of the environmental coalition opposing Antelope Run, one of Curtis's projects, filled in more details. Several groups are involved in the battle to save Butterfly Hollow, where Curtis planned to put Antelope Run. The Hollow is an unbelievably beautiful area, complete with animals, birds, wildflowers, and butterflies. They deserve to be protected. It would be a shame to lose all that, and Curtis's efforts to develop the area earned him a lot of enemies." I hope I didn't sound like an evangelist, but I felt strongly. "Who knows how many of them might be suspects."

KC remained silent a moment. "I hate to be discouraging, but all that sounds pretty far-fetched." She looked directly at me. "It seems like there would have to be something personal to goad a person to murder. Usually, I would say that sex has something to do with it, but in this case if you follow the sex, it leads straight to me. That's not right, you know?"

"I've just started looking," I said, defensively. I could feel KC's distress. "I'm waiting for a call back from the Scout who discovered the body. And money could be involved. Going back to robbery. It seems likely Curtis would have had a lot of donations in his collection basket, but they're all missing. And I met Curtis's nephew a few days ago. As the sole living relative he'll inherit everything, if there's anything but debts. He claims he didn't know about the murder 'til the lawyer called him, but he could be lying. I need to investigate him." I paused, waiting for congratulations that didn't come. Defensively I continued. "Who knows how many personal grudges Curtis stirred up?"

KC's smile seemed forced, and she fiddled with the latch on her flute case. "I've been thinking. A lot. Curtis's murder is almost all I think about, and I've thought about grudges." She paused. "Do you remember when I sounded out Curtis about whether he liked being a developer? We talked about it when I helped you with your case a couple years ago."

"I remember."

"He said he liked power. Being in charge. If he threw his weight around, maybe he made the wrong person mad, you know?"

I thought for a moment. "That's a good possibility. I'll follow all the angles and keep poking around."

KC's eyes filled with tears. "Any of the people at the concert would have had opportunity. In a crowd like that, the murder could have been an accident, with someone else the intended victim. Or, as you say, it could have been a routine robbery. And lots of people had motives to kill Curtis, as you've found from only a short search. Even the method of death isn't an issue. Obviously a gunshot killed him, but at the Fourth of July concert nobody noticed another loud noise. The cannon shots and fireworks drowned out the blast. Unless the police find the specific gun and match it to the bullet that killed Curtis, it's a totally anonymous crime. And the circumstantial evidence points at me, you know? How can I prove I didn't kill him?"

I said, "We don't have to prove you *didn't* do it, we just have to find the person who *did*." I put my hand on her arm. "Look, KC. It's true that there were thousands of people at the concert with opportunity. But even Curtis didn't have *that* many enemies. I don't think there's any reason to be discouraged. The people who didn't like him were legion. It should be easy to find someone with a motive. All we have to do is find the unique gun, the one that killed Curtis."

KC looked at me hopelessly. "That's impossible."

She didn't seem to have internalized my reassurances. "This isn't like you. You're just seeing difficulties."

"It will take Lieutenant Gordon's cooperation to run tests if we find anything. I don't think he's all that interested in finding a suspect other than me." A single tear leaked from KC's eye.

She'd allowed her feelings to get the best of her. "The police are after the truth, not on a witch-hunt. The lieutenant's not really such a bad guy, even though he's been wrong a lot. He won't neglect anything that comes up. Besides, he won't be able to find a gun he can tie to you. That'll give him incentive to look harder."

At that she finally brightened. "That's true." She began to assemble her flute and changed the subject. "Since I haven't practiced, can we sight-read this time?"

"Sure." I went to my music cabinet and pulled out some duets. "I know just the thing."

I put my flute together and we played Telemann Duets for the remainder of the half hour. By that time, KC had relaxed. She even managed a smile and a goodbye hug.

Hoping we would find the solution soon, I put my flute away.

That evening I logged on to the computer to find out what I could from the internet about Darlene Taylor, Mel's friend, the one I had overheard at the birthday party berating Curtis the day after his death, and then seen again at the art show's gallery opening.

The internet wasn't a whole lot of help, although I could put two and two together. Mostly what I found were news articles on her appointment by the mayor to the position of president of the Tourist Bureau. The articles mentioned that she'd been the first black female appointed to the position, and expressed optimism about her goal of protecting natural surroundings in the area from unbridled growth. They quoted her as saying, "We are fortunate to be able to lure tourists to the area with our spectacular natural attractions. We cannot allow those attractions to be damaged by economic predators."

"Economic predators." Pretty strong language. But you'd find Curtis's picture in the dictionary next to the term. He and Darlene would be on opposite sides of the battle for just about everything. I'd have to add her to my ever-growing list of Curtis's enemies.

THIRTEEN

TUESDAY, JULY 16, 2013, 9:30 A.M.

T HE NEXT MORNING MY APPOINTMENT with Harvey Rice was at ten. I fed Golden and headed to the Environmental Responsibility Foundation. Located in the ritziest part of town, a beautiful old two-story mansion had been converted for the purpose of serving as the Foundation's headquarters.

When I got there, a white bus marked "City of Monroe Recreation" took up most of the small lot behind the building. I assumed a group of kids was visiting the mansion. Sure enough, when I went into the building, I saw that the children were younger, maybe between five and eight years old, and were seated cross-legged looking up at a puppet stage crowned with the words, "Protect Our Local Wildlife."

Apparently, the kids had already seen the show and moved on to the question-and-answer period. A little red-haired girl with pigtails and freckles raised her hand. "I had a soda last night. I didn't see any plastic rings. Did I hurt a bird? I didn't mean to." She started to cry.

The puppet, a bird, answered. "Squaaak. Don't cry." He pointed to the plastic ring on a demonstration soda can. "If you cut these rings apart before you throw them away, it won't hurt us birds. It won't wrap around our necks and beaks. Or you can ask your mom to buy soda in bottles with a cardboard carrier. That'll help protect me and all my friends."

A small black boy responded with compassion and patted the girl's shoulder. "'S'okay. Our moms can fix it. They always do."

A wriggling boy raised his hand. Speaking loudly he announced, "I have to pee."

The bird puppet looked to the left. "Maybe Miss Gail can help with that." A young girl who looked to be in her late teens rushed to reach the boy and led him away.

The bird raised a wing to call on a girl dressed in pink baseball cap, pink shorts, pink blouse, pink socks, and pink shoes. I guess she liked pink. Before the girl could speak, a boy called out, "I'm hungry. We're s'pposed to have a snack. Will it have peanuts? 'Cuz I'm allergic to peanuts."

"Yeah," one of the older children agreed loudly.

Chaos broke out as the kids asked for their snacks.

Glad I wasn't one of the puppeteers, I skirted the group and climbed a wide marble stairway with a carpet runner to the second floor where Harvey's office was situated.

In what must have been a corner bedroom suite once, built-in bookcases covered one wall. A gigantic cherrywood desk holding a single folder sat in front of the shelves.

Harvey stood, left the desk, and crossed the room to greet me. A handsome man in his fifties, he hugged me and kissed my cheek. "Good to see you. How's Golden?" He and Jane, his wife, were devoted animal lovers. They had four dogs and three cats of their own, and Jane served on the Board of the local Humane Society. As my fellow Planning Committee member, Jane had avidly followed Golden's progress through obedience school and therapy dog school and passed the news of our progress on to Harvey.

"She's fine. A godsend with the visitation kids. They love her."

"Who wouldn't? She's super friendly. Everybody's ideal dog." Harvey had met Golden briefly at a symphony picnic and, apparently, fallen in love.

He took my elbow and escorted me across the room to an antique chair upholstered in red velvet close to the desk. He continued to hold my elbow as I seated myself. "Can I get you anything? Coffee? Iced tea? Water?"

The fuss he made embarrassed me. "I'm fine. Thank you."

He seated himself behind the desk and pushed a dish of candy toward me. "Help yourself."

They were melt-away mints. I had never been able to resist them so, diet or no, I popped one in my mouth and put three in my purse for later.

"You said on the phone you had some questions about one of our projects. What can I help you with?"

"It's Butterfly Hollow, or maybe you know it as Antelope Run."

A cloud passed across Harvey's face, and his professional and perpetual smile disappeared for an instant, so fast I wasn't sure I had seen it go. "Yes?"

"I heard about it and visited for the first time last week." Skipping over the part about Golden's unearthing the body, which didn't seem germane, I enthused. "What a wonderful area! The peace of nature in spades. I understand it's in danger from developers."

He nodded. "You heard right. That's how the Foundation got involved." He leaned back in his chair. "The owner needed money to pay medical bills after his wife died, and he put the property up for sale. Butterfly Hollow has been a part of my life since I was very young, and I encouraged the county to buy it. Even offered funding to help." He paused and thought a moment, and I saw the cloud come and go again before he continued. "Unfortunately, C.H. Strange Development outbid the county. The seller needed funds as soon as possible. He sold to the developers when they made an offer."

"Did he know Strange Corp.'s plans for the area?"

"He owed a bundle. I think he took a what-I-don't-know-won't-hurt- me approach and never asked."

A frown creased Harvey's forehead. "Curtis had the nerve to ask the Foundation to help support development with a grant. He argued that it would be a win-win. He would use our name in advertising, and we could monitor things. Make sure no one did environmental damage in the building process. No damage! How can you take out a stream, pave a natural area, and not cause damages? And you can bet he wouldn't allow us to truly monitor things. Add to that it's a profit-making business. Naturally, I laughed him out of my office."

He took a mint and picked at the wrapper. "We've been involved in a fight ever since. We're part of a coalition of interests trying to block development. We didn't have much hope until the Colorado Water Conservation Board got involved. They're asking for a court injunction. They have a better claim than the coalition ever did."

"I don't understand the ins and outs of the law, but wouldn't the courts consider the damage Strange Development planned?"

"Damage is just imaginary until it actually happens." Harvey sighed. "Landowners downstream would have to prove they had actually suffered erosive damage before the courts could get involved. By then, it'd be too late. The stream'd be gone, along with the ecosystem it created. The concrete ditch would be in its place and the increased flow speed would have caused injury to the landowners' property. In the meantime, birds and beavers don't bring lawsuits."

A depressed silence followed.

The smile returned to his face. "But as I say, things are looking up. The Water Conservation Board's well-funded, with a good claim. And I hate to be a ghoul, but Curtis's murder has helped, too. Right now Strange Development is frozen until whoever inherits the property takes over."

I weighed my words carefully, but decided I had to know. "How would it affect things if a body was discovered in the Hollow?"

Harvey looked at me curiously. "A body?"

Since the Sheriff had already notified Joe's family, I explained about Golden's discovery.

"Hmm. I guess it'd depend on how law enforcement handles it. I can't imagine it being more than a temporary delay, though."

I tended to agree.

"There's the possibility that, if the court nixes destroying the stream, Strange might be open to reselling to us. In that case, depending on how much they asked, we'd try to buy back the land."

A stunning brunette in her late twenties opened the door. Petite, she had a spectacular figure that wasn't hidden by her tailored skirt suit. "Mr. Rice, your eleven o'clock is here."

Harvey went to the door and, standing *awfully* close, took her hand, put his arm around her, and drew her into the room. "Danielle, I want you to meet Ms. Wilson. She plays flute with the Symphony and is on the Planning Committee with Jane. Danielle is my intern."

I stood and put out my hand. "Nice to meet you."

He hadn't removed his arm from around Danielle's waist.

She blushed and stepped outside Harvey's reach to shake my hand, but not before giving him a sensual glance, punctuated by a wink I was certain I wasn't supposed to see. "Nice to meet you, too." She dropped her hand and lowered her gaze. "I didn't mean to interrupt."

I picked up my purse. "It's okay. We had finished." I turned to Harvey. I guess it was kind of snarky of me, but I felt it necessary to remind him he had a wife. "I'll see you later. Say hello to Jane for me."

There was an awkward silence, and his Adam's apple bobbed up and down.

Danielle turned her face away.

I didn't rescue them and waited for an answer.

Finally, Harvey said, "Sure thing."

Whew! Something was going on between those two. As I got into my car and turned the key, I wondered if Jane knew.

I'D GONE HOME, HAD LUNCH, and basked in that luxury of luxuries, a practice session without obligations. I could play both the Concert in the Parks programs and the trio sonata music easily. After I'd done my scales and daily exercises I gave myself permission to play anything I wanted, for fun. I had gotten to the middle of a Telemann Unaccompanied Fantasia when the phone rang.

"Emily, I need to know whether I'm being unreasonable."

Kathleen was upset. From her tone this would be a long conversation. I laid my flute on the kitchen counter and perched on a stool. "What's going on?"

"I'm really annoyed. Maybe angry is a better word." She paused. "I don't want to sound like a witch, but I need to vent."

"Your feelings are always important, Kathleen. You shouldn't be squelching them, whatever they are. What's up?"

"It's Paul. We were at the movies last night when his cell phone rang. I begged him not to take the call, but he said it was work and he had to answer it. Sure enough, he told me, 'Duty calls. I've gotta go,' and gave me two choices. Either I could sit there alone and finish the movie and a squad car would pick me up; or I could leave with him and he would drop me off on his way to wherever he went."

Sounded like a tough choice to me. For Paul, too. But he had considered Kathleen's feelings and given her a choice, including a plan to let her finish the movie. About the best that could be done under the circumstances, in my opinion. "What did you do?"

"Half the fun of going to a movie with him is sitting in the dark and holding his hand while the world is a million miles away. Well, *that* wasn't happening. Besides, there's no telling how long it would take the squad car to get there, and by that time I was pretty upset, even though I didn't say so. I picked the second option. He dropped me off, then didn't call."

"What bothered you most? That he interrupted the movie, or that he didn't call?"

"Both, I guess, but mostly that we couldn't have one uninterrupted evening to ourselves. And after I bought a new sweater and had my nails done! It's not the first time it's happened. Until the day he died, Bill would *never* have treated me like that. Scrapping our plans and leaving me alone!"

True. But Bill had a different kind of job. Kathleen needed to learn to be more understanding, more flexible.

I don't know that I was the best person to give relationship advice, but I tried. "Well, why don't you talk to Paul? Maybe he could get someone else to be on-call, or not attempt outings with you when he's likely to be called away. Beyond that . . ." I hesitated.

"What?"

"You have to understand he has to give his job priority. Even over you. He's in a position where he has to be available. Maybe he can work some things out. But you can't interfere. Not if you want to have a successful relationship, anyway." Listen to me. I sounded like I knew what I was talking about.

"Easy for you to say."

"True."

She sighed. "You think I should have a calm discussion of the alternatives when the time is right?"

"Definitely calm. Otherwise you *will* seem like a witch." I'd shared all the wisdom I had, such as it was. After a short pause I changed the subject. "How are Charlie and Ana doing?"

"Whenever I've talked to him he sounds gloriously happy. That's good, but I kind of feel like I'm unnecessary now."

"Pish tosh. You're his mother. No one will ever replace you."

"I guess."

I didn't have any other wisdom to offer. I tried a different tune. "Have you heard from Mom?"

"I talked to her a couple days ago. She's excited. Her boyfriend is flying out on Friday. She's looking forward to it."

"She's cute." I chuckled. "She's like a teenager about him."

"About as serious, too. Her family's her real concern. Or at least I think it is. She's always interested in my problems."

Personally, I wished Mom would get serious about something else. She needed some interests in her life that weren't vicarious.

"What about you, Emily? What's new?"

"I've been busier than I like. Committees, volunteering, gigs, symphony concerts. All the usual stuff. But the really important thing is helping KC. She's worried, and I can't stand to see her upset. Curtis's murder could have been as simple as a robbery gone wrong. I'm gonna have to leave that to the police to investigate, since I don't have the resources. Other than that, I've found proof that Curtis was a real sleaze, as if we didn't already know that." I moved into the living room and a more comfortable chair. "His business practices were pretty shoddy and environmentally unsound. He had a lot of enemies."

"That sounds hopeful, as far as proving KC's innocence, I mean. Is there anything I can do to help?"

"Not that I can see. I just have to keep at it until I narrow the suspects down to the killer. You'd better stay out of it. I don't want to add complexities to your relationship with Paul." Sounded like she had enough to deal with in that area.

"Thanks, Emily. That's considerate."

I didn't have anything else to say. "I really have to get back to practicing . . ." a lie, ". . . and I'll let you go. Remember I love you." That was the truth, even though sometimes we fought like dissonant notes.

"Thanks for talking to me, Emily. You always make me feel better."

"I'm glad."

FOURTEEN

I HAD FED GOLDEN AND FIXED MY BREAKFAST when the phone rang.

"Hey, lady."

"Barry! What's up?"

"I've been thinking about Matlow."

"So have I. Can you suggest to Paul that he test Matlow's guns against the bullet that killed Curtis?"

"Great minds think alike. I planned on it. It's an important case. Paul should be able to push the tests through. Hopefully, they'll only take a few days. Maybe Matlow's our man."

"What about Lila?"

"She's not such a good possibility. The motive is flimsy, and we don't know anything about her and guns." Barry sounded skeptical.

"Still, nothing disqualifies either Matlow or Lila from suspicion. They both were at the concert. They both had opportunity. Matlow had his own gun, according to him. Lila's a mystery as far as gun possession goes. Do you think the police will do a search?"

Barry didn't answer right away, and I heard the sound of computer keys tapping.

"Don't know, Em. All I can do is ask."

"Maybe ballistics'll match up Matlow's gun with the fatal bullet and KC won't be the suspect anymore. Or they'll find the murder weapon in Lila's possession. Good luck with the police. Let me know how it works out."

"Will do. I'll get right on it."

About an hour later, in the midst of a practice session, the phone rang.

"Hello. This is Elena Pascal. I understand you want to talk to the scout who discovered Curtis Strange's body."

"That's right. Thank you for calling. I know that night can't have been pleasant."

"That's putting it mildly. My son, Kevin, is the one who found Mr. Strange. I called instead because the whole incident distressed him in the extreme, and I don't want him dragged through it again. I don't think he's ever seen a dead person before, let alone one who died violently, and seeing the body and talking to the police disturbed him enough. I don't want him to relive it." She paused a moment. "Scooter said you're working for a 'friend.'" I heard the air quotes around the word. "I don't know if you're truly working for a friend, in which case you're true blue, or if you're really the one under suspicion, but I don't want Kevin upset again."

"I understand. No doubt I'd feel the same way. Maybe you can help me, and I won't have to bother Kevin."

"Well." She hesitated. "I'll try. I do want the truth to come out."

"I'm trying to find out who approached Mr. Strange's volunteer table, and who might have seen something."

"I'm afraid I won't be much help. My husband and I were chaperoning the outing, along with the Listers and Scooter, the scoutmaster. Mr. Strange's donation booth was ahead of us and to the left. The boys had gotten more and more antsy before the concert started and while the orchestra played the early pieces. We chaperones were busy trying to keep the boys quiet and occupied. I remember how relieved I felt when it started to get dark knowing the fireworks would start soon. I figured that would occupy the boys."

"Could you see Curtis? Was he alive?"

"As I say, the boys kept me busy—not just busy, but frantically busy—keeping them engaged. I really wasn't paying attention. I was vaguely aware of a person at the booth just before the *1812 Overture* and thought it odd they weren't settled for the fireworks. Anyway, Mr. Strange must have been alive then."

That must have been immediately before the murder. Maybe she'd actually seen the killer. "Did you notice any details?"

"Sorry." She hesitated. "Just a red, white, and blue shirt. I'm not even sure if the person was male or female. By that time it was dark, and I had focused my attention on the boys."

That didn't help. It would describe most of the people in the city on the Fourth of July. "Do you have contact information for the other chaperones? Did you say 'Lister' is their name?"

"You can understand this has been traumatic for everyone concerned." She paused only a moment. "I'll handle it the same way Scooter did. I'll give your phone number to them, and they can call back or not."

"That would be fine. Thank you for your help."

Without replying or responding, she hung up.

THAT EVENING MY TRIO HAD BEEN HIRED for a garden party at Diane Gelbart's. She had set up chairs for us outside next to the patio wall, sheltered by the eaves and an awning. The solid wall would help us hear each other better, and we were out of the way and protected from the weather if any storms developed. I would rather have been inside since the sound would carry better, but that wasn't Diane's plan. "I want to tempt people to come outside. It's such a beautiful night!"

I set up stands, and we'd been playing for about half an hour when we paused to get the next piece up.

"Emily!"

I should have known that Jane and Harvey would be here. The Symphony Board is a small world. The Planning Committee is an even smaller world, and Diane and Jane belonged to both.

"Jane!" I stood and we hugged.

"It's always such a pleasure to hear you all play. Soothing." Jane was dressed to "kill" in a clingy red floor-length evening gown with a mermaid neckline. Glittering diamonds dangled from her ears, and a huge diamond solitaire pendant blinded me. Her outfit overshadowed her, but I could see, even in spite of my ignorance of high fashion, that the dress had to be expensive, almost as pricey as the diamonds, maybe made just for her. I thought she'd looked better when I'd seen her in forest green with fewer jewels, but what do I know? I'm an orchestra member. My whole wardrobe is black.

Right then Diane appeared at her side. "Jane, you look fabulous. What a gorgeous dress!"

Thankfully, she relieved me of the burden of conversation. The trio got back to playing.

The two women didn't move away and I heard Diane clearly. "Where did you ever find it?"

Jane smiled and blossomed at the praise. "I have a seamstress who creates these things. She's a treasure."

I'd guessed right. The dress had been specially made for her.

While the two friends were oohing and aahing, Harvey had melted away.

The trio played for another twenty minutes before our first break. I went in search of a rest room and found one in a long dark corridor.

Harvey and his intern, Danielle, were having a tête-à-tête near the end of the hall. He stood close, bending over her, holding himself with his forearms pressed against the wall. She responded sensually, shoulders against the wall, hips pressed forward touching him, totally absorbed, looking up into his eyes.

Danielle didn't really fit in here. She knew all these people, but wasn't one of them. I couldn't help thinking that she looked much more elegant in her simple royal blue dress highlighted by a tiny sapphire solitaire, than Jane did in her expensive, specially made gown and diamonds. Intern's salaries being what they were, I'd bet Danielle had found her dress on the rack, on sale, at a local department store after prom. Her looks, personality, and youth made the inexpensive gown and almost invisible pendant sizzle.

Harvey and Danielle were on the other side of the rest room and several doors down. Since they were totally absorbed in each other, I pretended not to see them and ducked quickly into the bathroom. I spent a long time, not wanting to run into them and figuring that they would have time to clear the area if I waited awhile. Finally, I exited, poking my head out cautiously. They were gone, but I wondered once again if Jane suspected they had a closer relationship than CEO and intern.

During our second break, between hours two and three, I saw Jane, alone, searching. "Emily, have you seen Harvey? I'm ready to leave. I've looked around, and I can't find him." She seemed annoyed.

"I haven't seen him for a while. Have you checked inside?"

"I will. I just thought he'd be out here. It's much cooler, and the music's out here, too."

"Sorry I can't be more help. Good luck finding—oh! There he is."

He had come out the French doors, his eyes above the crowd, on the nearby mountains.

Jane headed for him without another word to me. They talked quietly, Jane gesturing, Harvey soothing, putting his arm around her, stroking gently. Jane calmed and they went inside, presumably on their way home.

Twice in one day I'd had the impression that Harvey and his intern didn't have a strictly business-like relationship. It wasn't up to me to tell Jane, though. I only had one day's observations—no other facts, and no desire to interfere.

FIFTEEN

THURSDAY, JULY 18, 2013, 9:00 A.M.

As I fed Golden and dressed, I realized that I had looked forward to both OPO's meeting on Monday, and the Symphony Planning Committee meeting today, even though I couldn't continue my inquiries into Curtis's murder for the moment. Two meetings in the same week that I not only reluctantly attended, but anticipated. For an apolitical sort like me, that had to be history. Both committees were getting the details of adding extra paid services for the musicians nailed down. It had been a long time coming but now, in my opinion, the Symphony moved cautiously in the right direction, with my help and the help of my colleagues.

After the Planning Committee approved the minutes of the last meeting, I proudly presented the results of OPO's deliberations. ". . . we approved everything."

"Excellent!" Mel's eyes were shining and he smiled. "That's all wrapped up, then. We're making good time on this. I'll be able to submit a proposed schedule next meeting. How 'bout you, Jane? What kind of progress were you able to make pinning down soloists?"

"I talked to the cellist's agent, and we were able to work out a date for the fundraising concert. We're working on the details of travel arrangements and such."

"Great! Anything else?"

Jane lifted her chin. "The administrative staff has been a problem. I've been making slower progress than I expected."

Mel narrowed his eyes. "Let me have names. I'll see what I can do."

"It's okay." Jane gave a crisp nod. "I took care of it. Stella is no longer with us. We'll have a new aide Monday. The office manager helped me after I made him aware." Jane smiled sweetly.

Whoa! Stella had been with the symphony for years, and she had been dismissed just like that? I wanted to ask why, but the atmosphere didn't encourage unscheduled questions. I made a mental note to give my condolences to Stella.

Mel didn't even twitch. "Okay. Thanks for handling it, Jane. What's next?"

Diane brought up the increasing cost of auditorium rental. For a while we discussed possible other venues. Finally, Susie suggested an outreach program, using the auditorium for our core concerts but investigating other locations, possibly in the suburbs, to woo those people who didn't want to brave downtown traffic.

We spent some time making suggestions before Mel agreed to look into it. "Too bad Curtis isn't with us. He would have had connections that would make this a little easier." He tapped something into his laptop. "On the other hand, he wouldn't have wanted to see growth in the Symphony. He would have squelched the whole idea."

There were a few moments of silence before Mel moved on to problems with parking.

I found this kind of thing incredibly boring. I tuned out, reflecting on the dislike Mel continued to exhibit for Curtis. Mel didn't even cut Curtis some slack now that he was dead. Tyler might have carried a grudge against Curtis, too. Remembering his unexplained absence during *1812* the night of the murder, I wondered if he could possibly have killed Curtis. He seemed such a nice guy most of the time, but because of his bitterness and anger during arguments in committee I knew he had another side. My mind whirled round and round. I didn't refocus until Mel dismissed the meeting, almost an hour later.

SUSIE, TYLER, AND I HAD OUR USUAL post-meeting luncheon at St. Pierre's.

"Do you believe Stella's gone with no notice?" I couldn't keep the surprise out of my voice. "I always got the feeling she wanted to lend a hand any way she could. She helped me a lot. Remember at the beginning of the year when we needed figures on musician's salaries? Stella got me the info I needed. Why would Jane get her fired?"

"Don't know. But I know there's nothing we can do about it. Might as well forget it." Tyler believed in choosing his battles.

I knew he was right, but Stella's situation bothered me.

Tyler shrugged and moved on. "I wanted to invite you guys to my birthday party the 26th. I'll be grilling in the backyard."

"Sounds great, Tyler."

Susie asked, "Can I bring the husband and kids?"

"Sure. The more the merrier."

But I found myself considering Tyler's words with suspicion, wondering if a murderer would say them. He was, or had been, a good friend. Would I ever take anything he said at face value again?

After considering a moment I changed the subject. "Susie, great idea about finding other venues for concerts. I bet there are lots of people who'd be interested. Even I wouldn't go downtown if I didn't have to."

Tyler nodded and lifted his iced tea. "To expansion in all sorts of ways."

I lifted my water and Susie her lemonade. "To expansion!" We all clinked glasses. I dismissed my unease and allowed myself to feel encouraged.

I NO SOONER GOT HOME THAN KC CALLED. "Em, I think I'm in trouble."

"What do you mean you 'think' you're in trouble?"

"It's Paul."

Now I understood.

"He hauled me in for questioning. From work, no less. I was mortified!" She sobbed just once. "I called Barry. The wonderful man didn't ask questions, just dropped everything to meet me at the station. There wasn't much he would let me answer. The lieutenant wanted to know about my background and about guns. He must have talked to Madeleine—"

"Remind me. Who's Madeleine?"

"She used to be my boss. The one who handled scheduling when I was an escort."

Now I remembered. Madeleine the Madam.

"Anyway, it sounded like he knew all about what I used to do for a living, and he asked if Curtis had been one of my clients. He asked about our three dates again, but this time he called them 'assignations.' Barry didn't let me answer any of those questions. When Paul asked me again if I had any experience with guns Barry interrupted, wouldn't let me answer, and pointed out that the lieutenant had asked the same question before."

She sighed. "In the end, I didn't tell Paul anything new, but I missed a couple hours of work. My people, Tommy and Julie, had to finish the pastries and get ready for the lunch rush without me, and they suddenly turned *very* quiet and started working *very* hard when I came back. The working hard isn't unusual, but we're always laughing and joking around. Not today. And Julie asked me if everything was alright. I told her it was, but really, how could it be? I can't believe this is happening to me. I don't think the police have given up the idea that maybe I murdered Curtis."

"Okay, KC. Don't worry about it. Your job is to cook for the patrons of the Articulate Artichoke. I know you can't get much time off." Or at least she told me that. In reality, I didn't think she could cope with the idea that Paul wanted to throw her back in jail, given her previous experiences there. "Don't stress." Easier said than done. "Barry and I will figure out what's going on. It'll be okay." I tried to sound confident, but I worried.

I called Barry right away. It wasn't the first time I thanked my lucky stars that KC had given Barry written permission to talk to me about her case.

"Yeah. I've already got a call in to my source at the PD. I wanna know why they're bedeviling KC. I'll let you know when I hear anything."

Now I could do nothing but wait.

I FOUND THAT STELLA'S SUDDEN FIRING CONTINUED to bother me. I owed her for her kindness to me. She didn't deserve to be summarily fired. I decided to call her.

"Stella, this is Emily Wilson. I just heard you're leaving, and I wanted to wish you well. How does coffee and a delectable dessert at St. Pierre's sound?" I didn't want to bring up unpleasant topics over the phone, and didn't mention I knew she'd been fired. I didn't want any interruptions either. I'd chosen St. Pierre's instead of the Articulate Artichoke, where KC worked. I wanted to say, "I think you're special" without have to explain.

She paused, and I heard something like a muffled sob. "That would be wonderful! I didn't expect . . . that is . . . I'd love to."

"Is tomorrow afternoon good for you?"

"Great, Emily. And thanks again."

SIXTEEN

FRIDAY, JULY 19, 2013, 10:00 A.M.

The next morning I spent a couple hours practicing absentmindedly, unable to keep my mind on the music. I wondered about the delay hearing from Barry. Finally, the phone rang.

I was rewarded with his voice. I laid my flute on the table, then flopped in a chair.

"I heard from my source at the PD."

"And?"

"The police still think KC's a good suspect."

"Why can't they go for the simple robbery explanation?"

"They learned about her background and immediately assumed she'd lied when she said she didn't know anything about guns."

"Geez Louise! Do they think she's some kind of gun moll?"

Barry chuckled. "Unless they connect a gun belonging to her or with her fingerprints on it, she's fine. Otherwise, all they have are theories."

"Thanks. Call her and give her some perspective and reassurance, okay?"

"I've already done it." Barry allowed a silence before he changed the subject. "All work and no play make Em a dull girl. How 'bout a movie tomorrow?" His voice had become teasing and intimate.

"I have a concert then. Can we make it tonight?"

We picked a movie, coming to terms quickly, then added dinner arrangements.

"See you tonight." His voice held laughter and promise.

After we hung up, I thought about what Barry had told me. KC *could not* have murdered Curtis. It simply wasn't in her.

I looked at my watch. Only late morning. I'd make a trip to the Tourist Bureau before my lunch with Stella. I'd ask for a schedule of coming events, saying I wanted to plan a flute recital. That sounded plausible. But I'd really be looking for info on Darlene Taylor.

The Tourist Bureau was downtown, just off the interstate, in a beautifully restored brick building. I probably would have been shopping in it back in the day, or on my way to buying war bonds. As it was, I meandered into cleverly arranged displays of Monroe's and Colorado's past, some of them interactive, and picked my way to the information counter.

"I hoped you might be able to tell me about upcoming events."

"What are you interested in? We have schedules of art shows, concerts, science fairs, job fairs, dances, train rides, museum attractions and operating hours, and more. You name it." She was young and eager, beautiful and delicate, with her long dark brown hair and upturned nose. Too bad about the nose ring.

"Actually, I'm not a tourist. I'm a symphony member, and I wanted to find a good date for a recital."

"Then you don't want our current schedule. You'll want a future date, right?"

I nodded.

"Let me see if there's someone in the back who can help you. They do future scheduling there." She lifted the phone and buzzed a number. Buzzed another number. And another. "Sorry. It's lunch time. Everybody's stepped out."

I glanced at the clock on the wall and saw that it showed twelve-ten.

"Let me try one more person." A pause. "Sorry to bother you, but there's a symphony member here who needs a schedule of future event dates." Another pause. "Okay. I'll tell her." She hung up the phone and looked up at me. "She'll be right out."

"Who will I be talking to?"

"Darlene Taylor, our president. She doesn't usually help clients, but she *loves* the symphony. She'll be glad to meet you. She said to give her a couple minutes."

In the flesh. What a stroke of luck.

After a short wait, Darlene appeared. She seemed to sway as she walked. Older than I expected, she had touches of gray at the temples. "Come on back. Ms. Wilson, isn't it?"

"That's right. How did you know?"

"I've seen you often. I have season's tickets to the symphony, and I've heard you perform at a couple of parties. I enjoy your trio. The group lends such an elegant touch."

We had reached a door at the back of the building with a frosted glass transom over it. Inside, it seemed I'd walked into nineteenth century luxury. In a palatial office, a floor to ceiling wall of books welcomed the visitor. It adjoined brick walls on both sides. A birchwood roll top desk stood catty corner on the left facing the visitor with two matching birchwood chairs, one behind the desk, and one out to the side. A red velvet sofa and matching antique armchair sat to the right and balanced the decor. A Persian rug in the center pulled it all together. Only the computer monitor on the desk gave a hint that we were in the twenty-first century.

"Thanks. It's wonderful to be able to make a living in music. You didn't mention the Concerts in the Parks, though. Do you go to any of them? Maybe the Fourth of July concert?"

"Oh, no." She waved a hand. "They're usually such a mob scene. I can't get enthusiastic. When I'm outdoors, it's usually to get away from people. The Fourth of July concert is especially bad. I went to the mountains with a friend this year, instead of the concert." Darlene seated herself at the desk.

I parked myself in the chair opposite. "It's pretty horrifying that one of our own was murdered there, right out in the open." Maybe Curtis wasn't one of *my* own, but I didn't think it'd do any good to bring up his attitude and really, in a broader sense, especially to outsiders, he *was* one of our own.

"Yes." That wasn't much of a response, but Darlene concentrated on the screen. "What dates were you interested in?" She punched keys on the computer and brought up a page as she spoke.

"I thought September would be good, if that's not too soon. My students will be back from summer break by then, the weather will still be good, and if we do it late in the month they'll have time to prepare."

She pressed a key and the schedule printed, almost instantaneously. "Here you go. Looks like we're pretty well booked. There are a few spaces, though. Did you want to schedule a date now?"

"I need to check a few things first. When do you need to know?"

"As soon as possible. There isn't much time. We'll be printing the new schedules the first week of August." She swiveled away from the computer screen and stood. "I'd love to talk to you some more, but I've got to get figures ready for the donors meeting."

I didn't have any choice but to stand, too. "Thanks for printing this out for me. I hope it wasn't too much trouble."

"Not at all. I'm glad to do it. Let us know if we can be of any more help." She walked me down the hall and to the front door. "Take care, now."

"I will. And say 'hello' at the next concert."

"I'd love to." She opened the door for me, and I found myself in the street enjoying her lingering aura of charm and grace. If she hadn't attended the Fourth of July concert, she couldn't be Curtis's killer, unless she lied. My intuition didn't seriously consider her a suspect. I couldn't visualize the elegant woman doing anything as uncouth as either lying, or firing a gun.

ST. PIERRE'S WAS NEAR THE TOURIST BUREAU. As a result, I arrived early for my meeting with Stella. I found us a table and waited until she appeared. A middle-aged woman, Stella was tall and full of *joie de vivre*. I had expected that she would show some sign of sorrow, maybe at least a lack of enthusiasm, but she displayed only her positive, cheerful self.

"I've been drooling over the thought of pastries all morning." St. Pierre's specialty. "Let's go make a choice!" She beamed at me.

I paid for the two coffees, a crème brulee, and a crepe caramel, then we returned to our table.

"Mmm. I haven't had one of these for ages." She took a bite of her crepe, then washed it down with a sip of coffee.

"Really? I have one *way* too often."

We both laughed.

"They said at the Symphony Planning Committee meeting yesterday that you were leaving." I thought I'd leave it up to Stella to tell me the circumstances. "You've been with us forever. It took me by surprise."

Stella looked serious for a moment. "I'll definitely miss the people I've worked with, like you." She smiled at me and seemed to choose her words carefully. "I thought I'd work at the symphony until I retire, but I suddenly realized, if I want to travel, I'd better do it while I can."

She'd put a positive spin on it. Typical. "You aren't that old."

"You're sweet, but I'm old enough to feel like it's time to enjoy life. I've wanted to go to New Hampshire to visit my sister for years. From there, I don't know." She hesitated and sounded unsure. "I haven't thought much about it. I may do more travelling if I can afford it."

"Well, I wanted you to know how much I've enjoyed working with you. You're always such a pleasant presence at the office, ready to lend a hand to a technophobic flutist at any time."

Stella's eyes filled, the only obvious hint that she felt less than happy about leaving. "Thank you. I needed to hear that. It's nice to be appreciated."

She'd inadvertently confirmed my information. Stella wasn't retiring willingly, and hadn't been given a parting gift. Suddenly I wished I'd invited her for a nice dinner instead of only dessert.

We chatted more about her sister and her plans, without mentioning the Symphony again.

It wasn't like Stella to badmouth the people she worked for or with, and I didn't press for any further explanation, respecting her decision not to complain. The exact details of her firing would remain a mystery, and Jane's role unknown.

I HAD STUDENTS ALL AFTERNOON.

In the middle of Kay Lemberton's lesson, the phone rang.

An annoying interruption. Kay was one of my better students. A beginner, she bubbled with enthusiasm, followed instructions carefully, and laughed a lot. The caller ID said "Elena Pascal," though. The scouting mom. I answered.

"Hello?"

"Hi. This is Elena Pascal. We spoke earlier about Curtis Strange's murder?"

"Of course."

"I wanted to let you know that I spoke to the Listers, the other chaperones?"

"I remember." Since they weren't returning my call, I feared I knew their position, but I asked anyway. "What did they say?"

"They don't feel they have anything to add. They were further away from Mr. Strange's booth and they didn't see or hear anything. Then after Kevin discovered the body, they were busy keeping the other boys in line while my husband, Kevin, and I talked to the police. The Listers said they won't be calling you back. I did give them your number, though, in case they change their minds."

"Well, thanks for following through and for letting me know how it came out."

"You're welcome. Good luck with your 'friend.'"

I returned to Kay's lesson feeling a sense of resignation. I hadn't expected much information from the scouts, but I found myself disappointed, anyway.

SEVENTEEN

SATURDAY, JULY 20, 2013, 8:00 A.M.

Barry spent the night after our movie date. In the morning I rose with the sun, unable to sleep any longer. Absentmindedly attending to my chores—making Barry's coffee, letting Golden into the backyard, boiling water for my tea—I considered the problem at hand. To my knowledge, nobody had a good word to say about Curtis. My to-do list only got longer and longer. I needed to investigate Curtis's nephew, Roland Strange. Mel had denied he attended the concert, but his explanation, or lack thereof, had been unconvincing. And Tyler looked ever more guilty. I wanted to know what he had done when he left the stage during *1812*. But I couldn't investigate any of it today. I had to get to the Visitation Center by nine, teach all afternoon, and play a Concert in the Parks tonight. I sighed. No rest for the wicked.

Wrapped in a terrycloth robe he kept at my house, Barry entered the kitchen. "Hey, beautiful."

He always made me feel twenty-seven, an age I hadn't seen for a long, *long* time.

I curled into him as he kissed me, then smiled and ruffled his hair.

He grabbed a mug, poured from the percolator, and sat on a barstool at the counter. "Thanks for the coffee."

"My pleasure." I poured hot water over my tea bag and sat next to him.

"You have a lot of pleasures, don't you?"

I could feel the heat rise into my face. "Mmmmmmm."

"What are you going to do today?"

"It's a full one." I recited my plans.

"Mind if I come to the concert?"

"That'd be great. Why don't you come over when we're done?"

He waggled his eyebrows at me. "Love to."

Golden and I left for the Visitation Center soon after. I wondered if the Martins were doing well, and who would replace them on my schedule.

Mr. Briggs seemed to have forgotten our brief row last week and discussed the weather with me as he waited for Melissa. Melissa, too, seemed unafraid and only anxious to talk to her dad.

As usual the mom and her baby had an uneventful visit; Mom was totally involved with the baby, who cooed and giggled. The infant followed a bright pink rattle with interest, reached for it and explored it with her mouth. Mom tried peek-a-boo then, which made the baby laugh, which made Mom laugh in turn. A successful and touching visit.

As it turned out, the Martins had been replaced by a mom with a three-year-old, the Stolzmans. Trying to relieve her obvious tension, I talked to the mom about casual topics while she waited for Ashland, her daughter. She seemed nice enough, but no matter what I did, Mrs. Stoltzman continued to twist her tissue into knots, then twist the tissue back the other way. I hoped it relieved her because the tissue was a mess. By the time Mr. Stoltzman brought the child and Mrs. Stoltzman burst into tears, the tissue couldn't be used. When Ashland started crying, too, I brought a full box of Kleenex®.

Golden and I worked with them. The little girl stopped her crying when Golden snuggled against her for a pet. I showed the toddler how to pet the dog with the fur instead of against it, then took Mrs. Stolzman aside. "I know it's easier said than done, but you can't get emotional when Ashland comes. Children only know Mom is crying. They don't know why. It upsets them."

"I know. It's been a long time, though. Three months. And she's my life."

A contentious divorce? Substance abuse? Mine was not to reason why.

"Now that you've had a first visit, maybe next time you can focus on the delight of seeing Ashland."

She sniffled and blew her nose with a tissue she had loaded into her pocket. "It is a joy to see her. I'll certainly try. And I'll remember what you said."

She returned to play with her daughter, who had quickly forgotten the trauma of meeting her mom and pulled out dress up clothes from the Center's supply of costumes. Mom helped deck her out in a ballerina outfit, then donned a princess outfit herself. Soon they were laughing together. A wonderful thing to see.

By the time Mr. Clearwater arrived, I was in high spirits. He, however, had obviously not forgotten last week's confrontation. He scowled at me and didn't respond to friendly comments on the weather. Okay, fine.

Travis arrived sulky, and Constance quietly moved to Golden and hugged her.

I made notes.

Mr. Clearwater made no effort to dispel the tension, and instead shot hostile looks at me.

I made more notes, then brought a pack of cards to the table. "Can I interest anybody in a friendly game of Go Fish?" Golden sat close to Constance, leaning against the girl's knees.

Mr. Clearwater looked daggers at me, Travis rolled his eyes, but Constance petted Golden and seemed relieved. "Sure, Miss Emily. I love Go Fish."

We played a game, but I left when Constance suggested War next. "I don't know how to play War. I'll just watch for a while." Golden stayed with Constance.

Mr. Clearwater didn't speak to me and nodded curtly, but he and Travis humored Constance.

I breathed a sigh of relief when the children left and Mr. Clearwater's waiting period ended, freeing him to leave. If this situation didn't improve, they wouldn't be in the program long.

BARRY HAD GONE BY THE TIME I GOT HOME.

As I fixed a salad for lunch, I thought about Curtis's murder. It seemed that the frustration of the residents of Homes at Skyridge must be at the max by now—mine certainly would be—and it could have boiled over. But they had a vested interest in keeping Curtis alive. Their lawsuit seemed destined to succeed, at least in my opinion, and there'd be no point in slowing things down by killing him. They might not have realized his death would bring the lawsuit to a halt, though. And it wasn't as though murder was rational to begin with. One of the most frustrated among them, Travers, had been cleared. But, according to Barry, another, Matlow, had been turned over to Lieutenant Gordon's not-so-tender-mercies. Paul's ballistics tests would determine whether Matlow's gun had shot Curtis. I had nothing left to do there. Hoping KC's ordeal would soon be over, I considered. Should I just wait for Paul's results? No. KC depended on me. And Matlow might not be the killer. In that case, where should I focus my efforts next?

As it had that morning, my mind whirled with the possibilities.

My students provided an escape. I concentrated on them and the best way to help them, and they responded with youthful enthusiasm.

I should have been tired by the time the concert rolled around, but I felt energized. Although my questions about the murder weren't answered, it had been a good day. With Golden's assistance I had eased Constance's visit with her dad, and been able to apply my musical knowledge to benefit my students. All in all, a day well spent.

IT WAS A BEAUTIFUL NIGHT for an outdoor concert. The sky was cloudless, and an afternoon thunderstorm had cooled the temperature just enough to need a light jacket. The sun cast its rosy glow over the mountains as I waited to get the all clear from the stagehands to have access to the orchestra shell. Our concertmaster, Peter Hall, stood beside me, making small talk.

A short, balding man detached himself from the crowd and handed Peter a violin case. "Should be good as new."

This must be his violin repairman.

Peter opened the case. The instrument was there but, "I don't see a bill."

"I assumed you wouldn't want to deal with it at a concert. I mailed it. I knew you'd want the instrument back as soon as possible, though."

"Thanks, George." Peter closed the case. "Appreciate it."

As the little man lifted his hand in farewell and blended into the crowd, Peter told me, "I couldn't be happier. The violin's been gone for three weeks. I've been practicing on my outdoor fiddle."

String players and wind players who played wooden instruments often had a spare "outdoor" instrument to protect their good instruments from the weather. "It must be a relief to have it back."

"Can you hold the violin for a minute while I make space to store it under the stage? It'll be safe there 'til I can get it after the concert."

"Sure."

Peter disappeared under the edge of the raised orchestra shell for a moment before he returned and took the instrument. "Thanks."

"No problem." At that moment we received word that we could use the stage. "Have a good concert."

"You, too, Emily."

BARRY'S LOVING PRESENCE AFTER THE CONCERT was, as the saying goes, the perfect ending to a perfect day. We tended to Golden and I sighed with contentment as all three of us fell asleep. Barry and I didn't even mind that Golden took up two-thirds of the bed.

EIGHTEEN

SUNDAY, JULY 21, 2013, 7:00 A.M.

BARRY HAD LEFT IN THE WEE SMALL HOURS of the morning to meet with a client who had been arrested. I hadn't been able to get back to sleep. I'd tossed and turned, unhappy that my commitments had delayed investigating Curtis's murder, and turning over questions in my head.

So, when the phone rang, I answered on the first ring. A disguised voice—male? female?—whispered. "Mind your own business."

"What? Who is this?"

"I have pictures. You and the stolen violin."

"Stolen? Violin?" There were lots of violins in the symphony. I might have been with any of them, but none of them were stolen as far as I knew. "What?"

"If you don't back off, the police and the Board will get the pictures."

"But I—"

Click.

I punched in star 69, but only "blocked call" appeared in the display.

Disappointed, I crawled back into bed, my eyes wide open, and speculated about the identity of the caller and the meaning of the call. When the phone rang again, I glanced at the clock. Eight a.m.

"You'll never guess!" Alice Smithson, the cellist in my trio, gleefully greeted me. Alice, a scandal junkie and my connection to the grapevine, considered it her duty to keep me in the loop.

I felt violated and afraid, and Alice's gossip was the last thing I was in the mood to hear. I sighed. "Just tell me."

"Somebody stole Peter's violin! Last night at the concert."

Abruptly I sat up in bed. Now it made sense. I had held Peter's violin for those few minutes last night, and someone had shot pictures. Now they were bullying me—threatening to accuse me of stealing the instrument. Knowing my history with the police and the Board's aversion to negative publicity, I wasn't confident that anyone would believe my version of events.

"That's awful." I answered mechanically, thinking furiously.

The caller had told me to mind my own business. The only thing I'd been asking questions about had been the murder. I must be getting close. "Does anyone know who did it?"

"No details. I'll let you know as soon as I hear." Alice said her husband needed her, and rang off.

"Mind your own business." Who had I been asking questions about? Matlow came to mind first. He didn't conceal his fury at Curtis, he had no alibi, owned guns, and knew how to use them. I'd even suggested Barry ask Paul to run ballistics tests on Matlow's guns. What else? I had asked questions about Darlene Taylor and Travers, but they had alibis. Presumably they wouldn't be concerned about inquiries. I'd asked about the body Golden dug up, both of the police and of Harvey Rice. I'd questioned Mel, Tyler, Darlene, and Lila as to their whereabouts during the July Fourth concert. I'd questioned Lila about Roland, who claimed to have an alibi which I hadn't checked out yet. And I'd asked John Reeves about Antelope Run.

Given all that, Matlow likely made the phone call. I breathed a sigh of relief. The whole thing had already been turned over to

Paul. There wasn't an issue as far as I could see, or not one I could do anything about, anyway.

As I began to recover my peace of mind, I had second thoughts. Matlow wouldn't have had access to the stolen violin. I supposed he could go backstage if he was determined, but it would be difficult. It would behoove me to consider the other suspects as serious possibilities. Only Mel as president of the Board, Harvey Rice as the husband of a Board member, and Tyler as a player would have easy access to the stage area.

What had Steve learned? I decided to find out. KC would be at the restaurant getting ready for Sunday brunch, but he should be home. I'd call him and learn the latest developments.

Before I could do that, though, Kathleen called. I wouldn't tell her about the threats. She'd overreact. Besides, I needed to think the situation through myself before I shared with anybody else. Instead, I made oatmeal following package directions as I talked.

"I managed to catch KC and talk to her yesterday. She seems awfully discouraged. She didn't kill anyone. She's the victim here. Curtis stalked her, and now the police are hounding her. She's being victimized twice."

She preached to the choir, or actually the orchestra, as it were.

"I keep trying to put in a good word for her, but Paul won't even discuss it. He tells me to keep my nose out of his business. We had an awful fight over it last night."

Uh-oh. "Kathleen, you'd better keep out of it. You might end up doing KC more harm than good if you make Lieutenant Gordon—I mean Paul—mad."

"I suppose so, but Paul knows I only want the best for KC. I think this shows a complete lack of trust."

"He can't afford to be biased for KC. If she's a murderess, he'll need to arrest her."

"A murderess! KC couldn't hurt a fly." She sounded outraged.

"I know that, and you know that. Paul will discover it for himself."

"If he'd trust me, I could help. I know KC about as well as anybody but you and Steve."

Kathleen's intuition often hit the target, but if Paul didn't want to talk about the case, his wishes should be respected. "It's not a good idea to mix business with a home life. Where would Paul go to get away from it all?"

Kathleen didn't say anything for a moment. "I guess you're right. I want him to be able to relax with me." She sounded squelched. "You're always level-headed. But I want for everything to be okay for KC."

"It will be. She didn't kill anybody, and Paul's investigation has to show that."

"You're right, Emily. It'll be fine." She sounded like she tried to convince herself.

I hurried to change the subject, hoping she felt better. "Have you heard from Mom lately?"

"She calls every week. That guy she's been seeing? The one who jets out every couple weeks to see her?"

"Um-hmm."

"When he came a few days ago, he asked her to marry him. He tried to talk her into it by saying they could be together and that she could move back east to be with him. Well, of course Mom blew up. She told him if he could ask her to move he didn't know the first thing about her, and turned him down, not too politely. She wants to stay close to her family. That's you and me."

I sighed. There went my hope that something, anything besides us, would hold Mom's interest.

"What about you, Emily? You never tell me anything about your life."

"It's practicing, students, trio performances, Concerts in the Park. And I want to help with KC's problems if I can. Nothing new." Not counting the threat, which seemed like the *only* thing in my life right now, but not suitable for discussion with Kathleen.

"She's lucky to have a friend like you with the interest and know-how to lend a hand."

"I don't know about 'know-how,' but interest, certainly."

She repeated, "Well, she's lucky."

My oatmeal started to burn and I wanted to get off the phone before the conversation got mushy. I excused myself and we hung up.

After I finished eating and cleaned up the pan, which had a layer of burned oatmeal stuck to it, I called Steve. "Hey. I wanted to get, and maybe give, an update. How is KC doing?"

"I'm really worried about her, Emily." His voice was solemn. "She's discouraged. She doesn't see how she can prove she didn't kill Curtis, and doesn't know how to prove somebody else did. There were a hundred thousand people with opportunity and Curtis had a boatload of enemies. Anyone could have murdered him, but KC's the only one he stalked. I have to admit, it's a gloomy picture."

I quit pacing and sat crosswise in the easy chair. "Have you found out anything?"

Steve sighed. "Nothing helpful. I played golf yesterday with Don Norton. He owns Norton Plumbing and Heating. His company got stiffed by C.H. Strange Development. Strange owed them over a million dollars for the work they did on that new shopping center. Don has been hard-put to meet payroll. He's scrambling and he needs Strange Corp. to pay him. He had to sue. For a few minutes I thought I'd found the answer. But no. He and his wife were on a cruise to Alaska and were gone during the murder. She can't take hot weather, and they make a point of going someplace cool every Fourth of July, rather than sweltering in the heat."

"I'd say that's helpful. It eliminates one possibility, and what we've got now is too many suspects. We have to find some way to narrow them down. It's as useful to eliminate innocent people as to find new suspects."

"What about you? Have you had any luck?" Steve sounded hopeful.

"Yes and no. I've found lots of folks who were mad at Curtis, and a nephew who lived in another state and claims not to have known him. Specifically, there are five lawsuits. You know about Don Norton. Another was brought by an organization called Homes at Skyridge consisting of thirty families, all with a bone to pick with Curtis. There are a couple of people on the Symphony's Planning Committee that might have motives, and I suspect that his assistant, Lila, wasn't real fond of him either. She attended the concert on the Fourth. She had opportunity. There are lots of possibilities."

"That seems hopeful for KC. Better than not having suspects."

"The big news is that I think I may be getting close. I've been threatened."

"Threatened! What happened?" Steve sounded dismayed.

I explained, downplaying my worry and emphasizing the potential progress it represented. "The trouble is I don't know which suspect made the call."

Sounding worried, Steve said, "I have to say you're taking the whole thing calmly." He sounded hesitant.

"No other way to take it. It doesn't do anybody any good to get upset."

"Shouldn't you at least report it?" He sounded concerned. "You know, just in case."

"It's sweet of you to fret about me, and I *will* report it. I promise."

Steve cleared his throat. "How can we learn who it is? When we find the blackmailer, we find the murderer, is my guess."

"I'm not sure, but if we keep nosing around we'll find an answer. It's been true in the past, and it'll be true again." I sounded confident, but I understood why KC and Steve were disheartened. "Let's stay focused on what we know. KC did not kill anyone."

"Now that's something I'm sure of."

"Give KC a hug for me when she comes home from work. Tell her we're working on it, and I'll talk to her at her lesson tomorrow."

We hung up and I sat down to think. Golden lay down beside me and sighed deeply. I knew just how she felt.

NINETEEN

MONDAY, JULY 22, 2013, 8:00 A.M.

WITH ONLY ONE CONCERT LEFT THIS SUMMER, immediate business dealt with, and President Rex Minoa's wife on vacation, OPO was on hiatus. That left me free to do some more sleuthing on Curtis's murder. I decided to investigate Roland Strange. It seemed too coincidental that the inheritance provided such a strong motive for killing his uncle, but that he also had the best alibi—if he hadn't lied.

Strange Corp.'s attorneys or Lila, as Curtis's assistant, would have the best information, but I wasn't sure which lawyers Curtis worked with. Besides, I didn't have an excuse for approaching them.

I started by going to the offices of C.H. Strange Development Corporation. Lila was there.

"Hi," I greeted her breezily, pushing open the office door. "I wanted to let you know I found my phone." I held it up. Even I cringed, but I hadn't thought of a better excuse to drop in on her.

Lila sighed. "That's great." She sounded anything but excited.

"I feel like we've gotten to know each other and I didn't want you to worry." I sat in the deskside seat. "Some papers at home covered it."

"I'm happy for you." Her voice reflected total disinterest.

"How's the new boss working out?" Chipper and cheery. That's me.

She rolled her eyes. "Pretty early to be making judgments."

"Oh, well, you just *know* when you work with a person. It doesn't take long."

"I wouldn't say I've really worked with him. I've just filled him in on what we do, and . . . oh, yeah . . . on the lawsuits."

"It's been, what, ten days, then?" I tried to narrow down his time of arrival.

"Maybe two weeks. I picked him up at the airport on Monday, the eighth."

Lila saw him arrive personally, then.

"Why you? Doesn't he have any family or friends here?"

"I followed instructions from the attorneys." Her words were clipped, showing her growing annoyance. I'd better get as much information as I could, as fast as I could.

"You've only seen him a few times?"

"Maybe. Why does it make any difference?"

"I'm curious. Antelope Run would be the most ideal place if the surroundings aren't ruined." I sounded wistful. That part was true. It radiated the beauty of nature.

"We haven't gotten anywhere near discussing it. Be reasonable. Give Roland a little time to get oriented. He has to take care of funeral arrangements, sort through personal effects, all that stuff, besides taking over the business."

"You're right. I shouldn't be eager. Not only is it rude, it's not good from a bargaining standpoint. Maybe I should contact the company attorneys and ask them to let me know when Antelope Run becomes available."

Seizing an opportunity to get rid of me, Lila showed her first enthusiasm of the morning. "You should."

"Can you give me their names and contact information?"

Lila turned to her computer and called up a screen, then printed out the name of the firm, their address, phone number, a contact person, and email. "There you go."

"Thanks. I hope you're in a better work situation now. If I ever get a chance, I'll tell the new Mr. Strange to give you a raise."

Finally, she laughed. "Thanks."

As I got in my car I reflected. It looked like Roland's alibi held true. If Lila had met his plane the Monday after the murder, it was unlikely he killed his Uncle Curtis in Monroe four days earlier. Strong motive or not, I'd have to look elsewhere. Fortunately, I had plenty of suspects, and wasn't a bit discouraged.

WHEN I PULLED INTO MY DRIVEWAY, I picked up the mail. Besides the usual junk, I immediately saw a 9x12 manila envelope which obviously had not gone through the post office since it had neither postage nor postmark. To appease my curiosity, after I entered the house I opened it first thing.

Photos. Printed on someone's computer on ordinary paper, showing me, holding a violin case. The pictures must have been taken from a distance with a telephoto lens because I would have noticed if anyone near me had been taking photographs. My picture was sharp and clear, but other people in the photo and the background were blurry.

I called Paul right away. Maybe the cops could get fingerprints.

"Hi, Paul. This is Emily Wilson."

"Emily."

I told him about the phone call first.

"Nothin' we can do about phone calls. Not unless it's a criminal case. Call the phone company. See what they can do for you."

Frustrated, I sighed. "I thought it might be connected with me asking questions about Curtis Strange's death."

"I told you not to interfere. Leave police matters to the police."

I kept trying. "Today, I found an envelope in the mailbox. It contains photos of me holding a violin, later stolen."

"That's important. Detective Copland'd be the one to call. He's the head of Robbery." With efficiency in mind, Paul supported me. "He'll know who's working the case. He can help you fastest."

"I thought they might want the fingerprints on the photos and envelope."

"If we need the prints, Copeland'll get 'em. In the meantime, better not touch 'em."

"Great. Thanks for your help, Paul."

"No problem. Tell Copeland I told you to call."

I did as Paul had suggested. After several transfers I got in touch with Detective Copeland's division, where the aide said he was out, but transferred me to his office. I left a message on his answering machine:

"This is Emily Wilson. I have information regarding the violin stolen from the symphony concert Saturday. Lieutenant Paul Gordon advised me to get in contact with you. Please give me a call." I left my phone number.

Afraid the neighbors' observations would be forgotten by the time I got hold of Detective Copeland, I pondered questioning them myself. Hopefully they had seen something, or someone, drop off the envelope. Mrs. Warren would be a good bet. She was retired and usually stayed home, at least in the mornings. The neighbors on either side of me worked bankers' hours, and the neighbor catty corner across the street was out of town.

I crossed the lane and rang Mrs. Warren's doorbell. A widow in her seventies, she had a lot of energy. She usually gardened in the front yard, and I'd met her when I walked Golden and admired her flowers. Over many walks and years we'd gotten to know each other.

"Hi there."

"Emily! Come in. I haven't seen you in a long time."

Despite Mrs. Warren's friendly welcome, I worried, unsure if the socializing required would get the information I wanted. I followed her down the entry hall into her beautifully maintained living room: pale blue carpet, lots of plants, not an ounce of dust, and books lined up exactly according to size. The room could have been featured in House Beautiful.

"Can I get you some iced tea? It's herbal."

"Yes, thank you. That sounds wonderful."

"Lemon or peach?"

"Peach, please." She and I shared a tea fetish. "Can I help?"

"Oh heavens, no! Just come along and keep me company." She led the way into her kitchen, bright yellow, and also beautifully clean and orderly.

I sat at the table while she filled two glasses with ice, poured the tea, and brought the drinks to the table. She crossed the room to the breadbox and loaded a plate with slices of cinnamon coffee cake, then brought it to the table, pulled out a chair, and joined me.

"How have you been?" I sipped my tea.

"Pretty good for an old cookie." Her standard response. We both laughed.

I asked her about her life first. Mrs. Warren expected her grandchildren to arrive in a week. She would keep them while her daughter and son-in-law cruised the Caribbean. Then she planned her own cruise with a travel group, starting in Seattle and moving north along the coast of Canada. She asked me if I'd be able to take care of her cat, to which I happily agreed.

"Now tell me what's new with you." She leaned forward and pushed the plate of coffee cake slices toward me.

I selected one. "Oh, you know. Same old, same old."

"I haven't seen KC around lately."

"She's not living here anymore. She's a good friend, head chef at the Articulate Artichoke, but she's engaged to be married now and lives with her fiancé. She's not around as much."

"Engaged to be married! How wonderful! She's such a sweet young thing. I remember her help after I had my hip surgery. All those meals! Wish her the best for me. I hope she has a delightful future with her young man."

"I'll let her know. And I'll tell her you missed her." Remind her to send a wedding invitation, too.

I thought for a minute, uncertain how to proceed. "I know you have such a keen eye for the goings-on in the neighborhood. I wondered if you saw who delivered a large manila envelope earlier today to my place. I didn't expect it, and I don't know who to thank."

"Oh! Is it your birthday?"

"No. That's why it took me by surprise."

"Well, I did see a van parked in front of your house, but it wasn't from a business. There wasn't any name on the side. It was silver."

"Silver? Did you recognize the make?"

"No. That's all I can tell you about it. It didn't stay long. I didn't see anyone get into or out of it. It might have been in front of the mailbox." She thought for a moment. "I don't remember seeing the mailbox. It's likely the van blocked my view."

"That's very helpful. I'll have to think about which of my friends have silver vans."

We chatted a little longer, and while I adored getting back in touch with Mrs. Warren, I excused myself a short time later. I had to get back to sleuthing. Someone else may have seen something, too, despite my pessimistic expectations.

"Come back soon, you hear? Don't let it be forever and a day again."

"I won't."

"And scratch Golden's ears for me."

I laughed. "I will. Take care."

As I suspected, none of the other neighbors who might have a view of my mailbox were home. I'd spent too much time getting the information, and my first student pulled into the driveway as I returned. I wouldn't even have time for lunch.

I'd been teaching all afternoon, and I was starving by the time KC arrived for the last lesson of the day.

As Steve had said, she seemed discouraged, and silently put her flute together.

I forgot my hunger and all the social niceties in my concern for her state-of-mind. "Is anything wrong? Didn't Steve fill you in on the latest?"

"No, he didn't. When I came home from the restaurant, I went straight to bed, too exhausted to talk. Then he left early this morning. Why? Did something happen? The last I heard, neither you nor Steve had made any appreciable progress, and the MPD still suspected me."

"Yes. Something did happen. Something encouraging." I paused to give the news dramatic weight. "I've been threatened."

"Threatened!" Her eyes filled with tears. "No! Please don't. I can't stand it that the people who care about me are endangering themselves."

"KC, don't take it that way. I'm encouraged. I'm getting close. I'm making someone uncomfortable enough to make threats." I patted her hand. "We'll prove that you didn't kill Curtis. I don't know how right now, but we will." I tried to sound my most confident.

KC rubbed her arms and sounded stressed. "I can't think about anything else. I know that I'm always harping on sex as a motive, but that doesn't make sense here. Curtis and I were never intimate, and it had been a long time since we'd seen each other, even on casual dates. I hadn't thought about him in ages. Sex is a dead end in this case, even if he obsessed over me."

"I follow."

I could hear the pads of her flute open and close as she nervously fingered the keys. "There's got to be another way to look at this." KC sounded baffled, like she had to improvise without knowing the tune.

I couldn't think of anything to say.

She didn't speak for a moment. "How about this? What about the murderer? Maybe he, or she, obsessed over Curtis. Even though that's kind of hard to imagine, every lock has its key. Or maybe Curtis interfered somehow with his, or her, relationship."

"KC, be careful. That makes it sound like Steve killed him."

"Steve?"

"Think about it. Curtis fixated on Steve's fiancée. That is, you. Steve can't have been happy about that."

"That's ludicrous! Steve could never kill anyone, he didn't know about the stalking, and he and Lieutenant Gordon were together all night at the concert." KC sounded outraged.

I shrugged.

"You can't believe that."

"Of course I don't believe it. I like Steve. And I believe in you."

We looked at each other, both puzzled.

"I do know someone else that might fill the bill."

"Yeah? Who?" KC sounded hopeful. "Tell me."

"Curtis's assistant, Lila, obviously didn't like Curtis very much. And she attended the concert. Not only that, I've questioned her. She might be the blackmailer. As you suggested, her job with Curtis could've been keeping her from her love life. Maybe long hours and low pay? More likely, he abused her once too often."

"Abused?" KC perked up.

"Mental abuse. We know Curtis was a jerk, and Lila implied that he was a difficult boss. She could've had enough and killed Curtis."

"That's a stretch." KC didn't sound convinced or even hopeful. "Shouldn't a motive be more emotionally involved than disliking a job?"

"Who knows what's in a murderer's mind?" I paused and smiled. "Anyway, back to the threats. They're a good sign. I must be getting close."

KC laughed. "That's certainly putting a positive spin on things."

"You should know. You're the one marrying the spin doctor."

She chuckled. One of the things I liked best about KC was she always laughed at my jokes, even when they were bad. "Okay, tell me. I want all the details."

I described the blackmailer's threats since last Saturday's concert.

"We have another clue then, too. A silver van." She sounded thoughtful. "It seems like I know someone with a van like that, but I can't quite connect the dots."

"Think about it, KC. I have the same feeling. That I know who it is, but it's just out of reach."

"Maybe it's someone we both know."

"It's possible. I'll have to think."

She smiled. "You always make me feel better, Em."

I put my arm around her. "I'm glad. For now, let's forget about it all and have a lesson. Let's start with scales."

We'd talked for most of her lesson time, but I had time to hear one movement of the Concerto. I accompanied her by transposing the bass line. She left looking calmer.

I felt better, too. Even if KC didn't think much of their motives, one of the suspects was worried. I could feel it. Why else would I get threats?

No sooner had KC left than Barry called.

"Hi, Em. I hoped to catch KC before she left."

"Sorry, Barry. You just missed her. What's up?"

"I wanted to tell her that Paul just finished questioning Steve. The lieutenant showed up at his office. Steve called me, I joined the party, and the three of us talked privately. He asked me to call KC. I don't think he wanted to break the news that Paul questioned him."

"Oh, lord! That's going to upset her more than being questioned herself."

"Yeah, I know. Steve invited me over to discuss it with KC after supper. I'd like it if you came, too. She could use your moral support."

"Okay, meet you there. What time?"

"About seven. I'll see if it's okay that you come, get an exact time, and call you when I find out the details."

"Thanks Barry."

"One other thing. Oneida got the information you wanted on Curtis's court cases."

"Awesome! How did she do it?"

"One never asks a magician to reveal her secrets. I make sure to give her a vast Christmas bonus, is all."

I laughed, amused by the comment, but not by the situation.

He gave me the information and we hung up. I slumped dejectedly. KC and Steve were such a beautiful couple. They deserved unrestrained happiness. Not this.

AT SEVEN WE GATHERED AROUND THE KITCHEN TABLE at KC and Steve's. I'd brought Golden, hoping she could provide some comfort for KC.

The perfect hostess, even as upset as she was, KC had put out a plate of homemade zucchini bread and boiled water for tea. She filled mugs, each with a bag of chamomile, at the stove. Steve helped her bring them to the table.

She bypassed the empty chair and settled on the floor between Steve and Golden. When Golden laid her head in KC's lap, she stroked an ear.

Steve started things with a request. "Barry, why don't you tell everybody what happened."

Barry cleared his throat. "Lieutenant Gordon, Paul that is, came to Steve's office and asked questions. The lieutenant's theory is that when some other fellow stalks your fiancée, it's a darn good motive for you to murder him."

Barry shrugged halfheartedly. "Basically, one of the theories Paul has to look at is the possibility that you two acted together to kill Curtis."

"Just when I thought it couldn't get any worse . . ." KC put her head in her hands without waking Golden, who had fallen asleep under her ministrations.

"You notice Paul has not arrested anybody. He has no fingerprints and hasn't proved that you and Steve had more opportunity than 99,998 other people. All he has are some photos and a cockamamie theory. He has to have more probable cause than that." Barry sounded angry "I don't want you to worry about it. We'll find the real killer."

"He's toying with the idea that we did it together?" KC seemed unable to believe her ears. "He knows Steve never left his side the night of the concert."

"True. But in his professional role he's forced to investigate the possibility that Steve may have served as a distraction, while you committed the murder. Paul kept saying he knew you would understand, since his job required him to get at the truth, and he couldn't ignore any potential solution. He asked lots of questions about how the two of you did it. I think he knows it's pretty farfetched. He pushed Steve for facts, but I didn't let him answer, of course, and reiterated that Steve had already said that neither you nor he killed Curtis."

KC's tea sat neglected on the floor in front of her. "Bringing Steve into this is the last straw." You had to know her to see her anger but, for me, her high chin and flaring nostrils gave her away.

She spoke to Steve. "If Paul won't accept the fact that you were with him all night as an alibi, I don't know what we can do except solve the case for him." Her voice wavered. "I'm sorry to bring all this on you. You'd be better off never to have met me."

Steve bent to KC, captured her hand, and pulled her up to sit on his lap, waking Golden, who gave KC a disgusted look and moved to sit by my side. "Don't say that. You're the best thing that ever happened to me. We'll deal with this and put it behind us. We won't let the crazy theories of one police lieutenant jeopardize our future happiness."

"Thanks." KC leaned back against him. " I just wish this was all over. I'll do my best to help."

She looked angry and miserable. KC had always been a clear note in my world. Her distress pulled at my heart strings, and I rededicated myself to solving this—quickly.

TWENTY

TUESDAY, JULY 23, 2013, 8:00 A.M.

I ROSE EARLY, THINKING I COULD WORK on Curtis's murder from a different angle, now. As Steve had said, "when we find the blackmailer, we find the murderer."

Barry had informed the police about Matlow and requested that they test his guns. But likely Matlow couldn't get access to the backstage area and take the pictures that were used to threaten blackmail. I'd also questioned Mel, Tyler, and Lila. Lila looked more and more improbable as a suspect. Unless the police found the murder weapon and somehow linked it to her, nothing connected her to the killing, and it was doubtful that she could get backstage to take the blackmail photos.

Most plausibly, either Mel or Tyler tried to blackmail me, and was therefore the killer. But I needed more information. Where was Mel the night of the murder? His response had been too evasive for me. And what had Tyler done when he left the stage during *1812*? He, too, had avoided answering my questions.

Almost certainly I had gotten too close to the murderer with my questions, but I didn't know how. The only answer seemed to be to continue my investigation, and there were areas I hadn't looked into yet.

Five lawsuits were pending against Curtis. Presumably the Colorado Water Board had no personal axe to grind, only a legitimate beef with Curtis's treatment of the stream at Butterfly Hollow. I'd already talked to some of the residents of Homes at Skyridge. In general, they seemed to be better off to let their court case proceed. Murdering Curtis would only slow things down. Matlow belonged to that group, but he had begun to seem an unlikely possibility. I had to keep following other leads. I couldn't let KC down.

Besides the Water Board and Skyridge, there were three other suits against Curtis. Steve had eliminated Don Norton, whose plumbing and heating company sued Curtis for unpaid invoices at the shopping center where they had been subcontracted. Norton had been out of town at the time of the murder. The only two legal actions left had been brought by the tenants of an office building, Mountainside Medical Tenants Association, and a private individual, Brian Conan.

I needed to question these people.

Before I decided what to do next, Barry called. "Hey, Em."

"Hey."

"Bad news. Paul checked out Matlow's guns. Ballistics tests proved none of his guns fired the bullet that killed Curtis."

I groaned. Matlow had been proved innocent. He hadn't killed Curtis and wasn't my blackmailer. My disappointment sent me into a black pit.

"Sorry, Em. We'll keep at it. It'll work out."

"I know. See you later."

Mentally, I squared my shoulders and put my discouragement aside. I taught a few students, then returned to pondering how to continue my investigation. I didn't know anything about Mr. Conan and his complaints or his lawsuit. Oneida had passed along contact information for all the plaintiffs. When I called Conan, unfortunately, I got a recording and had to leave a message.

Plan B involved a drive out to the Mountainside Medical Building. I found it perched on the side of a hill on the west side of town, with a wall of windows facing north.

On the ground floor were a dermatologist, an OB/GYN, and a general practitioner. The dermatologist looked the least busy. I entered there.

"Do you have an appointment?" The receptionist peered over the rims of her glasses at me expectantly. Her smile welcomed me.

I tried to give the impression I served in some kind of official capacity, without actually saying so. "I'm looking into C.H. Strange Development. Is the doctor available?"

"I'll check. Your name?"

Again, I felt it best to use my maiden name, in case the doctor had season's tickets to the symphony. "Emily Rizzuto."

"And what organization are you with?"

Faced with a direct question, I decided honesty was the best policy. "I'm asking questions on my own."

The receptionist pressed a few buttons and I heard, "There's a woman here wanting information on C.H. Strange Development. Do you want to speak to her?"

Silence, broken only by a garbled electronic voice on the other end of the line.

The receptionist covered the receiver with her hand. "She says she'll see you, but she has a patient right now and another after that. She wants to know if you can wait."

"Of course."

The receptionist turned back to the receiver. "She'll stay."

More incomprehensible speech on the other end of the line.

"I'll tell her." The receptionist replaced the receiver and addressed me. "Dr. Beal will see you on her break."

"Will she be long?"

"I'd plan on at least an hour."

I looked at my watch. "Okay."

"Help yourself to the coffee and tea over there," she motioned to a corner table. "The restrooms are down the hall."

I took a seat next to the tea and looked around. Although the office was on the first floor, its windows hung out over the cliff and had a spectacular view of the foothills to the north. The table holding the coffee and tea, and also some mints, rested in the corner between a side wall and the windows. The window wall had no seats, open to the view. Scenery became part of the décor, and evergreens seemed to cross the threshold of the waiting room. Plush furniture with cushy armchairs striped in green, gray, and black faced the windows. The carpet picked up the colors in its tiny speckles.

Incongruously, the area below the windows showed water trails, the carpet was stained, and the paint peeled. I suspected I would hear the same story I'd already heard many times. Strange Development had left the building with problems it never should have had in the first place.

I pulled out my ever-present book, a whodunit, and read for about fifty-five minutes, my patience increased by the fact that the fictional detective had almost found the solution. If only turning a few pages brought answers in real life.

"The doctor can see you now." A nurse showed me down the hall and into the doctor's private office. A small room, the view revealed by two adjoining walls of windows made it seem spacious. The doctor's desk sat to the left. Behind it a built-in bookshelf bulged with books. Being enfolded by the view had to make it easier to receive news—good or bad—here.

The doctor was fiftyish, with smile lines and silver hair streaked with black.

Sitting in one of two armchairs in front of her desk, I started the interview. "Thank you for seeing me on short notice."

"No problem. I understand you have questions about Strange Development. My receptionist didn't have details."

"I'm looking into the organization for a friend. Mr. Strange treated her very badly, and she is hoping for more information, possibly to be used in legal action."

"Do you have a card?"

I looked through my purse as if searching. "I must have left them in my other purse. Stupid of me!"

We laughed. In that moment we were two women who understood the challenges of changing purses. "I can give you my contact info, though." I wrote it on a post-it note she gave me, being careful to write my name as "Emily Rizzuto."

"I have plenty to say about Strange Development." She leaned back in her office chair, but she didn't look relaxed. "I'm grateful for a chance to vent."

"Vent? That doesn't sound good."

"It's not." The doctor sighed. "I have a private practice here. It's a life-long dream. When I saw the plans for this place, I thought it was perfect. The windows and the view create a relaxing ambiance, and the parking in back and below doesn't interfere. I planned every detail right down to the atmosphere and the decorations."

Dr. Beal removed a sack from a lower desk drawer. "This is my lunch break. I hope you don't mind if I eat while we talk."

"Of course not. Thanks for making time for me. I'm sure you're busy."

I waited while she dipped a carrot stick into what looked like hummus and chewed it thoughtfully. "The building *would* be perfect if the windows didn't leak, the outside light bulbs were replaced as needed, and the elevator from the parking garage worked consistently."

"It's pretty obvious in the waiting room that the windows are leaking."

"You should see it after a rainstorm from the north." The doctor's jaw muscle twitched.

"Hasn't the Development Corporation resolved any of the problems?"

Dr. Beal tsked. "The last I heard, they claimed they'd hired a management company, Vista Management, to handle repairs. But when you call Vista Management, they tell you that Strange Corp. hasn't paid them and they can't help until it does. When you call Strange, they tell you that it must be a mix-up and say they'll call back, which they never do. I'm frustrated because the windows have never been right. Strange should have fixed them as part of the original contract. A lawsuit seemed the only recourse we have." She sounded beyond disgusted.

"We?"

"The Tenants Association." Dr. Beal dipped a piece of cauliflower and popped it into her mouth, then chewed and brooded before she spoke again. "Everybody, or almost everybody, has similar problems. We all chipped in to pay the lawyers. Really, this building is *almost* perfection. It shouldn't be hard to get problems like these fixed, although I guess the offices on the top floor have leaky roofs. Those might be more serious."

"You must've heard that Curtis Strange, the owner of Strange Development, has been murdered. Has that affected the progress of your case?"

"Not that I know of. How do you get slower than a standstill?" Dr. Beal's voice rose in irritation, I assumed.

"Do you know of anybody who might have killed him?"

She shook her head and shrugged. "Everybody's angry, but as to who might have killed him . . . I don't know how frustrated or angry or whatever you'd have to get to commit a murder. That's a pretty extreme reaction. It seems like it wouldn't be worth it."

"Do you know of any of the tenants who went to the concert in City Park on July Fourth?"

Dr. Beal leaned back in her chair. "I'd guess no one. We have a magnificent view of the fireworks from here. The building's closed for the holiday, of course. All the tenants get together and have a private party in one of the larger suites on the top floor. Everyone brings their significant others and kids, and we don't have to fight the crowds."

I could understand not enjoying the crowds. But she had bruised my musician's ego. "Don't you miss the music?"

She chuckled. "I've heard *1812* before."

I stopped myself from responding that she'd seen fireworks before, too. "Well, I guess that takes care of my questions." I stood and excused myself. "Thank you again for seeing me on such short notice."

She stood and shook my hand. "I hope your friend has better luck with Strange Development than we've had."

"Me too. If you think of anything else, please call the police department. They can get to the bottom of this."

Dr. Beal had guessed that no one from the building would have been at the Fourth of July concert. Driving home I reflected that didn't definitively eliminate everyone in the building from suspicion, but the doctor had convinced me my efforts might be better spent elsewhere first. She'd also mentioned Vista Management. I'd look into that.

I TREATED MYSELF TO A LATE LUNCH at the Articulate Artichoke. When I waved at KC through the kitchen window, she pointed to her watch and mimed zipping her lip. I got the point. Back at the table, I checked my messages; nothing from Brian Conan. Taking my time, I ate my salad and finished my tea, then waved good-bye to KC before I went home to teach a few more students.

I didn't hear from Mr. Conan for six hours. When he finally called, I explained that a friend needed my help. It felt uncomfortable to use my real name, but the caller ID would have revealed it anyway. I just hoped he wasn't a symphony goer. He worked as an investment counselor and told me he could only meet me in the evenings. Not wanting to waste any time, I arranged a seven-thirty meeting at his place.

He owned a large house in a development of equally impressive homes. He appeared to be in his early sixties and greeted me in shorts, flip-flops, and a polo shirt. He must have been an exercise devotee because he sported a flat stomach and muscular legs, though no bulging muscles. Running maybe?

"You must be Emily Wilson. Hope you don't mind if I made myself comfortable. I've been hot all day—suit you know—and I couldn't wait to cool down."

"You're fine. I appreciate you meeting with me on such short notice."

He opened the door wider and waved me inside, then led the way to the living room. Generously proportioned, it had built-in bookshelves on one wall, a fireplace on a second wall, and western windows overlooking a stream and the mountains—a sensational view. What could be wrong here?

"Have a seat."

I sat in an angular wooden chair of modern design. "As I explained on the phone, I'm trying to help a friend. We're looking for information on Curtis Strange and his murder, and I wanted to interview people who had any sort of dealings with him. I got your name because you have a lawsuit with Strange Corporation."

Mr. Conan sat on the sofa, his right arm along its back. He raised his chin and gazed at me intensely. "Darned right I have a lawsuit with them. This is my dream home. Designed it myself."

"It's beautiful."

"It should have been a perfect location, too. Great view and all. But it turns out the whole development rests on an old mine." Mr. Conan tsked. "I know because I'm already having problems. I've had to become informed."

"Did Strange know about the old mine?"

"Had to have. While researching the case, my attorney found out about the mine. Apparently, a huge scandal erupted just before Strange bought the land. Twenty-some miners were killed. All the papers carried the tragedy and the trial. You had to have lived under a rock to miss it."

"Why aren't the other residents of the development suing?"

"Haven't had problems yet, I guess. Maybe they won't ever. But my foundation started crumbling right away. Another company told me they could shore up the foundation, but if the mine doesn't remain stable, I'll continue to have problems. They're willing to try the repair, but say they can't make guarantees it'll last. Their paperwork absolves them from responsibility. If I don't want to gamble on that, they recommend I buy a new plot of land and start all over. Either way, it's way more expense than I planned on."

"Wow. Unless you can get Strange to pay, you're . . . well . . . in a bad position."

"You're right. It's a matter of principle, too. This place is brand new. Actually, two years old now. But I started having problems six months in. It's not right. I think Strange should pay, rather than foist off their mistakes on buyers. The development never should have been built here in the first place, though I'm sure he got the land for a song. I'm suing Strange Corp. for the price of a new house and land, plus aggravation."

"I've heard a lot of people have the same type of problem. Curtis Strange, the owner of Strange Corp., was recently murdered. Do you know of anyone who would have been angry enough to kill Mr. Strange?"

"No. I'm angry, but not angry enough to kill. I don't know if anything could make me that irrational. Makes me feel better that other people have problems, too, though. Like I'm not crazy. I've been the Lone Ranger, trying to deal with this myself."

"Did you go to the Fourth of July concert in City Park?"

"No. We're not in the city here. The wife and I can have fireworks. The kids and grandkids came over and we made a day of it. We played games, I showed off my barbecuing skills, and we finished off the day by lighting fireworks in the driveway." He gave me a curious look. "Why do you ask?"

"I need to keep complete records. Curtis was killed at the concert. It doesn't sound like you or anyone in your family went, though."

"No."

"Well, I know you've had a long day. I won't take up any more of your evening."

Mr. Conan showed me to the door and I left, reflecting that he didn't sound like a good possibility. His wife and their kids and grandkids would support him. I felt I could eliminate him as a suspect.

In fact, the last three of Curtis's court cases had led to nothing. Mr. Conan's family would back up his story, Don Norton had been out of town with his wife, and Dr. Beal could prove she wasn't at the Fourth of July concert. Probably none of the other residents of the building were either. Had Paul looked into the lawsuits and come up with the same results I had? He checked into things thoroughly, although sometimes he came to wrong conclusions. Surely he wouldn't have neglected such an obvious step as investigating the plaintiffs. I had gotten only one new clue. Dr. Beal had mentioned Vista Management. I'd see what I could find out from them.

My interview with Mr. Conan hadn't taken long. I arrived home by eight-thirty, in time to receive Barry's call.

He got right to the point. "The cops found the gun."

I pictured KC's relief. "How come they didn't find it before?"

"They were both lucky and unlucky. Lucky that the Boy Scout discovered the murder before the trash was hauled away. But 100,000 people spent at least four hours, sometimes all day, in the park. The police had to sift through pounds and pounds and *pounds* of garbage, and I imagine it wasn't a high priority. They had other things to investigate."

"But they found the gun in the trash?"

"Yeah. That's a mixed blessing, though. The murder weapon was registered to Jane Rice."

"Jane Rice? The Jane Rice on the Symphony Board and the Symphony's Planning Committee?"

"That's the one. There were marks on the gun indicating a suppressor had been used. The weapon was wiped clean of fingerprints. Jane had reported it stolen the day before the concert, on July third. Some other things were taken in the robbery, too. Jewelry mostly, worth a bundle. Some cash, no electronics. It seems like the burglar knew what to look for and didn't want anything bulky. Just what he could carry. No windows or doors were broken or jimmied. She suspected construction workers who were remodeling her kitchen."

My knees were weak with dismay, and I flopped down in the easy chair. "I remember Jane mentioned it at the Symphony Planning Committee meeting, the day after the Fourth of July concert. Mel had gone to check on Curtis, who hadn't appeared, and we talked about the robbery while we waited for Mel to return, before we found out Curtis was dead. What's the mixed blessing?"

"The cops are trying to pin the murder on KC. Since the gun had been wiped clean and might have been tossed there by anybody, they're saying it must have been KC."

"That's ridiculous." I guessed wrong when I thought the discovery of the gun would let her off the hook.

"I know, but that's what they're trying to prove." Barry sighed, silent for a moment. "KC is Steve's fiancée. She'd seen Jane at various Symphony events. Concerts, fundraisers, that kind of thing. KC would have seen Jane's jewelry and been in Jane's house."

"But why would she take the gun? She doesn't know anything about guns. Paul already asked her about it." I heard myself whining, feeling his continuing suspicions of KC were unfair.

"If she had murdered Curtis she would have lied."

"Okay. I see the *mixed* part." I pleaded. "*Please* tell me about the blessing."

"Since there were no prints on the gun, they're still looking. They can't tie KC to the murder. She's not under arrest, for now."

"Pretty small blessing." I slumped, dispirited.

"I'll take what I can get."

I thought out loud. "If one of the workmen did steal the gun, like Jane thinks, robbery would be a credible motive for the murder, especially with the donation basket missing. You said the police had discounted that, though."

"Yeah. Because Curtis didn't draw his gun."

"I've thought from the beginning that the murderer could have taken Curtis by surprise."

"Seems possible to me, too, and I'll suggest it to the cops." Barry rustled some pages and didn't talk, as if he were writing.

I tried to think of any hole I could find in the police theories that implicated KC. "Or, if a workman took the jewelry, and in the process saw and took the gun, he could have sold it."

"That fast? One day? Unlikely."

"Did Jane discover the robbery right away? Maybe it happened earlier. I wouldn't think she'd be wearing expensive jewelry every day."

"I don't know the answer to that." Barry paused. "I'll talk to the cops. It's another thing I'll suggest."

"What about Jane herself?" I thought a moment. "She could have been planning the murder, reported the gun stolen a day early, then wiped it and thrown it away after she killed Curtis."

"What would the motive be?" Barry sounded thoughtful.

"There's the problem. Curtis and Jane disagreed over the future of the Symphony, but not violently, like Mel, Tyler, and Curtis. Curtis disagreed with everyone on the Symphony's Planning Committee at one time or another but, speaking personally, that didn't move me to premeditated murder. I wouldn't think Jane would be that angry, either." I remembered. "She seemed devastated by the murder, too."

"Okay, then." Barry paused, and when he continued his thoughts were organized. "It seems like the best possibilities would be either a thief, or someone who had a grudge against Curtis and had enough of a connection to the Symphony that he or she knew Jane, knew her jewelry, had access to Jane's house, and maybe knew she had a gun."

I groaned. "Except for the last one, that fits KC to a tee. I don't know that KC had a grudge against Curtis, but she sure didn't like him. She'd seen Jane's jewelry at various social events, and she and Steve were invited often to Jane's house. All those pictures the police found aren't helping KC's case."

Only the buzz of the phone line broke our silence.

Thoughtfully I continued. "Plenty of people had grudges against Curtis. He had truly inflammatory business practices, but I don't know about the connection to Jane."

"Any of them have ties to the Symphony?"

"Mel and Tyler. Beyond that, who knows? With a concert hall that seats two thousand, and three concerts per series, that makes six thousand people with ties to the symphony. Then add in the musicians and employees, and we're looking at about sixty-one hundred people."

"Well, at least the fat lady hasn't sung yet."

I wasn't amused. "Are you trying to be funny?"

"Sorry, Em. Did I make you smile?"

"No. But I guess I do need a little perspective."

I didn't tell Barry about the threat or the blackmail photos. He'd worry and go into protective mode. I knew him too well. He'd make more noise than a timpani at the climax of a piece, and try to get me to stop investigating. He'd done it when I looked into my own case a few years ago, and also when I helped Charlie. I didn't want to deal with his reaction.

I no sooner hung up with Barry than Steve called. He had been to the Board Meeting that morning, then had lunch with a few of the other members, and called to tell me about it. "This was the first Board Meeting since Curtis's death. The murder topped the list of discussion topics. Generally, people thought he deserved it, if anybody ever did. No specifics, other than general dislike. Almost everybody was at the concert on the Fourth. I can't even help narrow down suspects. There really wasn't much I could learn other than Curtis didn't have any loyal friends. We suspected that. After I got home from the meeting, Barry called. He said the gun belonged to Jane and told me how the police theorize KC took it. All of it's discouraging." He paused, then continued hesitantly. "There's another thing that's been bothering me, too."

"What's that?"

"The Police Chief, Howard Dare, came to the meeting." Steve sounded uneasy.

"I didn't know he was on the Board."

"We invited him to join during our community outreach." He paused for a moment. When I didn't ask any more questions, he continued. "Anyway, he took me aside and told me it didn't look good for KC. He suggested I drop her for the sake of my 'good name.'" Steve rarely used sarcasm.

Awkward. "You think it's because the police are building a case against KC?"

"Yeah, and in the process they've uncovered her past. I haven't told KC about it because she's already despondent over the news about the gun. I managed to stop myself from hitting Howard or making a scene, but I let him know he couldn't talk about my fiancée that way, and that I wouldn't be dumping KC." He made an odd noise in his throat. "He shrugged." Steve sounded angry. "Shrugged. Like it wasn't important, or like he didn't care."

I didn't know what to say. "Sorry, Steve. Thanks for defending her."

The subject needed changing. I thought a moment. "Jane thinks one of the workmen remodeling her kitchen stole the gun. A lot of strangers would have been traipsing through the house. Robbery seems like a strong possibility. Or one of the workers might have stolen the gun and sold to a dealer." I told him about Barry's doubts.

"I can't agree. What makes sense to me is that nobody would want to have the gun in their possession for long. Too dangerous. They'd unload it on a dealer as soon as possible. Then the dealer would feel the same way and get rid of it quickly, too. Maybe all the ducks need to line up for it to happen quickly enough, but I think it's possible."

For KC's sake, I hoped Steve was right.

I thought a moment. "Besides the workmen, can you think of anyone who would know about Jane's jewels and her gun, and have entry to her house?"

Steve huffed. "Everybody who ever saw her at a Symphony performance would know about her jewelry, since she never stinted on bling. She entertained a lot. Plenty of people were in and out of the house. They were nice people, though: me, KC, people on the Symphony Board, the members of the governing bodies of the Humane Society and the University. And as for knowing about the gun . . . I don't even have a guess. Why would any of those people want to rob Jane or steal her gun?"

I thought about the answer. "Her jewels were worth a lot. And if anyone planned a murder . . ."

"None of those people need money as far as I know." Impatience quickened his speech. "Besides, *killing* Curtis? I know Don Norton had a financial beef with him, but killing Curtis would make it harder to get his money. Their court case would come to a rapid close. Curtis's estate might even declare bankruptcy rather than pay. Besides, Don and his wife were out of town on the Fourth. Curtis wasn't popular, but as far as *killing* him? I haven't a clue."

"I have a couple ideas." I summed up my conclusions. "Mel Harmon, president of the Board, knew Jane, knew her jewels, and often visited her house. Ditto for Tyler Washington. He played string bass in the Symphony and is a member of its Planning Committee. He does need money. And both of them argued fiercely with Curtis. His assistant, Lila, kept his schedule, knew about the Board and Planning Committee meetings, knew Jane maybe only slightly, but had seen her jewels and didn't like Curtis either."

Lila seemed more and more unlikely as a suspect. How would she get into Jane's house? And how could she have gotten backstage to take the blackmail picture? But I couldn't eliminate her altogether, and I mentioned her to keep Steve's spirits up. "Lila could have been in Jane's house on some errand for Curtis and stolen her gun." I paused. "I've questioned all of them. Any one might be behind the blackmail threat."

"Maybe." He sounded doubtful.

"I don't know, Steve. I don't have all the answers. Only theories." I realized Steve might be able to be more help. "On another tack, do you know anyone with a silver van?"

"A silver van? Why?"

I explained that I'd questioned my neighbor, who had seen a silver van in the right time frame to have delivered the blackmail photos.

"I can't think of anyone off the top of my head, but I'll mull it over."

My concern for my friend couldn't wait any longer. "Can I talk to KC? Maybe I can cheer her up."

"You can try. Good luck."

I heard muffled rustling as KC took the phone. "Emily?" Her voice was thick and almost unrecognizable.

"Barry told me the police found the gun. I'm sorry that didn't exonerate you. I know you were counting on it. We all were."

It sounded like KC cried softly, and it took a few moments for her to pull herself together. "I'm discouraged." Her voice wavered. "The theft of Jane's gun makes all our theories seem laughable. You have to ask yourself, who could get into Jane's house? Who would know about her gun? The police think Steve and I are the answers to those questions. Steve and I both knew Jane and both of us, occasionally at least, were invited to her house. The last time we were there, though, was her May Day party, long before the murder. Of course, they'd think we were lying about that, you know?"

I didn't know what to say, but my heart ached for her.

She didn't speak for a moment. "I don't believe anyone had a strong enough motive for murder. I keep coming back to the theory that sex must be at the bottom of it somehow."

"But that's a dead end. We've talked about it before. The only person we know Curtis fixated on was you."

"Unless he interfered in someone else's relationship. But then there's the problem of access to the gun."

"KC! You're a genius!" I had suddenly seen the whole problem with different eyes.

"What? What did I say?"

"Sex and access to the gun. There's something I haven't mentioned." KC started to say something, but I continued. "When I visited Harvey Rice's office, he and his intern were obviously intensely attracted to each other. Shortly before the murder, Curtis visited him, requesting funding for Antelope Run. Maybe Curtis saw the same attraction I did. Maybe Harvey's fascination with his intern and Curtis's visit and subsequent murder are all tied together."

The hopeless energy shifted.

"Could be. If he wanted to keep the affair from Jane . . ." KC sounded excited. "Steve wants to talk to you again."

"Okay. But don't forget that we're getting close."

I heard rustling sounds.

"Emily. I can see KC's cheering up. What are you saying to her?"

"I told her about all the possibilities you and I have already talked about that." Slowly I gave voice to my theory. "But I also had an idea about Jane's husband, Harvey." I explained my thinking. "He's a respected member of the community and all . . ." I slowly continued, ". . . but it seems beyond coincidental that Curtis, a man Harvey had disagreements with, a man who disagreed with his values, and a man who possibly uncovered his love for his intern, was murdered with his wife's gun."

"Uncovered his love for his intern?" Steve hadn't heard about that part.

"It's pretty obvious if you see them together. And Curtis visited Harvey's office shortly before the murder."

"In order to accuse Harvey you'll need unassailable proof. He's got pull and power. On top of that, he seems like a nice guy. You've got to have a motive beyond committee disagreements. Proof he loved his intern, or strong proof of something else. Just as long as it leaves no doubts." Steve sounded puzzled. "It's hard to see him hauling off and shooting someone, even a lonely, unlikable sociopath."

Sociopath. Pretty strong term. I made allowances for Steve's anger, then asked myself, was Curtis a sociopath?

I wasn't a psychologist, but Curtis certainly didn't care about others' rights and feelings, and didn't attend to his own financial obligations. The residents of Skyridge, Mountainside Medical, Don Norton, and Mr. Conan could all attest to that. He also engaged in repeated illegal acts, as he had in stalking KC.

But regardless of what Curtis may or may not have been, we were discussing Harvey Rice. "You can't always judge a book by its cover." I remembered the heat between him and Danielle. "I'm going to look into him a little more thoroughly."

"Be careful. Jane is extremely protective of Harvey and her boys. She has a reputation for getting her own way, too." Steve sounded reluctant.

"A reputation?"

"Among anybody who's ever served on a committee with her. They say she expects to be in charge and expects to be obeyed. In general, a person like that is exceptionally useful as the head of a committee, but you have to handle her with kid gloves. She's easily offended."

"Ass kissing?"

Steve laughed. "To put it plainly."

"I'm not too worried. Jane and I get along well, and I won't be making accusations unless it looks like something can be proven."

"I can see KC is a different woman than before she talked to you." Steve sounded surprised and relieved.

"We inspire each other. She made me think of Harvey in a different way."

"It's good she helped. She keeps telling me how unhappy she is that she can't lend you a hand. The restaurant is at a crucial turning point, though, and she can't take time off now." Steve's voice descended to a whisper. "Or at least that's what she says. I think there's a part of her that's in denial—insisting that she didn't kill Curtis and it must be only a matter of time and patience until the real murderer is found." Steve's voice returned to normal. "She knows we're working for her. She's confident we'll find out the truth." I could hear Steve's smile when he said that.

"Give her a hug for me. I'll update her as I find out more."

TWENTY-ONE

WEDNESDAY, JULY 24, 2013, 9:00 A.M.

I STARTED THE DAY BY TALKING TO JANE. I had considered how to investigate Harvey, who, in my new way of thinking, seemed the best possibility. I didn't know him well. But I did know Jane. I could think of countless excuses to talk to her. Enthusiasm driving me forward, wanting to do something this minute, I called.

"Hi. It's Emily. How are you?"

"Oh, same as ever. Keeping busy with committees."

"And Harvey and the rest of the family?"

Jane laughed. "They've left for another camping trip. Since the boys were teenagers the four of them have been off at every opportunity. Nowadays the boys have their own kids and it's unusual that Harvey, the boys, and the grandkids can all get together at once. They didn't hesitate to seize the chance. They'll be back later today."

"You haven't been lonely?" She wouldn't admit it if she was. We weren't that close.

"Oh, no," Jane responded, amused and tinkly with pleasure. "I've had plenty to keep me busy, and it's nice to have the house to myself, and to keep my own schedule without worrying about anyone else."

Enough small talk. I changed the subject. "The reason I called is that I wondered if you'd be free for lunch after the Symphony's Planning Committee meeting. I hoped to run some ideas for soloists past you. I know I could bring it up with the full Committee, but I wanted to make sure you thought they were good ideas first."

"Of course, Emily. How 'bout the Vegan Village? It's close, we can eat healthy there, and have a good talk. The atmosphere is wonderful."

"Sounds great. I'll see you tomorrow."

As we hung up, I reflected that the coincidences around Jane were glaring. They had been bothering me since Barry told me that her gun was the murder weapon. But in spite of my instructions to Steve not to judge a book by its cover, I couldn't see Jane as a murderess; too wispy and insubstantial and controlled. More importantly, she didn't have any motive that I could see to kill Curtis. But Harvey . . .? That made sense.

Satisfied arranging lunch with Jane had prepared me to investigate Harvey as much as I could for now, in the interest of helping KC I decided to look into other angles, rather than sitting on my hands. Dr. Beal had mentioned that Strange Development Corp. had told Mountain Medical lessees that Vista Management would handle repairs in her building. I got the address for the management company from the computer. They were located on a quiet street behind the library in a building of therapists and dentists.

To keep my chops in shape, I played a short practice session consisting of the twelve scales, arpeggios, and crucial daily exercises, a routine I could do in my sleep, then headed for the address I'd found.

In the small office, one person sat in the lobby area, with a nameplate inscribed, "Pam Martinez." The sign on the closed inner office door read, "Mark Martinez; Service Director; Computer Specialist."

A family business?

"Hi. Welcome to Vista Management." A middle-aged woman, Pam had graying red hair and a welcoming smile.

I again used my maiden name to avoid any association with the symphony. "I'm Emily Rizzuto. I'm interested in Strange Development Corp. and understood you might have information."

She gestured at the chair in front of her desk. "Why are you interested?"

I seated myself. "You might have heard that Curtis Strange, the owner and CEO of the company, was recently murdered."

She nodded her head.

"I'm helping investigate."

"Are you with the police?" *A logical question.*

"No. The police are investigating a friend of mine in connection with the murder. I know she's not capable of killing anyone, and I'm looking into things on my own. I'll turn any information I get over to the police."

She smiled at me. "Pretty supportive friend you are. I'll help if I can."

I thought a moment. "To start, maybe you can tell me what you do here, and what you know about C.H. Strange."

"I answer the phones and do accounting." The light in her eyes spoke of sincerity. "Mark wouldn't have had any dealings with Strange Development, but I remember the company very clearly."

"Could you tell me about your experience with them?"

She hesitated only a moment. "Who could forget? Their office manager . . ."

Was that Lila?

". . . lined up our services for Mountainside Medical. We received a few calls requesting repairs, but never a deposit from Strange. We have a strict policy that we won't begin service until we get money up front. We learned that the hard way years ago. Anyway, we never really started work for Strange. But we did get irate calls from tenants of the building complaining about leaky windows and roofs, non-working elevators, security lights that were out. Stuff like that. Initially all the calls were from different people, but later they were repeat calls, and the people on the phone were increasingly rude and angry."

"That must have been upsetting. What did you tell them?"

"I told them all the same thing. We'd be glad to initiate repairs as soon as we received payment from Strange."

"Was there anyone who seemed particularly angry?"

Pam thought a moment. "No, I don't think so. They were all irritated, all angry, but no one more than any other. I felt for them. They weren't getting service from Strange, and they certainly weren't getting help from us. It must have been maddening."

"I've heard hints from other people that there were financial problems at Strange. I wonder why they would take on a new commitment."

She tilted her head. "Maybe they thought we'd be cheaper than being responsible themselves. Or maybe they wanted to distract the tenants? I don't know."

"You might be right." I stood. "Thank you for your help." We shook hands. "Have a good day."

"Thanks. You, too. And good luck."

In pursuit of further information on Strange Development's financial position, I headed for the company's office, intending to talk to Lila.

When I pushed open the door, Lila greeted me with, "You again!"

I decided to come clean. "Me again. I have to confess. I don't want to buy a home in Antelope Run, and I have my phone firmly in my grasp." I held it up. "May I sit down?"

"Why not? I can't stop you." She didn't sound happy about it.

"I'm really helping a friend . . ."

A door opened.

"I heard voices. I . . . Emily!" Roland Strange had come into the room. "What are you doing here?"

"You two know each other?" Lila sounded astonished.

Time to own up to the truth. "Neither of you know the whole story. Lila, I'm not looking for a house. And Roland, I'm not an innocent hiker. I'm trying to find out who killed Curtis Strange. The police suspect a friend of mine, but I know she wouldn't have done it."

"I think we'd better go to my office for this discussion." Roland sounded . . . what—distrustful?

I couldn't read him with any certainty, but I wouldn't blame him for being leery.

I glanced at Lila, who made a sour face.

"Okay. Lead the way." Fortunately, neither Roland nor I could hear Lila's thoughts.

We walked into an office around the corner.

Roland gestured at the only chair in the office. He sat behind the desk. "Explain."

"Curtis stalked my friend."

"Stalked?"

"There's detailed evidence."

He raised an eyebrow by way of inquiry.

"Unbeknownst to her, he'd been taking pictures of her for years. The police found the photos when they examined his house. Apparently they think that's a great motive for her to murder him."

Roland shifted in his chair.

"When you add that she attended the concert and admittedly talked to Curtis, the police start building a case."

"It sounds like she has reason for concern." Roland crossed his left ankle over his right knee.

"I've had experience with this police department before, and once they develop a theory, it's hard for them to accept other facts. I want to make sure all the facts are available before they settle on a theory."

Roland covered his eyes with his hands and shook his head. "Ever since I arrived, I've found continual confirmation that Uncle Curtis was an unlikeable and unprincipled man." He seemed worn out and beleaguered, older than I'd thought. "This stalking, though—this is the first I've heard of an actual crime. No wonder he and my dad didn't get along."

"Unlikeable and unprincipled?"

He raised his head. "Talk to Lila."

I had.

"She'll tell you. Lawsuits. Shoddy building practices. Environmental irresponsibility. Insensitivity. What's your connection?"

"I'm in the symphony. I served with Curtis on the Symphony's Planning Committee."

"And your friend?"

"About three years ago, she had a few dates with him." If only she hadn't volunteered to help me by dating him. "Most likely, he'd been stalking her since then. She's engaged to be married now. Her fiancé has been extremely understanding, but this is a development they don't need." I wanted info, too. "What do you know about Curtis?"

"I never knew about or met Uncle Curtis. But apparently I'm his last living relative." He chose his words carefully. "Now that I know him by reputation, I'm glad I never made his acquaintance. I had him cremated, but I don't think I can bring myself to have a memorial for him. Not unless there is an awful lot of alcohol served." His shoulders slumped. "I've been horrified not only by the way he treated people, but by the way he tore through the natural world. Maybe I'll just scatter his ashes instead. Butterfly Hollow would be a perfect place, if a trifle ironic. Then I can skip listening to a bunch of hypocrites say what a wonderful guy he was. Besides, I don't know if anyone would come to a funeral. Better to send him back to nature in solitude."

"Really?" Maybe Butterfly Hollow wasn't doomed after all.

"As I've told you before, I wasn't even aware Uncle Curtis existed until after he died. He and my father had a falling out before I was born. Dad told me the reason for the move to Montana is that he found an orange peel at the top of one of his favorite climbs in Colorado and decided there were getting to be too many people, even as few as there were then. Maybe it's true, but, in hindsight, I have my suspicions it isn't." Roland crossed his legs.

"How come?"

"Uncle Curtis and Dad were almost total opposites. They must have disagreed about all kinds of things." He shrugged. "All I know for sure is that Strange Development is in a shambles. Debts everywhere. It has to keep getting new loans, or the whole thing collapses. Dad would never have stood for it."

"Are you going to declare bankruptcy and go home, then?" I felt saddened by the thought, but recognized that to be the most likely scenario.

"I would, but then where would Uncle Curtis's customers be?" He frowned.

"Can you help them?"

"I hope so. I'm an engineer. In Montana I worked for an environmental engineering firm. The needs Uncle Curtis's clients have are pretty basic, and I feel like Strange Development has a duty to provide what it promised. If I'm going to be in charge, I'm going to try to do right by them." He hesitated. "It'll depend, though. They'll have to give me time, and Lila says they're angry. They might not give me a chance."

"I don't know if I can be of much help, but I'll do what I can."

Roland thought a moment. "If you've developed relationships with any of the people involved, maybe they'll listen to you."

I thought of Noah Wattle. "I'll try. That's all I can promise."

"That's good enough for me." He leaned back in the chair and changed the subject. "What about the body they found on my land? Did the sheriff update you?"

I told him what I knew. "The last I heard the authorities had identified him as Joe Connally. His family said he had a habit of dropping out of sight. They hadn't expected to hear from him and didn't know of any connection with Curtis. I don't either. It's a dead end."

"Not entirely. Sergeant Serna contacted me. Remember I said I had suspicions about why my father left Colorado? Apparently Strange Development incorporated as a partnership between the two brothers, that is, my dad and Uncle Curtis. The original documents registered Joe Connally as the treasurer."

I sat back in amazement. "There *was* a connection."

"Yeah. All three people who know the real story are dead, though. We can only guess at the details. The police theory is that the three of them had some kind of falling out way back when. Dad and Mr. Connally left at the same time. Then Mr. Connally came back after forty years and tried to blackmail Uncle Curtis, who murdered him." He paused and frowned.

"But you don't agree?"

"There are two things that bother me." He hesitated.

"What are those?"

"First, Mr. Connally showed every sign of being independently wealthy." He spoke slowly. "His daughter said he had been traveling all over the country, visiting beautiful and isolated places."

"So?"

"Those trips must have been funded somehow. He had a healthy retirement income, and owned part of the accounting business he started, which his son and daughter carry on. It's apparently doing quite well. He wouldn't have been hard up for funds."

"You don't see a financial necessity for blackmail?"

"That's exactly it." He frowned again. "Second, the coroner found trauma to the jaw. But he said the cause of death was a blow to the back of the head."

"What's your theory?"

"I think it's more likely that Mr. Connally decided to look up Uncle Curtis, maybe for old times sake, maybe to make amends, maybe to give Curtis a piece of his mind. But he said something that infuriated Uncle Curtis and my uncle struck Connally's jaw. Connally fell against something and hit his head. Uncle Curtis couldn't have been both *in front* of him punching him in the jaw, and *behind him*, hitting his head."

"I think you must be right. It accounts for the facts as we know them."

"Uncle Curtis buried the body in the Hollow. It would never have been found if Golden hadn't dug it up." He looked at me in what seemed like an appeal. "I'm holding on to the idea that it could have been an accident, because I don't want to believe there's a murderer in my family."

"We may never know what really happened, but that sounds like a good theory to me."

"Well, that's my truth. It'll keep me sane."

FROM THERE I DROVE STRAIGHT TO NOAH'S.

"Miz Wilson! Come in, come in."

He led the way to the living room and again reclined, feet up.

Wary of the depth of the sofa, I chose an armchair across from Noah.

I didn't waste time. "I wanted you to know that I've met Curtis's heir."

"Oh?" He looked up quickly.

"He struck me as a nice enough young man—an engineer. He's a little overwhelmed by all the homeowners Curtis let down, but he says he wants to make things right."

Noah grunted. "Actions speak louder than words. The homeowners have been duped by Strange Development more than once. I'll only believe promises if they're backed up by deeds."

"It's true that the new owner hasn't had a chance to do much of anything yet, but I did want to let you know that his heart seems to be in the right place."

Noah sighed. "We'll see. I suppose we can summon a little more patience. We've waited this long. Besides that, we want nice places to live. Not revenge. If there's a good chance of getting that out of this new owner . . . what did you say his name was?"

"Roland Strange."

"Well if Roland can fix things . . . we'll see."

We chatted a bit before I left. He had great stories about the Vietnam War and his buddies. He had served as a medic, and I loved to hear him talk.

As he showed me to the door I realized that I should also speak to Harvey Rice about Butterfly Hollow and Roland's more enlightened views. Maybe that would help. And it would give me an excuse to see Harvey again.

WHEN I GOT HOME A CALL on my landline from Detective Copeland returned my call. I called back, but missed him again. I left a message:

"Hi. This is Emily Wilson playing phone tag with you. Please call as soon as you can. I have information on the violin stolen at the symphony concert Saturday night."

TWENTY-TWO

THURSDAY, JULY 25, 2013, 9:00 A.M.

T HE NEXT MORNING THE DAY STARTED with the kind of
Planning Committee meeting I hated. We discussed parking
and Fleisher Center rental rates *ad nauseum*. I tuned out.

While Mel droned on, I considered him as a suspect. He disliked Curtis and disagreed with him passionately over almost every issue. He would have known about Jane's jewelry and been in her house often. Could he have known about Jane's gun, or discovered it, and stolen it? If so, he might be the murderer. By using her gun, maybe he had tried to frame her. It was possible, but not probable. I knew of no reason for him to want to embroil Jane in police investigations. And he could afford his own weapon. Surely there would be easier, less invasive ways to deflect suspicion than stealing her gun. Then too, he claimed he hadn't attended the Fourth of July concert, where Curtis's murder took place. That seemed a little unbelievable for a Board member, but, if true, meant he was in the clear. No one would have been surprised to see him backstage at the Concert in the Parks last Saturday, though. He could easily have taken pictures of me, with blackmail in mind.

Tyler also sat through the meeting. Though I didn't want to believe it, he might be the killer. He regularly quarreled virulently with Curtis and had been in Jane's house on Symphony business. He could have discovered her jewelry and gun. Then, too, he had left the stage during the July Fourth concert at the time Curtis had been killed. I couldn't even imagine what could be serious enough to call him away except possibly an illness, ambulances, or death—or an appointment to kill. But why wouldn't he have chosen a more private moment if that was his purpose? As a musician, it would be unusual if he *wasn't* backstage at all the concerts. That meant he could easily have taken the photos used to blackmail me.

My musings were interrupted when the meeting moved on to consider new venues. I cared about this subject and could participate in the discussion. Everyone had an opinion, and we had a lively discussion of possibilities and next steps.

After the meeting I excused myself from the usual luncheon with Susie and Tyler, and followed Jane to the Vegan Village. A trendy new restaurant I'd heard stressed the pocketbook, I reasoned that my budget could stand it for one meal.

Jane had taken the last spot in the parking lot. I parked on-street and met her inside. There were two parties ahead of us, which gave me time to enjoy the restaurant's open, airy feel and the numerous plants hanging about. After about ten minutes we were seated in the atrium, sheltered from those patrons at neighboring tables by trailing greenery.

"This is such a gorgeous place. I love it. Relaxing." Jane exhaled noisily and settled into her chair.

"I've never been here before." I echoed her comments. "It's a very soothing atmosphere."

"Wait 'til you taste the food."

We inspected the menus. I'd heard right—pricey. Obviously, Jane wasn't on a musician's budget.

The waitress took our orders before we turned to the subject that had ostensibly brought us here. "I wanted to talk to you about soloists. I wondered what you thought of Albrecht Vogel. He's an oboist. I know that's not generally a solo instrument, but he really impressed me with his musicianship and virtuosity. And there's a flutist, Sinead O'Flaherty. People would be more likely to have heard of her. Very showy. And flute's a popular instrument. It would give a more creative flavor to the programs. Different than the usual pianos, violins, and cellos. What do you think?"

Jane thought for a moment. "It would be an interesting new twist. But maybe not both of them in the same season. And they'd have to be approved by the conductor. I'll run it by him, then maybe approach the Board at the next meeting. We'll see what support we can get."

"You know how to get these things done. Thanks for your help."

"Oh, I have a lot of experience with committees and accomplishing things that way. I'm always interested in advancing good ideas."

"You serve on the Humane Society Board, too, don't you?"

"Yes." Jane smiled. "That's a joy. To think I'm being a voice for all those helpless animals. You know how I love them."

As an aside she said, "Don't forget to give Golden a pat for me."

"I won't."

"Harvey's interested in animal projects, too. You know what a fan he is of Golden's. And of course, our menagerie. He doesn't have time to volunteer at the shelter, but I've convinced him to commit some of the Foundation's funds to help the Humane Society. It works out well." She sipped her water.

I guess. It's not what you know, but who you know. "You two are a godsend to the world of animal lovers, and nature lovers, too." I thought of my last conversation with Harvey. "I talked to your husband about Butterfly Hollow the other day. He seemed dedicated to fighting development there."

The waitress brought our orders and Jane waited until we were both served before she responded. "That's where he took the boys and their kids camping. They love that place. They thought they'd enjoy it once more while they could all be together, before Strange Development destroys it. They came back yesterday, happy as golden retrievers."

I remembered Golden's "smile," and thought how appropriate Jane's simile was.

She took another sip of her iced tea. "I can't believe Curtis tried to get Harvey to support developing the Hollow. Of course, he turned Curtis down flat. Curtis's plan would have destroyed the ecosystem the stream creates and replaced it with a concrete run off ditch. It's crazy that he would even think of asking the Foundation, but I guess he was desperate. People were suing Strange Development right and left, and on top of operating debts, the suits were causing financial problems. The banks wouldn't lend to the company. I guess the Foundation was, you'll excuse the expression, a last-ditch effort."

We both laughed.

"It's hard to imagine that Curtis is dead, killed with my stolen gun. I guess it's a small world, but that's not the way you want to be made aware of it."

I shook my head. "The coincidences are bizarre. How do you think it happened?"

Jane put down her fork and gazed intensely at me. "It's weird. One of the workmen remodeling my kitchen must have taken the gun. From there it's hard to guess, though. Did the thief sell it? Did he kill Curtis and rob the donation basket, then throw the gun away? Did he know Curtis and hate him, find the gun, then conceive the plan to kill him? I guess any of those are possible. Curtis's corporation worked closely with construction companies. He might have known specific workmen and roused someone's hatred, but I don't think it's very likely. Curtis would have been dealing with owners and supervisors."

"I hadn't thought of his links with building contractors."

Jane picked up her fork again. "Other than that, I can't think of a thing. The police asked about July second and third, but Harvey and I had a quiet day both days. Darlene Taylor visited on the second. Mel Harmon dropped in for a while on the third. The soprano soloist for the Fourth had been in a bad car accident."

"I wondered why the soloist changed at the last minute."

"We either had to change the soloist or change the program. The conductor suggested an alternate singer, and Mel and I had to approve it. He came over and we discussed it, then I called the soprano and convinced her to come with no rehearsal. But to even think that Mel could have stolen my gun and murdered Curtis is ridiculous. I know they didn't get along, but really! He wasn't out of my sight except once, to use the restroom."

"That's crazy!" I leaned forward and, placing my elbows on the table, propped my chin in my hands, and wondered, though. Now Mel had motive, opportunity to steal Jane's gun, and, if he had stolen it, the murder weapon. Was it possible? Was he lying when he said he hadn't attended the performance? "Did you see Mel at the concert?"

"No. That doesn't mean he wasn't there. We had a big crowd."

"I didn't see him either." Maybe Mel *wasn't* lying about being somewhere else on the Fourth of July. "You said Darlene Taylor visited on the second?"

"She came to see Harvey. I didn't see much of them, beyond bringing some lemonade." Jane took a bite of her quinoa salad.

So, like Mel, Darlene might have had an opportunity to steal the gun. She claimed not to have been at the concert, though, and she seemed sincere.

"Did you see her at the Fourth of July performance?"

Jane laughed. "Why the twenty questions? You're like a dog with a chew toy. Same answer. I didn't see her, but that doesn't mean she wasn't there."

Figuring Jane's chuckle covered the beginning of annoyance, I decided to abandon the interrogation.

"I guess the police'll figure it out." Jane sounded confident.

They aren't showing signs of making any progress yet.

After a moment's silence I realized that if I didn't speak now, I wouldn't get a chance. The tables near us had been vacated and no one could overhear. "I also wanted to talk to you about one other thing." I leaned forward confidentially. "I know . . . that is . . . have you met Harvey's intern?"

"Yes, I have." Her smile disappeared and she sounded cautious.

"Well . . . she seems . . . very . . ." I didn't know how to proceed, and I inserted my foot firmly in my mouth. "Listen, Jane, we're friends. You've done a lot for the Symphony. You need to know . . ." I decided I didn't know any tactful way to put this. "She seems a little too friendly with Harvey."

Jane laughed. "Harvey can't help the silly girls who get crushes on him. He's a handsome man, you know."

At that point I gave up the hope of getting further information on Harvey. She didn't seem worried, and I had to get along with Jane. I conceded, "You know him best."

Jane smiled and looked as satisfied as a cat who'd just delivered a mouse to my feet. "I appreciate your concern, but Harvey loves his family."

I didn't know what to say, and I wanted to leave as soon as possible.

The waitress rescued us by clearing away our plates and leaving dessert menus.

"This is my treat. I'm always happy to introduce people to this restaurant. I think it's a wonderful place." She looked at the dessert menu. "I can't eat any more, but why don't you have something?"

Remembering the prices, I said gratefully, "Thank you. That's very generous, but I couldn't possibly."

Jane paid, and we went our separate ways.

In the car, I reflected on Jane's lack of hostility. She had been unambiguously positive in her defense of Harvey. Clearly, she wasn't worried about Danielle, unless her acting skills were extraordinarily good.

I HAD A TRIO GIG THAT NIGHT. A couple on the Board of the Humane Society, Mr. and Mrs. Cho, were celebrating their silver anniversary. They were having a party and Jane had recommended they hire my trio for the three-hour job of providing music. She and Harvey arrived early, while I set up the trio's chairs and stands.

Mrs. Cho seemed frazzled. Jane, with her talent for marshalling people, "helped," that is, took charge, while Mrs. Cho scurried uselessly from the kitchen, to the wait staff, to the bar, to the serving table.

When a waiter asked, "Shall we serve the drinks first, or wait until the hors d'oeuvres are ready?" Mrs. Cho put her hand to the side of her cheek. "I'm not sure. On one hand . . ."

Jane stepped in, addressing the waiter directly. "Let's wait until the two can be served together."

The waiter glanced briefly at Mrs. Cho, who looked relieved and nodded.

"That's what we'll do, then." The waiter turned and walked toward the bar.

Mrs. Cho hugged Jane. "Oh, thank you. You're good at entertaining. I don't do it often enough."

The other two members of the trio, Alice and Jen, arrived and we started playing, my attention necessarily given over to the music, starting with Haydn's *London Trio, number one.*

Later, I caught occasional glimpses of Mel, Darlene, Jane, and Harvey, sometimes together, more often, separately. I reflected on how frequently they attended the same parties, their social group well-defined.

During the first break Alice, Jen, and I helped ourselves from the serving table. Harvey, Darlene, and Mel were there, discussing Butterfly Hollow.

I eavesdropped on their conversation while I heaped my plate.

Harvey was talking. "My boys, their kids, and I just got back from a camping trip there. I wanted to see it one more time before Strange Corp. destroys it, but I ended up even more convinced that we need to save that place. It'll be over my dead body that Strange Development follows through with its plans!"

Over Curtis's dead body, or Joe's, would be more accurate.

Mel sipped his wine and said nothing.

Darlene responded with conviction. "I tried more than once to convince Curtis that the city's economic health depended on its beauty and ability to attract tourists and their money. He either didn't care or didn't agree. Butterfly Hollow is a case in point. I couldn't convince him that he could play a major role in 'greening' the city. He was horribly rude at the suggestion." She took a deep breath. "Frankly, I'm glad Curtis is gone. I won't have to deal with him anymore."

"We'll have to see who takes over the business. The new owner couldn't be harder to contend with than Curtis." Mel waved at someone.

"It can always get worse," Harvey observed gloomily.

I made a mental note. I needed to talk to Harvey about Roland Strange.

Knowing they were as aware of me as I was of them, I nodded to the group. "Harvey, Mel, Darlene. Good to see you again." I glanced at my watch. "I wish I could stay and talk, but I've got to get back to playing."

I didn't see Jane, but during the second break I spotted both her and Mrs. Cho earnestly listening to a group discussing animal rights and efforts to eliminate kill shelters.

Mel, Darlene, and Harvey were together, but they had moved to the bar and were joking with several other people. Had Harvey and Jane been together at any point in the evening? Not that I had seen, except for their arrival. Different interests—or were they avoiding each other?

On the ride home I relaxed. It had been a long day. Thankfully, it was over. I kept thinking about Harvey. On the one hand, he seemed likeable and concerned. On the other hand, he might be a murderer. Which was the real Harvey? Could I be imagining things?

With gratitude, I came home to Golden's wiggling welcome. In bed, I snuggled with her bulk. Her warmth and acceptance soothed my mind as I fell asleep. What would I do without her?

TWENTY-THREE

FRIDAY, JULY 26, 2013, 10:00 A.M.

Iwoke thinking about KC. She relied on Steve and me, but I didn't have the resources to follow up on the workmen Jane suspected of the robbery. I didn't even know who they might be. I'd have to make sure that Barry had mentioned it to his friend with the police. Hopefully the force investigated the possibility thoroughly, even though they didn't take it seriously. I wasn't optimistic, given their persistent view that KC had committed the crime.

Though Jane said both Mel and Darlene had come to her house shortly before she discovered the robbery, they both claimed not to have attended the concert. I wasn't sure if they told me the truth.

But Harvey would have had endless opportunities to take Jane's gun. He and I were both concerned about Butterfly Hollow, and I could, and would, tell him about Roland, but my connections with him ended there. How could I learn more?

Diane, our fellow Planning Committee member, had served on several boards with Jane and knew the family. Maybe she'd have some info. I gave her a call.

"Hi, Diane. I wanted to tell you again what a breath of fresh air you've been on the Planning Committee. We've gotten more done in the three weeks you've been with us than we did in the whole nine months before you came."

She laughed. "Oh, I just have a lot of experience on committees, and of course I love the Symphony."

"Yeah. I think we're all playing the same tune, now."

"It's a good group. You three musicians seem very positive and Mel runs things with a light hand, which gives Jane some independence."

"Is that important?"

"Maybe not important. I'd say 'wise' is a better word. It's been my experience that Jane works best if she's either in charge or operating independently."

"How so?"

"I don't want to say too much. It's only my opinion. She seems to have a need to be in control, is all."

"Why do you say that?"

"I've been in a couple situations where she *wasn't* in charge and had to work with other people. She insisted on her way until the rest of us gave in. Fortunately, she's also a smart woman. Not very flexible, though."

Jane had no control over her husband Harvey, at least when he was away from home. I wondered if a domineering woman would find that infuriating. Her behavior at lunch would seem to indicate otherwise. And what about Harvey? Did he escape Jane's influence through his relationship with his intern, Danielle, who clearly respected and adored him? I didn't want to be too obvious, and changed the subject.

We had a good chat about Diane's grandkids and vacation plans. Then she asked about Golden and I gave her an earful. I guess I'm as obnoxious about Golden as some people are about their grandchildren.

When we said goodbye I was smiling, and truly grateful that Diane's positive attitude had replaced Curtis's obstructionism.

I made myself a salad and had just started to practice when Kathleen called.

"We got the house! The inspection's all done and it passed with flying colors, except for a few little things that we can fix ourselves."

"Awesome! How long before you move in?"

"Paul's got to work this weekend, but next weekend we're planning to move."

"I'll help, and I'll see if Barry's free, too."

"Thanks, Emily. Paul's planning on asking the guys at work to lend a hand. We shouldn't have to do any heavy lifting, just boxes and house plants. Stuff like that. I'm already packing up the kitchen. Since I moved from Indiana fairly recently, I shouldn't have too much sorting and cleaning to do."

"You worked out a solution for your concerns about his cases, and especially KC's case?"

"Sort of. I imagine it's a work in progress, but I realized you were right. I want Paul to be able to relax at home. And, after all, KC won't be involved in anything else. At least, hopefully not. I can use some self-control and stay out of her case this one time."

"That sounds like a workable solution. Have you talked to KC lately?"

Kathleen sounded out of breath, and somewhat rattled. "I talked to her Wednesday after Steve came back from the Board meeting and she came home from work. She didn't sound any better. Barry's news about the gun discouraged her. I felt bad for her."

"I talked to her after that, hoping to cheer her up a little."

"I trust you succeeded. She doesn't deserve to have unfounded suspicions blow everything up when she's turned her life around successfully." Kathleen didn't even ask for any details. "I guess I'll let you go now. I just wanted you to be the first to know the good news. Thanks for letting me tell you all about it."

Whew! Both a lack of curiosity and a thank you—she's really keeping her word to Paul with respect to KC's case. "That's what sisters are for."

Contemplating Kathleen's news about the house, her relationship, and KC, I returned to practicing with mixed feelings. Playing my flute, a refuge and a safe haven, often helped me process my world.

With our last concert scheduled for tomorrow night and consisting of music I was familiar with, I didn't feel I had to practice symphony music. I did the daily *musts* (scales and exercises) then played some popular songs. I'm not very good at playing by ear, but I'm getting better, and I exulted in the improvement.

The ringing of my landline interrupted my playing.

"Hi, Em."

"KC? Shouldn't you be at work?"

"I am at work, but I thought you should know right away. It finally dawned on me. It's Mel! The silver van I know belongs to Mel."

"You're right. Now that you mention it, I've seen him in a silver van, too."

"I can't talk. I've gotta get back to work. Good luck! Be sure and let me know what you find out."

"I will, KC. And thanks."

If Mel had blackmailed me, he looked better and better as a murder suspect. I felt encouraged. I only had to place him at the Fourth of July concert to complete the case against him. But I couldn't investigate now. My first student had arrived.

A little while later, Barry's call interrupted my teaching, but lifted my spirits. "Hey, beautiful."

Love needs an optometrist, as Mom would say. "Hey, Barry." He was obviously in a great mood. Relief at reaching the end of the week, maybe. With an eye to privacy, I left the student in the studio and moved to the living room. "I'm teaching. I can't talk long."

"We have Tyler's birthday party tonight," Barry reminded me.

"Mmhmm."

"What time should I pick you up?"

"I don't know. What works for you?"

"The party's at seven, right?"

"Yeah."

"When did you want to get there?" Barry always took my wishes into account.

"How 'bout if we leave here at seven. That way we won't be the first ones there, but we won't be too late."

"Sounds good," Barry agreed.

"Thanks for picking me up. Do you want to spend the night afterward?"

"Always." Barry's voice held a smile. "I'll see you at seven."

TYLER HAD SCHEDULED HIS PARTY early enough that his kids could come, but late enough that they would go to bed and leave the adults to grown-up gossip and other pursuits. He and the boys lived in an older section of town, becoming fashionable once again, in a small house with an arching garden gate and colorful flowers to welcome the visitor. He told me his ex-wife had created that feature.

A fellow guest directed Barry and me to the backyard, where Tyler had prepared the grill. I'd guesstimate there were eight to ten guests already there. I recognized two of the members of the Symphony's bass section and their spouses, as well as Susie and her husband. Her kids hadn't come.

As invitees arrived, we all got acquainted. The rest of the Symphony bass players and their significant others arrived before long. The people I didn't know turned out to be Tyler's neighbors and his former co-worker.

Ready to grill, Tyler took orders. With a sizzle he started barbecuing hamburgers, hot dogs, and brats, with Beyond Meat burgers for the vegetarians.

The kids mingled, and adults made a special effort to include them. The wife of one of the other bassists sat on the ground and addressed the smaller boy. "How old are you, Joshua?"

"Five." He held up five fingers, four on one hand, one on the other.

Susie and I were in a small group listening to the conversation.

"You're a big boy, then." Was the bassist's wife Joanna? Joan? I couldn't bring myself to ask . . . again.

"Yeah, I am." He seemed to grow taller before my eyes. "I even went to one of daddy's concerts. We seen fireworks. Jason got losted, but daddy found him."

Tyler's head jerked up. "Who wanted burgers?" The resulting confusion distracted guests from the conversation. Was it intentional?

Joanna/Joan claimed a burger. Jason, Tyler's older boy, carried the plate to her. She rose and left to help herself to condiments and potato salad.

Undaunted, Joshua turned to the other adults. "It was kind of scary, but I was brave. Daddy said so."

I took up Joanna/Joan's end of the conversation. "Why were you scared?"

"Daddy left and Jason got losted and they left me all alone. It was spooky!"

"Joshua, I don't think Ms. Wilson is interested." Tyler's voice held a warning.

Not true. I was very interested.

Both Joshua and I ignored Tyler.

"What did you do?" I leaned closer.

Joshua must have sensed he had my full attention now, and moved closer. "Went to the door where Daddy was and called, 'Daddy, Daddy!'"

The stage door? I glanced at Tyler. "Did he come?"

"Not right away. That's when I got more scareder. But then he came and he picked me up and we found Jason. I think Daddy was mad at Jason for getting losted."

I'll bet.

Tyler was red-faced. "Joshua, it's time to get ready for bed. You, too, Jason."

"Awwww, Dad. Five more minutes? We haven't even had cake yet." Jason whined his plea.

"Okay." Tyler stepped in front of the boys. "But after cake, it's off to bed."

I looked at my watch: eight. Seemed appropriate for a five-year-old, but for an eleven-year-old? And on his father's birthday? Before the cake?

The boys were allowed to eat several hot dogs, then carried cake to the guests and had some themselves. By then the clock showed a quarter to nine.

"Okay, guys. Off to bed."

"Five more minutes?" This from Joshua.

Tyler couldn't be persuaded this time. "Go!"

"Okay." Both boys left and returned in their P.J.s for a hug from their dad and a final goodnight to the guests.

Barry and I were among the last to leave. I had lingered, helping clean the kitchen. I wanted to find out more if I could. When Barry went to the rest room, I finally found myself alone with Tyler. We were throwing paper plates away and storing leftovers.

"Why didn't you tell us what happened with the boys at the concert?"

"It's embarrassing." He flushed.

"Embarrassing? We're your friends."

Tyler pulled some plastic storage containers from the cupboard. "Leaving the stage during a concert is about the worst thing you can do as a musician."

"Yeah, but sometimes life happens. Why was Joshua alone in such a big crowd?" I had filled a trash bag with paper plates.

Tyler tied the trash bag and propped it against the door, then turned and frowned at me. "Look, Emily. It was Fourth of July. I couldn't find a babysitter. Jason swore he could handle babysitting. He's nearly twelve, and I suppose I wanted to believe him. I figured if I took them with me, it would be like I'd never left them. I'd be there. I spread a blanket for the kids right outside the stage door. I wasn't far away, on the other side of a flimsy piece of wood enclosing the performance platform. I left food and made sure the security guard knew the boys were with me." He took a breath.

"And?"

"I don't know how the boys got separated, but I heard Joshua calling for me during the break before *1812*, and . . . well . . ." Tyler cleared his throat. "The beginning of *1812* is quiet, exposed for the basses. I played the opening, but then I hurried as fast as I could to find Joshua."

"Your duties as a dad come first. Your boys are your main priority. We would have understood."

"You can't know that. What if some friend of my ex-wife's had called the police? I might have lost the boys forever, and my job, too."

Both Tyler and I were silent for a few moments.

"Well, for my part, I'll do my best to silence the grapevine, which has you packing a gun and killing Curtis." *Déjà vu.*

Tyler looked alarmed. "Please don't, Emily. It'll dredge it all up again. Let it die a natural death. I want people to forget. They will. The grapevine'll find some other bit of gossip to occupy it. It'll all blow over when the cops find Curtis's killer."

"I want to help." I thought for a moment. "But if that's the way you want to handle it, I'll respect that. If you change your mind, though, let me know." At the very least, I would take him off my mental suspect list.

On the way home, I told Barry all about it. In truth, I felt relieved. I'd never wanted to believe Tyler capable of murder. Finding out that he didn't kill Curtis, and why he left the stage, went aways to restoring my faith in good guys.

Even though I sometimes got annoyed with him, Barry seemed like a good guy, too. I clasped his hand, connected, and enjoyed the night sky and the drive home; at least, until Barry brought up a surprise topic.

"Em, have you ever thought where this might go?"

"This?"

"I mean us. You and me."

I pulled away, sat up straight, and answered, "No. I'm enjoying what we have. That's as far as I've thought."

Barry pulled the car over next to a small neighborhood park and shut off the engine. "I'm enjoying what we have, too. I think we make a good team. I'd like us to have more time together." He took my hand.

"I . . . I . . . What are you saying?"

"Life with you is never boring. And I think I can help you, take care of you. If we lived together, it'd be easier."

Ooooh, that scared me. *Take care of me?* What did that mean? Did he mean bring me chicken noodle soup when I felt bad? Or did he mean keep me "safe"? Because who would decide about my safety? If it was Barry, that could be stifling. He'd objected to the sleuthing I'd done in my own case, and in Charlie's case last year. Should I listen to the fear I felt? Or was the fear only the past expressing itself in the present? I didn't want to be molded, or trained, or taught to fit into somebody else's life. On the other hand, naturally his concern about the woman he cared for showed. And I truly appreciated his support. "I don't want to be afraid to be myself again."

"I know you had a rough time in your marriage, but this would be different. I love you the way you are. I wouldn't try to change you, or shape you, or force you to do things my way. Just let me love you."

"I don't know what to say."

He smiled, kissed me lightly, and leaned away. "Don't say anything. Think about it. There's no rush. But I want to be with you." Again, he kissed me, then started the car.

I guess I should have been overcome with joy, but I wasn't. I felt confused. It flattered me that Barry wanted a life together, and relieved me that his feelings weren't hurt by my indecisiveness. But awareness that my relief indicated caring warred with uncertainty about how much I cared. An even bigger relief—that I didn't have to make an immediate decision—overshadowed it all. For now at least, our relationship wasn't changing.

We made the trip back to my house in silence. Barry held my hand and glanced at me from time to time. I felt awkward, as if I'd let him down. I only relaxed when Golden greeted us, bringing a feeling of normalcy with her.

TWENTY-FOUR

SATURDAY, JULY 27, 2013, 9:00 A.M.

THE NEXT MORNING BARRY SAT IN A BATHROBE sipping his coffee and reading the paper when Golden and I left for the Supervised Visitation Center. He hadn't mentioned living together again. Everything seemed normal.

My day at the Center started uneventfully for the most part. Mr. Briggs and his daughter colored quietly, the mom rocked her baby and played with a musical stuffed toy, and Mrs. Stolzman had pulled herself together since last week and greeted Ashland with a smile. The two of them played dress-up and worked a simple puzzle, and both seemed to enjoy their visit.

Then Mr. Clearwater entered, a scowl on his face. He sat on the sofa, waiting for Travis and Colleen.

He seemed even angrier than when I last saw him, but we'd had no interaction, and I didn't take it personally. I greeted him. "Hello, Mr. Clearwater."

"I hope you're happy." His voice was as menacing as his scowl.

I sat in a nearby chair, to be on a level with him. As I did, Golden moved from my side and sat protectively in front of me, blocking the path between Mr. Clearwater and me.

"I don't understand." If he was upset, getting his gripes out in the open before the children arrived offered the best hope for a good visit.

"The judge didn't grant me unsupervised visitation. He said my visits 'weren't going well' because I 'had trouble with anger management and rule breaking.'" He made air quotes, sounding disgusted. "What did you tell him?"

"I took factual notes on whatever occurred. You control that. My notes were just observations which were turned over to the judge by the Center."

His fists balled in his lap. "My lawyer told me I could win unsupervised visitation with the kids by coming here and jumping through the hoops." His face turned red and his voice rose. "But you've screwed things up. I don't need this kind of aggravation."

"Instead of concentrating on me, maybe you should concentrate on your relationship with your children. I'll note any improvement."

He leaped to his feet and roared, "There is nothing wrong with my relationship with my kids."

The security guard moved toward us.

It wouldn't do any good to point to this example of Mr. Clearwater's anger problems. I stood. I didn't like cancelling a visit, but, in this mood, he wasn't likely to have positive interactions with his kids. "You don't appear to be calm enough for a visit with your children. I'll call Mrs. Clearwater and cancel."

"What? You . . . you . . . you can't." He stopped pacing and his mouth hung open.

"Sorry, but I think it's best."

He stomped to the exit, gave a final dirty look to Golden and me and said, "Nobody interferes with my visits to my kids. You'll pay for this!" Then he slammed the door behind him.

The security guard grinned at me. "Doesn't like us, eh?"

I collapsed in a chair. "Guess not." I made my best effort to smile back at him.

Golden licked my face, and I scratched her ear.

"Don't worry about it. I'll back you up. He was angry before you ever spoke to him."

"Thanks, Aaron."

I tried to call Mrs. Clearwater from my cell, but I'd forgotten to charge it last night and the phone's battery was dead. Instead, I used one of the Center's land lines and contacted her. I found her at home, though she should have left by now.

"Oh, thank goodness. Travis absolutely refuses to come, and Colleen keeps crying and saying, 'Daddy'll be mad. Daddy'll be mad.'"

I waited in the Center until the visit would have ended on the chance Mr. Clearwater might come back. He didn't, and by the time I left I wasn't shaking anymore, but the encounter had put a damper on my mood.

MY STUDENTS REVIVED ME, THEIR ENTHUSIASM spilling over and leaving me smiling.

I had also regained some confidence about my confrontation with Mr. Clearwater. He needed to dispel some anger before he would be able to visit his children safely. In the end he—and they—would be better off having good visits at a later date, rather than trying to force things now.

THE LAST OF THE CONCERTS IN THE PARKS series was tonight. On a clear, warm evening with a spectacular sunset, the audience responded with heartwarming enthusiasm to a bevy of old favorites: everything from Khachaturian 's "Russian Sabre Dance" to Sousa's "*Semper Fidelis March*" to "That Old Black Magic". Some people danced, and kids did cartwheels and summersaults in front of the stage.

After the concert, as I arrived home in the dark, a couple houses down from me I noticed someone forcing a dog into a light-colored SUV. The dog struggled—thrashing against the person's hold on its collar, jerking its head—putting its weight on its back legs. The person forced its front legs into the car, then pushed from behind, and not gently, either.

"Hey! You! What are you doing to that dog?" My shout didn't make any difference, and the person continued to push and lift the dog's hind legs, trying to get it into the SUV.

As the shadows thrashed, I pulled the phone from my pocket to call 911. The battery was dead. Damn! I had forgotten to recharge it. Angry with myself, I pulled into the garage and ran to summon police from the house phone.

But Golden wasn't there to greet me as usual. "Golden! Golden!" In a flash I realized the struggling dog was mine, and someone was stealing her.

I ran to the front window, my heart pounding, and looked out. The thief, and Golden, were gone.

Maybe if I hurried I could catch them. I sprinted to my Subaru and backed out of the garage. A quick glance showed taillights disappearing to the right.

I floored it and overtook the taillights; a compact sedan, not them. I drove for blocks, looking up and down side streets for the SUV, but no luck. I blinked away tears.

Backing into a driveway, I turned around and drove in the other direction.

After about a mile, now hardly able to see for the tears in my eyes, I realized I was wasting time. I couldn't find them, but maybe the cops could.

I had to go home to call 911 on the landline. I reported my emergency, then phoned Paul. He'd help.

"Golden? You must be devastated, but I'm not in that department. That would be robberies. Call 911. They'll get you help faster than I could, but be sure and mention my name."

"I already did. Isn't there anything else I can do?"

"Can't think of anything."

I covered my face with my hands. "Thanks for your advice." His words were more than a line. By the time I got off the phone, a squad car had responded to my 911 call and pulled up outside.

I let the two officers into my house. "I'm Detective Copeland. This is Officer Jaffe. How did they get in?"

"I . . . I'm not sure. I tried to follow them and haven't had a chance to look."

The officers searched the house and found a broken window in the back bedroom. "I think this must be the entry point."

Detective Copeland took a small notebook and pen out of his pocket. "Can you describe the dog?"

I took a deep breath before I could respond. "She's a golden retriever, friendly and obedient . . ." I swallowed before I could get my voice under control enough to go on. ". . . great with children . . . trained as a therapy dog. She has a red collar . . ." I remembered picking it out, trying to find a color that would set off her fur. ". . . and tags with her license number and my phone number and address . . ." My voice broke and I couldn't continue.

"Nothing else missing?"

I shook my head. "I don't think so."

"Can you describe the SUV?"

I tried to pull myself together. "I'm not much of a car person. I'm not sure of the make, but it was big and light-colored, maybe white or beige."

Detective Copeland jotted down that information.

"Anything else you can tell us?"

I suddenly connected the dots. Excited, I told them, "I volunteer at the Supervised Visitation Center from nine to one Saturday morning. Golden goes with me. There's recently been some trouble with one of the clients, Mr. Clearwater. He was especially hostile this morning. He knows how much I care about Golden. We're a team." I sniffled. "He might have chosen this way to get even with me."

The cops exchanged a look. "Can you give us the names of all your clients? We can check them out."

"Sure. You'll have to get their contact information from the Center, but these are the ones I've been working with." I named them all as Detective Copeland took notes.

"We'll do our best." He handed me his card and cocked his head as if thinking. "Isn't there a message on my answering machine from you? I returned the call, but didn't get an answer. It couldn't have been about the dog."

"No. Everything's gone wrong. I've gotten calls threatening to blackmail me about a stolen violin, and copies of photos that the blackmailer said would be sent out if I didn't stop asking questions."

I paused to breathe. "Lieutenant Gordon—he's engaged to my sister—said to contact you, since you'd know who was investigating the stolen violin. My phone call was about that." I took another breath, deeper this time, and tried once more to calm down. "What about my dog?"

"We'll do what we can. The dognapping may be connected to the blackmail. Tell us more about that."

Slowly I continued. "One of the neighbors said the photos might have been delivered in a silver van." I paused. Should I give them Mel's name? He might not be involved. On the other hand, he might be a killer. "I know someone with a silver van. Mel Harmon."

"Mel Harmon the bank president?"

"That's the one."

Glancing at each other, the cops made no comment.

I felt a surreal sense that I was playing in the wrong key. They didn't believe me. "I asked him and several other people questions about Curtis Strange's death. It seemed to me that my inquiries might be connected with the blackmail attempt." I looked from one to the other. "But why take my dog?"

Neither cop said anything.

Maybe the photos would convince them. "I'll get the pictures." Sniffling as I went, I retrieved the photos from my desk where they were safe from harm. Carefully carrying the envelope by the edges, I held it out to the detective. He took a tissue from his pocket and used it to handle the envelope, placing it in a large plastic bag the other officer gave him.

"This puts the theft of your dog in a different light. Makes it more serious. Sit down. I'll get you a drink of water and then you can start at the beginning and tell us the whole story."

Detective Copeland fetched the water while I sank into a chair and tried to pull myself together.

"Now, why were you holding the violin?" Detective Copeland pulled a chair to face me and sat.

I took a deep breath, and told him all of it, occasionally interrupting myself with tears, sniffles, and nose-blowing.

When I had finished Detective Copeland said, "I definitely

agree that the blackmail might be connected to the theft of the dog, and they both may be connected to the murder case."

Finally! He sounded sympathetic, and like he took me seriously.

"We'll look into it and let Lieutenant Gordon know. Can you tell us the time of the phone call?"

"I think so." I got my phone and plugged it into the wall. The call history had recorded the phone call and number, along with the time and date, but it said "Unknown Caller." I read the information to Detective Copeland.

He pulled a small notebook from his pocket and wrote down the information. "Could be helpful."

"You seem skeptical."

"Yeah. I've been through too many investigations where the caller has used a spoofing app. The number's fake." He tsked. "When you think about it, a criminal'd have to be pretty stupid to make a call with his real number."

I know nothing about technology other than how to turn my computer on, use my cell phone, or cuss if they don't work. I figured it was his problem and returned to my real concern. I asked again, "What about my dog?" My voice broke. "She might be in danger."

The cops avoided looking at me. "There's more information here than usual with a crime of this nature. There's hope, but we don't routinely have very good luck with these types of cases." I guess they considered that comfort. Then they were gone, leaving me distraught and in tears.

Since I couldn't even think about sleeping, I went back to my car and drove the streets, up and down, up and down, in a grid, hoping to find the SUV I had seen. I had no luck, and by two in the morning I returned to the house, exhausted and heartbroken, and wide awake.

TWENTY-FIVE

SUNDAY, JULY 28, 2013, 2:00 A.M.

WHEN IT BECAME OBVIOUS I WASN'T GOING to find Golden and wouldn't sleep the rest of the night, I called Barry.

Bless his heart, he came right over. He helped me board up the broken window. While we worked, I told him about my search.

"Where have you looked?"

I listed all the areas I'd hunted.

"Em, there's got to be a better way. You're not thinking straight. There are any number of light-colored SUVs on the road. You don't know which direction the dog napper went, and it's . . ." He looked at his watch. ". . . four in the morning. You need some sleep. I do, too."

"The more I think about it, the more convinced I am the dog-napper is Mr. Clearwater. He's blaming all his problems on me. Taking Golden had to be his revenge. He's trying to hurt me, and make me take his side in the court case."

But what about the blackmail? The murder? My brain couldn't put it all together. I could only think about one thing. I shook my head, hoping to clear my thoughts. "If I had Clearwater's address we could go to his house. Check for Golden."

"It's Sunday." Barry paused. "I'll try my source inside the PD tomorrow, during business hours. He'll make sure officers check out Clearwater. Beyond that, you need to leave it to the cops. You gave them the information. I'm sure they'll investigate him, as well as Mel and his silver van. You don't have to take the risk. Whoever it is might be dangerous to both you and Golden."

I hadn't thought of that. A sob escaped me. "Golden needs me. I've got to do something."

"Right now you're sleep deprived and your head's befuddled. Let's get a little sleep, and then we can talk about it some more."

"But . . ." I realized Barry was right. "Okay. Will you stay?"

"Of course."

I gulped a cry of relief and blubbered into Barry's chest.

"C'mon, Em. Let me hold you."

He led me to bed, helped me under the covers, then crawled in on the other side. Lying on his back, he pulled me to him.

Lulled by the comfort of his presence and sheer exhaustion, I let my heavy lids close and almost instantly fell asleep on his chest.

I WOKE IN THE SUNLIGHT AND SAT up.

Barry's side of the bed was empty.

I'd had a dream about Golden. She whined, desperate for me to come for her. Feeling how miserable she was, my head sank to my knees and I sobbed until I had no tears left, then padded into the living room.

Barry was on the phone. "Call me if any dogs matching that description come in. Okay?" He paused and I heard a garbled voice say something on the other end of the call. "Thanks." He hung up and stood, crossing to put his arms around me. "I called the Humane Society. Now talk to me. How did you sleep?"

"I had a dream about Golden," I explained.

"How can I help?" He held me at arm's length and caressed my shoulders as he listened.

"I know the dream's a sign. We have to do something. Let's go look for the SUV."

"We've been over this. There are thousands of light-colored

SUVs in the city. Let's go to lunch, instead. Getting some food'll help us both think better."

My head burrowed into his chest.

He stroked my hair as he coaxed. "What else can we do right now? Maybe we can come up with some useful ideas."

Reluctantly, I responded without lifting my face. "Okay."

Now that he had ministered to me, what he said next pointed to Barry's possible sainthood. "Can I get a shower first?"

"Sure."

About an hour later we drove to Benny's. It wasn't until after we ordered that I spoke. "Barry, what am I going to do? She's my girl."

"Em, let the police handle this. They can get hold of addresses, sort through vehicle registrations, and gain entry if they suspect anybody."

"But they won't! To them Golden's just a dog. A dog that might lead them to a murderer, but still, a dog. That's all. They don't realize how irreplaceable she is. But she's important to me."

Barry didn't say anything for what seemed a long time. "What if I talk to my friend at the PD? Emphasize that Golden's specially trained and has unique skills. Maybe he can talk to officers in the K-9 unit. Get them involved."

I sobbed. "You'd do that for me?"

"Of course." He nodded. "You're worth it, Em. Golden is, too."

I couldn't stop the tears from escaping. "Okay. Thanks, Barry. I don't know what else to do anyway. I'd thought about posting 'Lost Dog' posters, but Golden's not lost. She's been stolen."

As we dawdled over the meal, Barry changed the subject. "Have you thought any more about Curtis's murder?" He was trying to distract me. I let him.

"Only to speculate about who could have stolen Golden. Why?"

"Well, I've been thinking. It seems awfully coincidental that someone Jane knows was killed with Jane's gun. I know she reported it stolen the day before the murder, but the thief didn't break in. Only her gun, some cash, and a few pieces of jewelry, although those were worth a fortune, were taken."

"I'm a step ahead of you, Barry. I *had* thought the coincidences were getting hard to believe. And there's one more thing you should know."

"Oh?"

"When I talked to Jane's husband about Butterfly Hollow, I noticed he and his intern were drawn to each other in a way that tempted me to call the Fire Department."

"Really."

"*And* Harvey mentioned that Curtis had been to see him."

"So . . ."

"Maybe Curtis noticed the same thing I did and threatened to tell Jane. Harvey's got a lot tied up in his relationship with Jane. Their finances, their children and grandchildren, their social standing. Jane wouldn't take a threat to her social position, let alone her family, lightly. It makes perfect sense to me that Harvey wouldn't have wanted her to know about his affair. He would have known about her gun and could have taken it at any time. Maybe he faked a robbery, killed Curtis to stop him reporting to Jane, wiped his prints from the gun, and threw it away."

Barry whistled. "It's a possibility. It covers all the bases, and it's simple."

"You think it'll save KC?"

"Maybe. It's one more thing I can talk to my friend about tomorrow. Thanks, Em." He hesitated and frowned. "But be careful. If your theory is right, you'd be a potential target for Harvey. You've reached the same conclusions Curtis likely did. If Harvey suspects . . . I want you to be safe."

I closed my dry, aching eyes. "I'll be careful."

Barry was frowning, but I had finished with this discussion. I felt desperate to eat lunch and get back home to bed.

MY EYES OPENED TO DARKNESS. I had gone to bed after lunch, around two. My odd sleep patterns had screwed up my biorhythms and I didn't have a clue what time it was. I glanced at the clock. Ten-thirty-five p.m. Barry, who hadn't gone to bed with me, was now in the bed, asleep. Tiptoeing out of the bedroom, I headed for the kitchen, poured myself a bowl of cereal with almond milk, and called it dinner.

It seemed a miracle Barry had stayed with me. I wasn't used to having this kind of support and had to admit, if only to myself, that I liked it. In fact, without Barry's calm and help, I might not be functioning.

On the counter, my cell phone rang.

Hoping it wouldn't wake Barry, I grabbed it, but didn't catch it 'til the third ring.

"I warned you," the disguised voice whispered.

Barry padded into the kitchen.

"Who is this?" My voice sounded strong and firm, even though my hands were shaking.

"You haven't quit asking questions."

"No. I haven't, and I won't. KC is my friend. She didn't kill Curtis and I'll prove it."

"The cops would love to see those photos of you with the violin. They'd cause you a lot of problems. Don't make me send them."

"Go ahead. Those photos show me holding the violin, not stealing it."

"Oh, yeah? It'll be our word against yours."

"Who else?"

The caller hung up.

"Who was that?" Barry rubbed his eyes. "You sounded upset."

"The blackmailer."

"Blackmailer? What's going on?" Barry was fully awake now.

I explained about the calls and the photos.

"Why didn't you tell me?"

"Because after Golden was stolen, I forgot everything else."

"Paul needs to be informed. And Detective Copeland, too."

"I've handled it. Paul pointed me to Detective Copeland, and he's working on it."

"They both knew before I did? You should have told me, Emily." Barry was obviously hurt. He had called me Emily.

Now I felt guilty on top of everything else. "I would have, but I knew it would upset you. I just dealt with it. I didn't steal the violin and the cops know that."

He took a deep breath. "I'll stay here tonight. I'll check the doors and windows to make sure they're locked and call my friend at the station tomorrow. I don't want you to be alone. You could be at risk." I took a deep breath, realizing he cared about me. But I wasn't used to help, or even caring really, from men. And I didn't want him to see me as weak. "You don't need to stay. I'm fine. I've been fine since the first threat a week ago."

"A week!" He glared at me. "I'm staying. You're not fine. What if the killer comes for you? And you're already distraught about Golden."

His last statement brought the whole situation home again, and it nearly doubled me over, like a gut punch. But there was nothing substantive he could do. "You have court in the morning. Just go."

"That's really what you want? To be alone through this?" His questions sounded like an accusation, and I knew if he walked out, it might be for a long time. It might be forever.

Time to be honest with myself. Did I really want him to leave? I wanted to be able and willing to act by myself, but I also wanted moral support. Yes. I had to admit, I wanted him to stay, especially now.

When I didn't answer right away, Barry continued. "I want to help you. You shouldn't be alone now. Let me be here for you."

When I looked deep inside myself, that was what I really wanted anyway. "Okay. And thank you."

He checked the windows and the doors, and then we went back to bed—together.

TWENTY-SIX

MONDAY, JULY 29, 2013, 7:00 A.M.

I COULDN'T SLEEP. GOLDEN HAD BEEN STOLEN, KC was a murder suspect, and I'd hurt Barry's feelings. All the underpinnings of my safe little world were wobbling. Everything felt wrong. The only bright spot was that Barry had stayed, in spite of my words and actions. I tossed and turned. Around seven in the morning I gave up on sleep. By eight I had taken a shower and was slicing fruit for breakfast. When the phone rang, I snatched up the receiver.

"I can't believe he doesn't trust me!"

I had to guess at the caller's identity. "Kathleen?"

"He . . ."

I knew the "he" had to be Charlie or Paul. They were the only men in her life.

". . . won't tell me the smallest thing about KC's case."

Ah. Paul.

Kathleen continued. "I talked to KC, and she seemed depressed about the case. When I got off the phone I just asked Paul if he still suspected KC. Instead of an answer I got a lecture on privacy and confidentiality and the 'sanctity of the rights of the accused.' He asked me if I wanted to screw up his case. Really. As if I would. I only asked a tiny little question. He could have answered it 'yes' or 'no.'"

"He didn't know that. From his point of view it might have been the beginning of a major inquisition."

Kathleen snorted.

"Seems like he's got a bee in his bonnet about this. Wouldn't it be easier not to ask about KC?"

"I didn't think I had."

"I get it. But he must be sensitive about it because you've already fought about it. And because he's worried." That thought hadn't occurred to me before.

"Why doesn't he trust me?" Kathleen whined. "I'm his fiancée. I'm on his side."

"I'm guessing it doesn't have anything to do with trust. But he doesn't want to be pressured from all sides. He must be stressed already because he knows KC is your friend."

"You agree with him!"

"I'm not agreeing with anybody. But it's awkward for Paul because KC's your friend. You're going to have to be respectful and understanding of his position, at least this time."

She sighed. "I suppose."

"Have you explained your feelings to Paul?"

"No. I got mad, and I couldn't think straight. How come I never had these problems with Bill?"

Bill was her deceased husband. "I don't know, Kathleen. If I did, I could make a bundle in counseling."

She sighed and didn't say anything for a moment. "Well, thanks for listening."

"No problem. That's what sisters are for."

We hung up. She hadn't asked about Golden, Barry, or the blackmailer, but I guess I couldn't expect her to. I hadn't told her about any of them.

Barry came into the kitchen in his bathrobe. "Who were you talking to?"

"Kathleen."

"At this hour?"

"It's not really early anymore." I went to his arms. "Thanks for staying with me."

"I'm just worried about you and Golden."

I snuggled into his chest. "I know." I kissed him. But it's almost nine. Don't you have a court case? You'd better get moving."

He glanced at his watch. "You're right. You'll be okay?"

"No worries. Now go."

DISTRACTEDLY, I TAUGHT A FEW STUDENTS. Barry had said he would talk to his friend at the PD, but by lunch he hadn't called me. I called him.

"I'm sorry to bother you, but I couldn't stop myself from worrying."

"Em, I know you're concerned about Golden, but you've got to be reasonable. I talked to Tom at eleven. Give him a few hours. He does have other business, and he has to be discreet about helping me."

"Barry," I pleaded. "There must be something I can do."

"My best advice is to be patient."

As I hung up I reflected. *Easier said than done*. Barry's calm stance soothed me into feeling he might be right, though.

After lunch and another few students Barry called back. "Tom talked to his friend in the K-9 unit. Officially, the guy can't work on Golden's case. That's Robbery's job. But he loves dogs and understands how concerned you are. He'll do what he can to light a fire under Robbery and make sure Golden's case doesn't fall through the cracks. And Tom'll make sure Paul hears the theory about Harvey, too. The blackmailing incidents should give it some weight."

The doorbell rang. That would be KC for her lesson.

"Thanks, Barry. I've gotta go, but I appreciate the help and the update."

He didn't have time to respond before I hung up and answered the door.

"Em! You look awful! What gives?" She stopped and glanced around the empty entryway. "And where's Golden?"

So much for not adding to KC's troubles by pretending nothing was wrong. I should have known she'd read my face and miss her canine buddy. "It's a long story."

We moved toward the studio. "Give. Did you get another threatening phone call?"

"Yeah. But the main thing is, somebody stole Golden."

KC's hand flew to her face. "Oh, no!"

"It happened after Saturday's concert. I had just gotten home when I saw someone force her into an SUV and drive off. I tried to follow, but I lost them." We had reached the studio and I slumped into my chair, tears in my eyes.

"Em, you must be in a state. Did you call the police?"

I collapsed in my chair, while KC sat beside me in the student seat. "Of course. It's Robbery's case. Like Golden is a thing. I told them about the threats and the photos, too, and how they might connect to the murder case." Even to my ears I sounded discouraged. "They say they'll investigate everything, but usually they can't solve missing dog cases."

"Great. They've accepted defeat before they even start. Par for the course, I guess." KC was understandably cynical about law enforcement.

"Barry contacted his friend in the department for extra help. And I told the officers about a man who has been confrontational at the Supervised Visitation Center—"

"We've got to find her." KC sounded energized and determined. "It'll be dark by nine tonight. Let's investigate the man from the Center. We can get his address from the internet and see if Golden's there."

My brain had reverted to pre-internet thinking, and I hadn't even thought about the possibility. "Don't you have to get up early tomorrow?"

"Whatever. This is more important. You're my friend. Golden is, too."

Her concern and confidence revived me, and I laughed. "KC, you're the best." I gave her a hug. "I haven't forgotten Curtis's murder, either." I told her about my lunch with Jane and her generally-recognized controlling nature. Then I filled her in on the latest on my suspicions that Harvey may have killed Curtis to hide his affair from Jane.

"I'm glad you're working on that. It's a real motive. I can see that, you know?" She sounded enthusiastic.

"There's something I'm confused about, though."

"What?"

"The blackmail photos were delivered by a silver van. As you said, maybe it belonged to Mel. He could be the blackmailer. Mel hated Curtis, had opportunity to steal Jane's gun, and evaded my questions about whether or not he had been at the concert on the Fourth."

"Yeah?" KC traced a circle in the air with her hand, urging me to go on.

"But Golden was taken by someone in a light-colored SUV." It didn't make sense.

"Maybe the blackmailer has two cars, or maybe he stole a car."

"Maybe. But the blackmailer threatened to deliver photos to the cops and the Board, not to take my dog. I'm thinking the two could be unrelated."

"Neither a blackmailer nor a dognapper would necessarily be a person who keeps his word. Besides, I don't believe in coincidence." KC sounded confident. "Surely one woman could not be unlucky enough to have two separate unrelated incidents of evil directed at her. Trust me. They're connected somehow."

I wasn't convinced, but I wasn't willing to argue, either. I wanted comfort. Like a true musician, I compartmentalized and changed the subject. "I'll keep looking into it, but for now, let's forget everything and play Mozart."

Before she left we found Mr. Clearwater's address on the internet and made arrangements to meet at eight forty-five that night. We'd take my Subaru. When we found Golden she'd have a familiar car to travel in. KC's support renewed my courage and confidence. I felt hopeful we'd bring Golden home. I ached for her soft fur and happy tongue licks on my face.

That night KC arrived right on time dressed stereotypically for a stealth operation—black T-shirt and black jeans—and I had to laugh. Then I realized I wore an identical outfit. At least my thrillers and whodunits were good for something.

Perfectly dressed, the two of us set out.

The address we'd gotten for Clearwater was on the north end of town on a corner lot. The house was a beige split level with a black Corolla parked in the driveway. Lights glowed from the windows on the first floor.

We parked across the street from the side of the house, avoiding the front door, and approached the backyard furtively. A six-foot wooden fence surrounded it.

KC and I hid in the shadow of the fence and tried to peer between the slats. Whispering, she asked, "Can you see anything?"

I squinted and whispered back. "No. You?"

KC had taken a breath to answer me when the sliding patio door opened and a black lab bounded out, barking his fury, followed by Mr. Clearwater.

"Who's there?"

KC and I sprinted for the car.

"Hey! You! Stop! I'm calling the cops."

By the time they turned up we'd be long gone.

We vaulted into the car.

KC watched the rear as I squealed off. The red and blue lights hadn't arrived by the time I rejoined traffic on the main road and breathed a sigh of relief. "Well, that was a bust."

"Not really. Now we know where Golden's not, you know?" Doing something must have helped KC's depression. She had regained her positive outlook.

"I'm at a loss, though." I thought for a moment. "If Mr. Clearwater doesn't have Golden, she must have been taken by the murderer-slash-blackmailer. Where is she?"

That was the million-dollar question.

TWENTY-SEVEN

TUESDAY, JULY 30, 2013, 5:00 A.M.

WHERE IS SHE? WHERE IS SHE? WHERE IS SHE? The question haunted me, and I spent all night tossing and turning. If Mr. Clearwater didn't have Golden, who did? Nobody but my students and my Supervised Visitation Center clients knew about Golden, unless you counted her obedience class and teacher, and her therapy dog trainer. Why would they dognap her?

If it wasn't someone who knew Golden, it had to be someone who wanted to hurt me. At the Center, after Mr. Clearwater, only Mr. Briggs had a contentious relationship with me. That seemed to have healed peacefully though, over time. That left Curtis's murder. The dognapping must be related to my investigation.

By eight that morning I had decided I'd call the cops and find out what progress they'd made. It had, after all, been over twenty-four hours. I didn't expect results, but at least it would keep Golden on their minds and make them aware she had an advocate. I rang Detective Copeland.

"Miz Wilson? I had just picked up the phone to call you. Apparently Golden has powerful friends."

Really. Who *was* Barry's friend Tom?

"I spent some time yesterday working on the case. We didn't have a search warrant, but both Mr. Briggs and Mr. Clearwater let us in to look around. We didn't see any trace of a big yellow dog. That'd be hard to hide. And Mr. Clearwater had a black lab that wasn't showing any sign of special interest in any area of the house or yard."

I didn't tell him I knew about Clearwater. "That's that then."

"We also investigated Mr. Martin, one of your former clients." Detective Copeland sounded encouraged.

"Why would he dognap Golden now? If he had any issues with me, they've been resolved."

"Hear me out."

I waited and felt my hopes rising, though I tried to steel myself for disappointment.

"We called Mrs. Martin. She didn't have a kind word for her ex, and thought him capable of any crime, including dognapping." He coughed. "When we went to his house Mr. Martin had a golden retriever that meets the description."

Golden! "Is she okay? Did he take care of her? How does she look?"

"She seemed fine to me. He claimed he got the dog as a surprise for his daughter, Sarah, who hasn't seen it yet. He calls it Sienna. We took both the dog and Mr. Martin into custody. We'd like you to come ID the dog."

I sobbed in relief. Why hadn't I thought of that? Sarah had always loved Golden, and Mr. Martin indulged Sarah any way he could. "I'll be right there."

"Fine. She's being held at the Humane Society. We'll meet you there."

I disconnected the call almost before he finished speaking and slid into my shoes. I pulled my car keys from my pocket, and broke my previous speed record getting to the shelter, halfway across town.

Detective Copeland met me there. "The dog's this way."

I followed him impatiently along a corridor lined with enclosures holding dogs, some of them excitedly poking their noses out of chain link pens, some sleeping motionless in a corner, as if resigned to their fate. The smell of urine assaulted my nose, and barks, howls, and whining battered my ears. What a horrible place! The atmosphere oozed canine misery.

Eager to be reunited with Golden, I caught up to the Detective as he slowed to a halt before a pen holding a retriever.

"But . . . but . . . that's not her." I wilted.

"It's not?"

"No." I shook my head. "I know my own dog. Golden's got a little bit of gray on her face, and she's more of a true gold. This dog is yellowish brown. Sienna's a good name." I refrained from asking why he hadn't checked her microchip when I realized, in my distress, I had forgotten to mention that Golden had one. My dashed hopes were my own fault.

Detective Copeland was red-faced. "Sorry. I thought we'd solved the case. We were sure."

Awkwardly, I tapped my toe and looked at the ground.

"We'll keep checking into the other leads you gave us. Have you thought of anything else? Something that might help?"

I felt like crying, though my voice didn't wobble. "I forgot to tell you about her microchip."

"That will help. Anything else?"

"No. I spent all night tossing and turning and didn't come up with a single idea."

"Well, if you think of something, let us know."

"Okay. Thanks for trying." I scuffed dejectedly to my car, shut the door, and burst into tears. I wasn't helping anybody with anything. My two best-loved buddies in all the world—KC and Golden—were in trouble, and I didn't have any clue what would help either of them.

Wait a minute! Maybe this wasn't about me, but about Golden. The body she dug up might be important. Joe Connally had known Curtis. His body could be a clue to the murderer.

I rushed out of the car and ran across the parking lot.

Detective Copeland sat in his car, making notes on a clipboard.

"I thought of one more thing." Panting, I waited until I could catch my breath. "Golden uncovered a body a couple weeks ago. Maybe that has something to do with the dognapping."

"She dug up a body? Really?" He sounded impressed. "She does a little of everything, doesn't she? I'll work that angle." He took the information I had and said he'd get back to me.

I thought more about that theory. Only Roland Strange and Sgt. Serna knew about Golden's involvement in finding Joe Connally's body. Could Roland be involved in the dognapping? Why? Golden had discovered the body. Her role was over, and it couldn't be reversed. Why would stealing her make any difference? Besides, Roland had been out-of-town the night of Curtis' murder. No, that didn't make any sense. I was tired, worried, and not thinking straight.

I told myself I did have an idea on KC's plight. Maybe if I worked on that for a while the solution to Golden's predicament would become clear.

Before I could get started Barry called. "I have some news about Golden."

"I know. I talked to Detective Copeland. No luck with Clearwater or Briggs. They had me go look at a dog they found at the Martins', but it wasn't Golden." Did I sound as discouraged as I felt?

"I have a confession to make. I never asked for Clearwater's address. I tried to avoid a situation where you could get into trouble."

"It's okay, Barry. KC got the address off the internet. We went to Mr. Clearwater's last night. I knew he didn't have Golden."

"You went there? Unprotected? What if something had happened? That's exactly why I didn't find the address for you. I didn't want you to risk your neck."

I wanted Barry to understand. "You have to consider the risk-to-benefit ratio. Golden's my girl. She needs me and I need her. I can't let her down."

"You said it. 'You have to consider the risk-to-benefit ratio.' You could have been hurt or killed, Emily."

I tsked and ignored his use of my full first name. "KC's the only one who understands."

Barry sounded angry. "Dammit, Emily. It's not about who you think understands you." He took a deep breath. "The consequences of your actions could have been severe."

In silence I tried to find the words to express what I felt, but before I could speak he said, "I know you did what you feel you have to, but I don't have to like it when you take risks."

"You should have told me you wouldn't help with Clearwater. I have a right to know where help is coming from and what needs to be done."

"You're right. I'll try to be more honest in the future."

We said our goodbyes with me feeling sick in the pit of my stomach. But I didn't know what to do besides put one foot in front of the other. If I couldn't help Golden, I'd try to figure out Curtis's murder and absolve KC. That might lead me to Golden.

Harvey Rice topped my list of possibilities to investigate. I wanted more time to observe him with his intern, and I had the perfect excuse. I called.

"Hi, Harvey. I have some new information on Butterfly Hollow, and I wondered if I could talk to you about it?"

"Sure, come on out. Looks like there's a gap in my schedule between one and three."

"Great!" I looked at my watch. "I'll be there as soon as I can." There wasn't time for lunch, but I didn't feel like eating anyway. My sick feeling intensified each hour Golden was gone. I couldn't twiddle my thumbs, doing nothing. I had to be active. This at least was productive—maybe.

By the time I got to the Environmental Responsibility Foundation it was the hottest part of the day. Despite the apparent luxuries, the building had no air conditioning. That was the tradeoff for converting a nineteenth-century mansion to a twenty-first-century business and the Foundation's home. Both front and back doors and all the windows were open, and members of the office staff were fanning themselves. I waved, then climbed the stairway to Harvey's office.

He had all the windows open, creating a nice cross breeze. The scent of evergreen blew through the room. He seemed as cool and comfortable in his suit as if he wore shorts and a t-shirt. He stood and put out his hand. "Emily! Good to see you. This is an unexpected pleasure."

Danielle, the intern, sat in a chair near Harvey's desk, her silk blouse unbuttoned to the point of indecency, though her almond skirt suit couldn't have been more proper. She slumped in the chair, fanning herself.

"I have some news about Butterfly Hollow." I paused and waited for Danielle to excuse herself.

Harvey reseated himself and leaned back in the chair. "It's okay to talk in front of Danielle. She's in training." The two exchanged a quick glance.

I'll bet. In training for what?

I seated myself in the other chair and glanced at Danielle, then continued. "I thought you'd be interested to know that I met Curtis's nephew." I hadn't told him about our encounter. "I went to see Butterfly Hollow and ran into him while he apparently inspected that part of his inheritance. He said he's Curtis's only living relative. I assumed the estate was substantial. Later, I went to the offices of Strange Development while he was there. He's taking over. His name is Roland Strange. He's an environmental engineer."

Harvey leaned forward, his forearms on the desk. "Interesting. Do you think he'd be interested in reselling Butterfly Hollow?"

"When we talked, he mentioned that his father and Curtis were estranged, and that he doesn't approve of Curtis's business methods or the way he treated people and the natural world. Roland is from out of town. He wants to 'make things right,' he says. Maybe after that he'll liquidate the business. In any case, it's quite possible he'd be interested in selling the Hollow."

"Hmmm. Danielle, get the figures on Butterfly Hollow. I want to know what we offered, and what price the owner got from Strange."

"Right away, Harvey." She left the room, her skirt swishing as she walked. Harvey watched every move until she disappeared.

"She's incredibly efficient. Such a gift." Harvey exhaled and shook his head. Released from her spell by her absence, he stood and began to pace. "This could be good news. We can solicit donations to save Butterfly Hollow. Given enough time, I'm sure we can get up to the price Strange paid."

"That would be wonderful. Places like the Hollow are becoming all too rare in modern life. I want to help preserve it—maybe volunteering? If people knew what they might lose . . ."

"I'm sure the county will support this. They did before." Harvey continued to pace, his speech faster and faster, sounding more and more enthusiastic, making plans. "We'll get the Hollow coalition to help us. Heck, we can even get the Scouts' support. Solicit donations from school kids. Maybe we can convince the school district to make a sizable donation, too."

Whoa! I could see why Harvey exerted such a force. His fervor would make a dead man leap in enthusiasm. Guiltily I thought of Joe Connally and mentally gave him my blessing. He'd approve of plans to save Butterfly Hollow.

At that moment Danielle returned with a folder which Harvey seized and opened while he returned to his desk, a ball of concentrated energy.

Danielle focused on him.

"Yes! Strange got it for $20,000 more than we offered. That's not much if we have time to mount a fund-raising drive." Harvey turned to me. "This is a great help. Now we know who to approach, and I think there's a good possibility we can convince Roland to work with us, especially if the Water Conservation Board puts the kibosh on Antelope Run."

Danielle pulled the chair she had vacated closer, then sat, shoulder touching Harvey, her attention on him. "I can get contact information for Roland and start on fundraising letters."

I could feel the energy crackling from one to another, growing. The two of them fed off each other.

No wonder something sizzled between them. They shared passion on several levels, and this project transcended the physical. Could Jane compete with this? I thought of her mousy personality and her stiff, unyielding presence. I guessed, no.

I left awed and unnoticed, while Harvey and Danielle strategized, heads close together, building on each other's ideas, passionately enthusiastic about their latest shared project. I concluded Harvey had sincere feelings for Danielle.

On the trip home I compared their enthusiasm and camaraderie with Harvey and Jane's interactions at their Christmas party last year. I had the opportunity then to observe the couple for a whole evening.

Jane had hired my usual trio, Jen Feifer on flute and Alice Smithson on cello, for the three-hour gig. We played the traditional repertoire: Haydn's *London Trios*, and works by J.S. Bach, Loeillet, Handel, Telemann, Quantz, and others.

When you play private parties there are two kinds of employers. Those who want you unseen, part of the servant staff. They feed you in the kitchen, if at all, and hide you in a corner. At the other extreme, there are those who treat the whole group as creative geniuses, kind to grace their humble gathering. They ply you with drinks and food, which they bring and place at your feet while you play, and engage you in long conversations when you take breaks. Harvey and Jane were the second type.

The trio had taken a break after the first hour and Jane had been immediately at my elbow, dressed in a shimmering forest green evening gown with matching emerald and diamond necklace, earrings and bracelet. She asked if she could get me water, soda, or something stronger. I hadn't had a chance to answer when Harvey also approached.

"Harvey, make a plate for each of the performers," she ordered, "and bring some water and drinks. And they've only got ten minutes. Hurry."

"Sure thing." Harvey had scurried off, and returned a few minutes later trailing waiters with three plates and a selection of beverages. Meanwhile Jane and several of their friends chatted with us. At the time I'd thought it sweet that Harvey helped Jane and wondered if she fretted about the party. Now I knew better. A party wouldn't have worried an experienced hostess like Jane. Which left me to wonder if she was always that commanding. The way she'd had Stella fired after all her years with the symphony would suggest—yes.

I could easily imagine why Danielle attracted Harvey. She admired him, gave him her full attention, and worked in harmony, rather than ordering him around. Add to that Danielle's swishing skirt and swinging hips, and Jane didn't have a chance.

I pondered the implications.

Curtis had been short of money, facing lawsuits on every side. If he had tried to blackmail Harvey, threatening to tell Jane about his affair if he didn't pay up, Harvey would definitely have a motive for the murder, given the financial and familial costs of splitting with Jane. He also would have had endless opportunities to steal Jane's gun. At the Fourth of July concert with Jane, he would only have had to excuse himself for some reason—to search for a Porta-Potty, speak to a friend, go back to the car—to be free to commit the murder. I was sure I had found the solution.

That night I had crawled in bed and was almost asleep when I got the call.

"I have Golden."

"Who is this?" Was it male? Female? The disguised voice gave me no clue.

"Come to City Park in half an hour, alone, if you want to see her again." Click.

TWENTY-EIGHT

TUESDAY, JULY 30, 2013, 11:00 P.M.

I WAS AFRAID BARRY WOULD NEVER APPROVE of what I planned to do. But I had to let him know where I was, in case everything went wrong. I called.

He answered the phone sounding groggy.

"The dognapper just called. He's got Golden. I have to go to City Park to get her. I wanted to let you know where I went and why, in case I don't come back."

"I'll get dressed and go with you. I—"

"The dognapper said to come alone. I don't want to risk his hurting Golden. Just say a prayer for me."

"I know you'd do anything to save Golden, but you can't take this kind of risk. This is crazy. I'm coming with you. Don't leave until I get there." He hung up.

If Barry was determined to stop me from going after Golden, I didn't have much time. I had to be gone when he arrived. I couldn't risk Golden by not following instructions. I knew I was doing something dangerous, but I had a plan to protect myself.

I took my cell phone and set it so I could be tracked, then thought a moment. The dognapper might be smart enough to take it from me, but I didn't want to lose contact under any circumstances. So,

I gave myself insurance. I tucked the good phone in my bra, put an old one in my purse, and, knowing he'd be here any minute, left Barry a note on the door including a code he could use to track me. As an afterthought I tucked bear spray from my camping supplies in alongside. It was the best I could do before I hurried to the car.

I'd only been to City Park with a hundred thousand people for our Fourth of July concerts. Now, it was deserted, in a not-so-good neighborhood, with tall pine trees casting moving shadows in the park lighting as the breeze blew. It was scary.

The dognapper hadn't indicated which parking lot to use. I drove the Subaru to the central lot. At this time of night, I saw no one. Reluctantly I exited the car. What now? I surveyed my surroundings.

On the opposite side of the parking lot sat a white SUV. *A Honda?* I hadn't noticed it until now. It was almost hidden behind a large evergreen growing in the far island. The driver's door opened, and Harvey Rice got out. "Emily?"

I hurried toward him. "Harvey?" At first I felt relieved to see a familiar face; then remembered the dognapper had a white SUV. So did Harvey and Jane. I put the pieces together. "I . . . I . . . Where's Golden?"

"Golden?"

When I didn't answer, Harvey said, "Something strange is going on." He hesitated.

"I got a call telling me to come here to get Golden. She was stolen after the last concert. Do you have her?"

"No, but Jane sent me to pick you up."

"If she knew I would be here and sent you to get me, then she must have made the phone call and knows about Golden. Let's go." I started toward my Subaru.

Harvey said, "Jane stated specifically that she wanted you to come in our car."

That made me uncomfortable. If Jane intended to give Golden back, she'd want me to have my car. She must have another plan, one that Harvey didn't know. "If I follow you, you won't have to bring me back."

"No. This is the way Jane wanted it. We'd better follow her directions. We don't want to annoy her."

That sounded like Jane controlled his every move. I clambered into the SUV, settled my purse beside me, and buckled my seat belt. Harvey climbed into the driver's side and steered the car west.

"Who would take Golden? She's such a good girl." Harvey looked concerned. "Things at the house have been a bit odd and getting odder. There was that robbery. And then Jane started taking long walks into the woods on our property at all hours. She's never liked to walk or hike before. I haven't seen a sign of Golden, but now Jane says she wants to talk to you. And at this strange hour."

"Why would Jane want to talk to me?"

"I can think of several reasons. But what I don't know is why it needed to be late. What does she have to say to you that she couldn't say on the phone? Why didn't she simply call and ask to meet you?"

"I don't know the answers, Harvey. But my main question is, why would she need to dognap Golden to get me to listen? None of this makes sense."

"I haven't seen Golden. Are you sure Jane has her?"

"She must. Otherwise, why would she know about the phone call that brought me here? She must have been the caller."

We sank into silence.

His route took him into the foothills on the nearest thing to a main road, a narrow ribbon of pavement twisting and winding, up, up into the hills. He turned off onto a side road, then into a private drive.

I'd been here before, when we had the occasional Planning Committee meeting at Jane's house, and of course there'd been the trio gig at Christmas. As we approached, I had time to scan the building again. The house was enormous, modern and flat-roofed with four stories, each of them way bigger than my little house. The house was opulent. Jane didn't work and I wondered where the money came from.

Harvey drove into the basement garage and parked.

"Follow me."

I caught a glimpse of a large kitchen before we entered an elevator and ascended to the top floor. Harvey led me past a bedroom and bath, library, an office, and a kitchenette before he stopped in the living room. With a three-sided view of the city and a wrap-around balcony, its sliders open to let in the evening's summer breezes, it spoke of comfort and money.

"I'll get Jane."

"First I want to see Golden."

"I don't know anything about Golden. But if that's why Jane called you, and why she had me pick you up, she'll bring her."

Harvey disappeared the way we had come.

I used the waiting time to investigate the room. Not wasting a second gazing at the paintings, I searched for an escape route. The leather-covered sectional had three sides for comfy conversations, but with a view. Off one side of the balcony an external flight of stairs led down to the third floor, which met the hill the house sat on. From there it looked as if a footpath led into the surrounding forest. That seemed to be the only way out, except for the elevator and maybe some interior stairs.

I heard footsteps in the hall and darted back to sit in the portion of the sectional facing the outside stairs, unclasped my purse, and, hoping the phone had tracked my location, made sure I could reach the bear spray.

"Emily!"

Oh, for heaven's sake. Jane acted like we were meeting in the conference room of the bank. But she led Golden on a short leash.

"Harvey, you can leave. This is between Emily and me."

He lost no time obeying Jane.

I breathed a sigh of relief. Golden appeared healthy and well-cared-for, and even better brushed than when I'd last seen her.

When she spotted me, she whined and strained at the leash.

Jane gave it a vicious jerk.

Golden quieted and tucked her tail between her legs.

"Hey! Careful! I'll take her."

"I don't think so." Jane smiled a self-satisfied grin. "I've always wanted a dog with Golden's special skills and training."

"Well, you're not her person."

"Oh, I don't know about that. She'll soon be looking for a new owner."

Her threat made my stomach tighten. I sat up straighter and moved to the edge of the sofa. "What do you mean?"

"That's a long story." She pulled a gun from her waistband, which had been hidden in the folds of her blouse, and trained it on me.

"I thought the police had your gun."

Jane laughed. "Oh, I have an assortment of guns. This is one of my favorites. It's feminine, small and light, but deadly." She waggled it at me. "Let me have your cell phone."

Grateful that I had the foresight to bring the old one, I gave it to her.

With a not-so-feminine smile, she dropped it to the floor and stomped on it.

Golden whined at the sound and the sudden movement, and again Jane jerked fiercely on the lead.

"You're hurting her!"

"I've never had to do this before. It's you. She's trying to get to you." Jane shifted the lead in her hand.

"Then let her."

"I'm sorry. Even though I like you, I can't let you go. You've been too curious."

"I don't know what you're talking about."

"Your questions upset the equilibrium of the status quo." Jane seated herself on the sofa opposite, pointing the gun at me, with the outside stairs at her back. I realized, too late, that she had cut me off from my escape route. Golden sat beside her but watched me.

"I don't understand."

"I've already been through one unimaginable scandal. I can't repeat the experience."

"Jane, you're talking Greek. What do you mean?"

"I guess we have time." Patiently she conceded, "After all, you'll never ask another question."

She paused and settled back into the sofa, never lowering the gun. "When Mother and Daddy first married years ago, he had nothing, but he went into mining and with ingenuity and luck found a rich vein of gold, then expanded and developed new mines until, when I was in my late teens, he had several that kept us nicely."

"I don't understand. That was years ago. Probably about the time I was born."

"You need to know the history." She looked at me, but I asked no questions. She continued. "When one of the mines collapsed, twenty-seven miners were killed. Daddy's enemies claimed safety violations were responsible. A huge scandal nearly ruined him. Oh, it was awful! Reporters camped outside our door for weeks before the trial, then again for the months of the court case. In the end, he was found guilty. He took the little he had left, sold the mines, and invested in drug stores, instead."

"Jane, that's all ancient history. I can't see what connection that could have with me or Golden."

"Curtis, who was just starting out, bought the land from him, ridiculously cheap."

Okay. I began to see connections with Curtis, but why me?

"Thirty years later, Curtis had run his business into the ground. He owed money to several banks, there were lawsuits from clients unlucky enough to do business with him, and he couldn't get a loan."

"I'd heard something about that."

Jane continued. "He had the nerve to ask Harvey to fund his latest development, Antelope Run. When Harvey understood that Curtis would drain and reroute the stream, turning it into a drainage ditch, he refused funding for the project."

Golden had calmed and sat quietly beside Jane. Apparently lulled by Golden's cooperative behavior, Jane dropped the lead and put her foot on it.

I saw Harvey come up the outside stairs behind Jane, approaching the living room, but he turned around and quickly descended the stairs. Had he seen Jane's gun?

I glanced at Golden. She sat beside Jane, whose foot remained on her leash.

Jane shook her head. "When Harvey told me Curtis had threatened to revive the scandal of Daddy's mine, I agonized. Apparently, Harvey didn't understand, or didn't care, how important it was to me to keep all that in the past. I didn't want my children and grandchildren traumatized, as I had been."

Movement outside caught my eye. Clutching a gun, Harvey had climbed the stairs to the west balcony, behind Jane, and now made signs to me to come. I scooched slowly closer to the edge of the sofa cushion. "What did you do?"

"I couldn't let it all come out again. All these years later, it's the worst experience of my life. My grandchildren don't deserve to go through it all, and Daddy's dead. He can't defend himself anymore." Jane pinched her lips together. "I faked a robbery and reported my weapon stolen, along with a few jewels. I knew Curtis would be manning a volunteer booth at the Fourth of July concert, as he always did. I found him and killed him under cover of darkness with the 'stolen' gun. I've heard *1812* often enough that I knew exactly when the cannons would fire and synchronized the fatal shot. My little gun went completely unnoticed. I used a suppressor just in case, but if anyone heard, it didn't stand out from all the other firecrackers and fireworks."

"Didn't Harvey notice you were gone?"

"Of course he did." Jane sounded annoyed. "I told him I needed to speak to the General Manager backstage about the fireworks display. Harvey knows I'm on the Board. He never suspected a thing."

"He doesn't know?"

"Harvey's a buffoon who thinks with the wrong part of his body." She paused and glanced at me as if expecting more questions, then continued. "To confuse police, I took the money Curtis had collected. I had plenty of time to wipe the gun clean of fingerprints and remove the suppressor. Then I discarded the weapon in a nearby trash can. Only Tyler's brat—what is his name? John? Jaxon?—saw me, but by then I'd killed Curtis and disposed of the gun. Publicly, the events horrified me as they were discovered. No one dared to disbelieve me."

She waggled the gun. "Except you. You're as bad as Curtis. You've been asking questions about Curtis's murder. You haven't threatened blackmail yet, but you would have. Instead, I was pro-active. I took Golden, hid her in the woods, and made the phone call that brought you here. I knew you'd come. You'd do anything for Golden. I'll bury your body on the grounds of the estate. No one will ever find it."

"What about Harvey? He'll figure out what's going on."

"He'll either go along with me, or I'll dispose of him, too."

Such callous contempt for her husband of years shook me, but I managed, "Besides, I wouldn't blackmail you. You're my friend, and it sounds like you were under terrible stress."

Then Jane's eyes teared. "I don't believe in friends. They only stay until it becomes inconvenient." One hand holding the gun, she wiped at her eyes with the other.

I sprang to my feet, already running, spraying the bear spray as I rushed past the sectional.

Jane howled in pain. Her foot moved as she furiously wiped at her eyes and struggled to breathe.

"Golden, come!" I called desperately.

She obeyed without hesitation, leash flying.

Meanwhile, Harvey had opened the screen door and motioned me to follow him. The three of us ran down the stairs. He waited for Golden and me to pass. "Go. Run."

He didn't have to tell me twice. I followed the path as fast as I could, running, no doubt helped by fear and adrenalin. Golden kept up with me stride for stride, though she coughed, as if she'd gotten a dose of the bear spray.

I lost track of Harvey in the darkness.

Behind me I heard a gunshot. Golden yelped, but didn't fall back.

I heard another gunshot, then another, but we had reached the shelter of the forest. Golden and I didn't stop running, afraid Jane followed right behind us, though we were necessarily slower now, paralleling the edge of the trees until we came to another house.

The lights were out. *Law-abiding citizens*, I thought, *in bed for the night*.

I pounded on the back door. "Help! I need help!"

The lights on the porch came on along with the lights in the house, but the door didn't open.

I heard no sounds of pursuit. I hid behind a tree, and with shaking hands pulled the cell phone from my bra and called 911.

"What is your emergency?"

"A killer is shooting at me."

"Your phone number?"

Oh, for heaven's sake. I gave her my cell number.

"What is the address?"

That I didn't know.

Just then I saw red and blue lights. Sirens screamed up to the house. The residents must have called 911. Bless them.

Two policemen with guns drawn began thrashing the bushes of the house.

I hung up and walked slowly toward the police, my hands held high, Golden wheezing beside me.

"I called. I need help."

The closest cop startled but didn't shoot. Both trained their guns on me.

Holding my hands high, I quickly explained the situation. I think it helped that Golden was with me and bleeding from a wound on her flank. She must have been injured by the first shot. The officers believed me and radioed for back-up, then disappeared, presumably to look for Harvey and Jane.

Relieved, I kneeled to love on Golden. She knocked me onto my back in her joy and licked my face.

I had stayed by the squad car, and it wasn't long before a second arrived. The officers in that car disappeared, and soon I heard a radio call for two ambulances. When the first patrolmen reappeared, they interviewed the homeowners, then took my contact information and a statement.

When I expressed concern for Golden and her wound, an officer offered to have the paramedics examine her if I'd wait for them to finish with Harvey and Jane. By the time they got to Golden, the bleeding on her flank had stopped.

"Doesn't look like there's a problem, but we can bandage it if you want."

They cleaned and dressed the wound while Golden patiently endured their ministrations with only a few whimpers, though she tucked her tail.

My next priority was getting home.

Barry and another man showed up while I negotiated a ride to my car with the officers.

"Em! Thank heavens! Do you know how worried I've been? Are you alright?"

I ran to his arms. "I'm fine. I can't believe you're here. I love you."

He held me and didn't say anything for what seemed like a long time before he said into my hair, "I love you, too."

He continued. "You were gone when I got to your place, but I saw your note with the code to track your phone and knew you were going to City Park. I followed. Your car was there but you weren't. I didn't know *what* had happened to you. I called Tom, my friend at the PD, for back-up. He came right out, but by the time we got to your location there were ambulances and squad cars, and I didn't know who was hurt. Thank goodness I found you, but don't *ever* do that to me again! Why did you leave when I clearly told you to wait?"

I had fences to mend. "I'm sorry I worried you. But Barry, the dognapper said to come alone. I couldn't risk her hurting Golden."

"Golden couldn't be more wonderful, but she's a dog. You're more important to me."

"I couldn't live with myself if Jane had hurt Golden or worse, because I failed to follow instructions."

Barry dropped one arm, the other pulling me close, and looked for Golden. "How is she?"

She sat patiently at our feet.

"She's fine, or she will be after a visit to the vet."

"The vet? What happened?"

I quickly recounted the events since my call. "The best news is that KC is off the hook and Golden is safe. Jane Rice killed Curtis."

"Why?"

"It's a long story. Bottom line, she killed Curtis rather than let him breathe life into an old scandal involving her dad. When I started asking questions about Curtis's murder, she feared it would all come out and took Golden. Jane knew I'd come after my girl. She planned to kill me next."

"Thank goodness she didn't succeed. Let's get your car and go home—I mean, to your house."

I wanted nothing more.

He and Tom had come in Tom's car. He dropped us off at the park, and we each drove to my house. Then he, Golden, and I snuggled together for what remained of the night.

TWENTY-NINE

WEDNESDAY, JULY 31, 2013, 10:00 A.M.

BARRY LET ME SLEEP IN THE NEXT DAY. When I finally opened my eyes, he had gone, maybe to an early appointment.

Golden's wound seemed to be alright—no redness, no swelling—but I took her to the vet anyway.

"What a brave girl!" the receptionist cooed. "We'll take care of it."

She escorted us back to the doctor, who removed the bandage the EMTs had applied, shaved Golden's hair around the wound, cleaned it thoroughly once again, doused it in antibiotic, and re-bandaged it. She was stalwart throughout—no whimpering from her—not in front of the vet.

"The news is all good. It's just a flesh wound. She won't be able to reach it. She won't even have to deal with a cone of shame." She treated Golden with dog biscuits the entire time we were talking. Golden came away happy, and I came away relieved.

Next, I wanted to update Paul, but I couldn't stand to let Golden out of my sight. I took her with me.

"Been getting into trouble again, eh?"

"I wouldn't call solving a murder 'getting into trouble.'"

Paul tsked. "A lot like your sister, aren't you?"

"I hope that's a compliment." The lieutenant *did* claim to like my sister. He was her significant other. That must mean he liked me, too.

He turned on his recorder and prepared to take notes. "Okay. Tell me what happened in your own words."

So I did.

After Paul turned off the recorder, I had some questions of my own. "What about the violin? How does that fit in?"

Lieutenant Gordon shrugged. "All I know about is the solution to Curtis Strange's murder. Maybe Copeland can tell you. He's in charge of the robbery case." He changed the subject. "You might be interested to know that Harvey is at St. Luke's. He'll be there a few days, but he'll be okay."

"And Jane?"

Paul shook his head.

"She's dead? What happened?"

"If you want details, you'll have to get them from Harvey. It's his story to tell."

"Do you know if it's okay for him to have visitors?"

"I can call and check."

"Make sure it's okay if Golden comes, too. They need to know she's a therapy dog who will be wearing her vest."

He nodded as he picked up the handset and rang the right people. It took a while, but eventually he received the okay to visit from nurses, doctors, and Harvey himself.

On the strength of his phone call, Golden and I headed to the hospital.

St. Luke's was in a quiet neighborhood. A large facility nine stories high, all its west side rooms had views of the mountains. Harvey occupied a private room on the seventh floor with a peak vista. When Golden and I got there, Golden wearing her therapy dog vest, Danielle was with him, holding his hand.

"Harvey, I came to thank you for helping us. You look a little the worse for wear."

He gave a weak chuckle and winced.

Danielle spoke for him. "He took a bullet in his left side. Luckily, it missed the heart and passed on through. He lost a lot of blood, though, and had some damaged ribs."

"What in the world happened?"

Harvey and Danielle exchanged a look.

She jumped up immediately. "I'll let you two talk. I'm going to see if I can find some coffee. Can I get anybody anything?"

"Nothing for me." I'd treat myself to a huge lunch when all my obligations had been attended to.

"If you can get chocolate chip cookies, no nuts and very soft, that'd be great. Otherwise, don't bother," Harvey whispered.

"You got it." As she left, she closed the door.

I claimed her chair. Golden sat beside me.

Harvey breathed deeply, then had a coughing fit, which made him clutch his side and moan.

I watched helplessly. "Are you alright?"

When Harvey could speak again, he answered in a soft voice, "I'm fine. You need to understand what happened." He coughed and clutched his side.

I moved closer, the better to hear him. "There are some gaps I'd appreciate understanding."

"When Jane and I got married, I came from an old family, well accepted in society, but struggling financially. Mom worried about keeping up appearances for as long as I can remember. Jane's father had money. He'd become wealthy in mining but switched to drug stores after some kind of scandal. I never asked Jane for details because it seemed to upset her. Her dad was retired and trying to marry her off. She was awkward, stiff, and shy, but she took a shine to me. I was ambitious, and I wasn't in love with anybody else. I figured, where's the harm? We married and had a family. I've made a good living and helped the community, if I do say so myself."

Harvey grimaced, and took a sip of water before he continued.

"When Curtis visited the office before the murder, he wanted funding for his travesty of a development, Antelope Run. When

I wouldn't give it to him, he threatened first to tell Jane about Danielle and me."

Harvey swallowed and paused a moment before he continued. "Well, I had thought about ending the marriage with Jane anyway, in order to marry Danielle. I hadn't done anything about it yet. I wanted to find the best way to lessen repercussions for Jane and me, and for our family. I laughed at him and continued to refuse funding.

"Then he threatened to unearth an old scandal involving Jane's father and the 'dirty money' we'd inherited when he died. When I told Jane about Curtis's threat, I didn't think any more about it. After all, it happened years ago, and her dad was dead."

"Jane told me she killed Curtis because she didn't want him to bring up the old disgrace again."

"Apparently." Harvey continued slowly. "But I didn't know she was troubled about it. The next thing I knew the cops were asking about the robbery and Jane's gun. I didn't know anything about any robbery, but she claimed her things had been stolen. That's the first time events seemed strange to me."

Harvey cleared his throat, then grimaced painfully. "When we found out about Curtis' murder, I began to suspect Jane, but I couldn't imagine a motive, except for her dealings with Curtis in the committee, and that didn't seem right. Didn't seem strong enough. When I put my suspicions together with her disappearance during *1812*, though . . . like I say, I had a strong inkling, even though I didn't want to believe it."

After a moment's rest, Harvey took another sip of water and continued. "Jane went to the final Concert in the Parks on Saturday by herself. Like I told you before, that's when the walks in the forest started. Then she told me to pick you up late Tuesday. I didn't get why she wanted you to come in our car, or why the whole thing had to happen late at night, but I didn't ask any questions or second guess Jane. We didn't connect at all. Doing what she wanted kept the peace as far as possible."

Harvey hesitated. "I was inexcusably blind, but I just didn't want to see."

His voice had been getting weaker. He sipped his water again and laid his head back on the pillow. "When I saw she had drawn a gun on you I figured it out. That's when I got my gun and circled 'round the back way, to guide your escape. When Jane started shooting at you, I fired at Jane. As she went down, she shot at me. My aim must have been better than hers. She bled out before the ambulance came." He closed his eyes, and a tear escaped.

"Harvey, I'm sorry."

"It's okay. We hadn't respected, let alone loved, or even liked each other for a long time." He hesitated and his face lengthened. "We were together a long time, though. We formed a family. I'm sorry it ended this way."

"I have one question. Did you, or she, blackmail me?"

"Of course not. Looking back on it, I'm sure Golden's presence was all the blackmail Jane needed."

"You didn't have a silver van?"

"No. Jane's SUV was white, and I have a silver BMW Z4."

At my look of confusion, he clarified. "It's a sports car."

He quieted a moment and seemed to be marshalling his strength. "The cops said I wouldn't be charged, pending an investigation, since it initially seems to be self-defense, but I'm sorry about the scandal the shooting is going to cause. It's going to blacken Jane's name. It'll be hard for our grandkids."

"I'm very grateful for your help. Let me see what I can do. Maybe Steve Palmer can hush things up."

"Thanks, Emily." His voice had gotten weaker and I could barely hear his stumbling words. "I think I'd better get some sleep now."

"Okay. I'll let you rest. Thanks again."

Danielle sat in a chair in the hall outside the room, chocolate chip cookies on a paper plate in her lap. "I didn't want to interrupt."

"I appreciate that. Take care of him, okay? He really loves you, and the community needs him."

"You couldn't keep me away."

Golden and I left then, on our way to Steve's office. I reported the events of last night. Steve hugged me, then held my shoulders at arm's length. "KC told me you'd find the solution, but I worried. Paul just wouldn't quit."

"Obviously, KC couldn't have murdered anyone. I knew if I didn't give up the answer would find me." To my surprise, I realized somewhere along the line I'd developed confidence the truth would come out one way or another, even if I had to help it along.

"Can I get you some coffee? Tea? Soda? Come over tonight and we'll have a real celebration."

I chuckled. "That sounds great. Can I bring Golden? And Barry?" The gathering would feel incomplete otherwise. They were both deeply involved. Golden had been a victim of both the dognapping and the shooting, and Barry was KC's lawyer, after all— and a good friend, well, more than a friend. He also cared—about me. My heart warmed. He'd been a terrific support when Golden was stolen. I wanted him in my life. I wanted to be there for him, and I wanted to know he'd be there for me. I'd tell him that, soon.

"Sure. The more the merrier." Steve sat in his desk chair and leaned forward.

I parked myself in the armchair to the left of the desk. "I do have a motive for bothering you."

"No bother. Anything."

"Harvey's worried about damaging Jane's name."

"If their marriage was a sham, and Jane's dead, why would Harvey care about her name?"

"I don't know. Loyalty. Guilt. Family." I paused. "The thing is, I told him I'd see if you could do anything."

Steve frowned. "Curtis, Jane, and Harvey were all socially prominent. Everybody in the city's going to be interested in this. It's not possible to squelch it from the police end."

"I know."

"The news people will, you'll excuse the phrase, *kill* to get the scoop." He pursed his lips. "Even if I called in a couple of favors, at this point it'd only keep the story off page one and move it to page three. I'll make sure it's not the lead on the evening news. If we're lucky the president will cooperate and declare war on some hapless country. Then the story'll get buried."

I laughed. "Thought I'd ask. Have a good day, and I'll see you tonight."

My next stop was Detective Copeland's office. I sat across the desk from him. Golden lay on my feet.

"I'm glad you got Golden back." He smiled.

"I have one loose end that's bothering me, though. The threatening calls I got and the blackmail photos?"

"Yeah?"

"I'm curious about who made them."

"Don't know. The call on your phone was spoofed. Number turned out to belong to a florist shop. The woman who answered the phone says she gets what she called 'prank' calls all the time. Call wasn't long enough to trace the real number. And there are lots of silver vans on the road."

"Don't you think it's important? Aren't you curious?" *My* curiosity operated overtime.

Copeland shrugged. "Nah. There's really no crime that's been committed that hasn't been solved. Maybe you don't know that the violin's been returned to Fleisher Hall. You have your dog back. Curtis's murderer confessed and then bought it, thereby saving the taxpayers a chunk of money on the trial. All's well that ends well."

I could see the cases were closed from his point of view. My curiosity unsatisfied, I left with Golden.

But the threatening calls bothered me. I wanted to know who had made them, and why? Since only Mel of the people I knew had a silver van, I called him.

I explained about the blackmail. "I know you have a silver van."

There was a long pause. "That's true." Another silence. "I heard you and your dog went through a rough time. I'm sorry for that."

The grapevine. It seemed a non-sequitur.

Another long pause. "Now that Curtis's murder is cleared up and you're home safe, I don't suppose you'll be asking any more questions."

That line sounded familiar. The blackmailer had been particularly insistent that I stop asking questions. "I don't understand."

Mel hesitated. "I'm trusting in your discretion. If I explain, it can't go any further."

"That depends on what it is." I didn't understand. "I won't commit to keeping quiet if something illegal is involved."

Apparently, Mel wasn't too worried. "Neither Darlene nor I came to the concert on the Fourth because we were together. In a discreet little bed and breakfast I know."

I sank into the recliner. "You're—"

"An item." Mel didn't mince words. "She's married. Her husband's the CEO of Ramsgate Corp."

"Ramsgate?"

"It's a high-tech company. Lots of government contracts. He's hardly ever home. When Darlene received her appointment as Tourist Bureau president we were together a lot, and one thing led to another."

He paused as if thinking how to proceed. "We're both well known. I'd be okay. I'm not married and I'm in charge of the bank, locally at least. It stays out of the personal lives of its employees. All it asks are first-rate work habits." He exhaled.

"But for Darlene, it would be awkward if people knew about us. Certainly, it would make her husband angry. And he's good friends with the mayor. Since she's a political appointee, she's afraid it might affect the mayor's future choices. When you started asking questions about where we were that night, we only wanted to warn you off. Scare you a little. We made a few phone calls, took a few pictures. We wouldn't ever have really done anything. We had no idea . . ."

I guess my silence worried him.

"We returned the violin along with a note. No one will be blamed." His words fell into an uncomfortable silence. "No harm intended. Can we let bygones be bygones?" A pleading note came into his voice then. "I didn't have to explain all this to you. I'm trusting you."

The words were gone. "Really. I'll have to think about it," I managed, before I disconnected the call.

The situation worried me. Mel had given his word, but could I believe him? On the internet, he could spread the photos with the touch of a button. I could trust Barry to be discreet. He would also have the know-how to help me.

I called him and explained.

"Don't worry about a thing. I'll take care of it." His voice sounded confident, but I fretted.

"How?"

But he had already hung up.

I SPENT THE AFTERNOON CLEANING. That's how I could tell I really worried. Cleaning is always at the absolute bottom of my priority list.

As I emptied the refrigerator prior to giving it the scrubbing it hadn't had since KC left, I wondered, when would Barry call?

After I finished the inside of the refrigerator, I moved it and cleaned underneath.

It wasn't until I'd reorganized my sock drawer, cleared out the old clothes, and made a donation pile for Goodwill that the phone rang.

"Hey, gorgeous."

"Hi, Barry." Obviously, he was in a great mood. Hoping he had excellent news, I held my breath. "What happened?"

Barry chuckled. "I talked to Mel. He didn't want to come to my office, but I made it clear I knew about the blackmail and would go to the police if he and Darlene didn't appear within an hour." I heard his office chair squeak.

"Bet Mel didn't like that."

"He made noises about it'd being your word against his, but both he and Darlene showed after forty minutes. I explained the situation—that you didn't want anyone to suffer needless consequences, but you needed to protect yourself."

"You put it in terms of self-protection?"

"Yup. I had both Mel and Darlene delete the photos from their phones while I watched. They swore they had returned the violin, and signed and dated a statement divulging their role in the crime.

My paralegal and a colleague notarized it. I promised Mel and Darlene I'd lock their testimony away and forget it existed unless the photos and lies against you resurfaced. They were relieved there would be no charges. You're protected. A good day's work."

As Barry spoke, my stomach knots untied themselves, and I laughed in relief. "I'll say. I can see why your clients love you."

"Most of them don't love me. They're just very, very grateful."

I laughed again.

THAT NIGHT STEVE GRILLED IN HIS BACK YARD. KC hugged me and thanked me for my help several times. I laughed and hugged her back.

Barry and I came separately. He seemed delighted KC's name had been cleared, winking at me and joining in the general good spirits.

I found an opportunity to take him aside, pulling him to the side of the house, sheltered by a soaring fir. We were alone there. "I was afraid you'd be angry with me."

"I don't like you taking risks, but I realize you wouldn't be you if you didn't. It's you I love, just the way you are."

He kissed me then, long and tenderly.

I didn't know I'd been on edge, but I felt physical relief at this proof of his understanding. "I've been thinking about your suggestion. I love you, and I want you in my life. I'm all for putting the past behind me and moving on. But I'm not sure you know what you're getting into. I can't give up defending the people and things I care about. And my record with relationships is beyond bad. And, no offense, but yours isn't great either."

He exhaled, as if he'd been holding his breath. "Your answer is no?"

"No, my answer is yes, but I think you're crazy, and I hope you don't regret it."

He grabbed me and swung me around in a circle. "Hallelujah! When you didn't jump for joy at the idea, I was pretty sure that 'no' would be your answer." He laughed like an excited little boy, and couldn't stop smiling.

He caught me up in his excitement, and I laughed too. Now committed to a new way of life, I let myself feel exhilarated.

He stepped forward, took me in his arms, and kissed me deeply. "You're sure you enjoy being with me?"

"Of course I do!"

Barry grinned. "We'd better get back before they miss us."

Holding hands we strolled into the back yard, neither of us releasing the other.

I told and retold the story of the solution to the murder and KC's proof of innocence over barbecued ribs, burgers, and veggie burgers.

Barry stood. "I propose a toast. To KC and Steve. May they enjoy each other and the fresh start the Monroe Police Department has given them. And may I never again serve them in a professional capacity."

"Hear, hear!" We all clinked glasses.

Steve and KC exchanged deeply intimate glances, and were never far away from each other, touching constantly.

As KC's substitute mother, I couldn't have wished for anything better.

Even Golden wasn't forgotten. Innumerable pieces of hamburger fell her way, and she was petted and pampered as befitted a wounded heroine. In short, a good time was had by all.

EPILOGUE

SATURDAY, OCTOBER 5, 2013, 1:30 P.M.

KC's sister Miriam, from Washington State, had come for the wedding. Miriam fixed KC's hair and applied her makeup without help from me, to my relief. My knowledge of girly things ended at hand lotion. In KC's case I didn't think the froo-froo made much difference. She was beautiful, whether she was fresh out of the shower or primped to the max.

Her mother had been invited, too, but the invitation had gone unanswered. I assured KC that was okay. She had taken the first step to heal the relationship. Now the next step would be up to her mom. KC had done all she could to mend the rift.

I zipped her into her wedding dress. "There you go."

She whirled around. "Do I look okay?"

I couldn't believe KC was insecure about her appearance, but I responded. "Radiant. And too gorgeous for words." I hugged her—carefully.

"Will I do Steve proud?"

"Now you're fishing. Of course you will. You're dazzling."

She laughed and hugged me again.

"I can see there's nothing more for me to do here. I'd better get downstairs and set up before the bride has a tizzy."

KC grinned.

On a raised platform in the chapel I arranged the trio's chairs, stands, and music folders.

"Jen! Alice!" The other two members of my trio had arrived fifteen minutes early to warm up. We greeted each other, then settled in. I always felt a slight relief when everyone showed up. *One less thing to worry about.*

Right on schedule the wedding coordinator, a short, motherly woman, whispered in my ear. "We can start now. Everything's ready." The trio had been waiting for this cue.

We began the prelude music and played several introductory pieces by Handel, Bach, and Vivaldi. The groomsmen, Steve, and his best man were all in place. The bridesmaids and KC's matron of honor, her sister Miriam, walked slowly down the aisle.

Golden held a basket in her mouth with both rings on a pillow. She was calm and dignified (and oh, so cute!) as she followed the wedding party down the aisle, then sat obediently waiting when she reached the altar.

Finally, KC entered.

Everybody stood as she floated down the aisle to Pachelbel's "Canon in D".

She was stunning, and both she and Steve seemed aware of nobody other than the two of them, exchanging private glances, not taking their eyes off each other. I barely kept from crying. The music, though, gave me a focus, and I managed to stay, if not dry-eyed, then at least functional.

We played an arrangement of a Bach Arioso for the candle lighting. I cried almost all the way through the vows. But the minister stunned me into recovery.

"Do you, Karen Carlotta Giroux, take this man, Stephen David Palmer, to be . . ."

Wait a minute. Karen? Her name is Karen? Who knew?

I didn't have time for amazement. A trumpet player from the symphony stood to play an arrangement of Purcell's "Trumpet Voluntary" for the recessional, accompanied by the trio. I gave myself to the task at hand, ignoring all distractions, including my feelings.

KC AND STEVE HAD HIRED A DJ FOR THE RECEPTION. The Articulate Artichoke had closed to all but the wedding party and guests. My job over, I set out to enjoy myself. I met Barry in the lobby. A tall, slightly pudgy man accompanied him, and I realized it was Tom.

"Em, I want you to meet my friend, Tom Hartley, officially. He's the Police Department's Deputy Chief of Patrols. We go way back. Met in a police procedures class in college."

I took his hand and covered it with mine. "Thank you for all your help over the years, and especially a couple months ago. It's been much appreciated."

"No problem. I wanna make sure justice is served, is all, and Barry and everyone he loves is safe." I blushed and lifted my eyebrows at Barry while the three of us exchanged a few more pleasantries.

When Tom went off to his seat, I saw my neighbor, Mrs. Warren, finding her placard, and waved. Barry and I were seated at the head table. Golden settled herself at my feet and went to sleep. KC and Steve sat next to his sister and her husband on one side and KC's sister Miriam and her husband on the other side. Steve's best man and his wife were across the table, next to Barry and me.

The happy couple received almost constant congratulations, and Barry and I managed to catch up as people passed by.

Kathleen and Paul were some of the first well-wishers.

They had moved to their new house a couple months ago, with the help of Barry and me, and half the police department. They were very happy, for the most part. Kathleen, being Kathleen, was spontaneous and impulsive, and occasionally I got a call which required a calm, cool outlook. She and Paul seemed to be working out their challenges, though, to the satisfaction of both.

I wanted an update on her son. "How is Charlie?"

"He's loving the new job and the time he gets to spend with Ana. I'm expecting an engagement announcement any minute."

As we hugged and she and Paul made their exit, the DJ put on "Annie's Song." Barry asked, "Pretty lady, can I have this dance?"

I felt heat rise to my face.

Checking that Golden slept under the table, I replied, "Absolutely," and surrendered to his arms.

As we returned to the table Harvey and Danielle, who had married after a scandalously short mourning period for Jane, finished congratulating Steve and KC.

Barry and I were both interested in Butterfly Hollow. We'd had several picnics there. We caught them before they returned to their seats.

"How goes the fundraising for the Hollow?" Barry asked.

Harvey flashed a smile. "Roland Strange gave us his enthusiastic support. Said he advocated environmental responsibility. Maybe it's cynical of me, but I think it helped that the Colorado Water Conservation Board won their court action and put the kibosh on Curtis's plans for the Hollow. Anyway, I spoke to Bill Harrison at the county. They came up with some money. Then the Foundation offered some funding to get things moving. Matching grants, you know. That motivated the Butterfly Hollow environmental coalition, and they helped raise money from scouting troops, school children, and individual contributors. Even the school district helped. Fifth graders will make a field trip to the Hollow part of their science curriculum, each of them paying a small fee to visit. To make a long story short, we met the goal and will finalize things with Roland next week."

Amid congratulations, both Harvey and Danielle practically glowed with pride. I happened to know that while Harvey recovered, Danielle had carried out the preliminary negotiations with Roland which made the whole thing possible.

I spoke up. "I have more good news." I couldn't help smiling. "Roland has started work with the residents at Skyridge to address their complaints. In return for dropping their lawsuit, he's signed an agreement to fix the problems, and pay damages if he can't. Ditto for the other plaintiffs. Noah Wattle is the president of the homeowner's association at Skyridge and he keeps me apprised of the latest."

Interrupting me, the best man tapped his glass in a ringing summons.

He rose. "I know that traditionally I should tell a funny story, but I'm not good at that. So, I ask instead, a blessing." He raised his glass toward the newlyweds. "May Steve and KC always be healthy and happy. May they handle concerns and problems easily, and may they always see the good in themselves and others."

It seemed to me that spoke for all of us, and to all of us. Golden woke and barked happily. Everybody laughed, and I wholeheartedly clinked glasses with Barry and savored the goodness of the wine.

Used by permission. © Lifetouch Nat'l School Studios, Inc.

B.J. BOWEN IS A MUSICIAN AND FREE-LANCE WRITER whose love of music was awakened by her mother, a flutist and civil engineer. After failing miserably as a flute player, at the age of eleven Ms. Bowen began studying oboe. She has since performed and recorded on both oboe and English horn with professional symphonies and chamber groups throughout Mexico and Colorado. Her inspirational articles have appeared in *Unity Magazine* and *Daily Word*, and she was a finalist and earned Honorable Mention in the 2018 Focus: Eddy Awards for her article, "Letting Go with Grace," published in *Unity Magazine*; Sept/Oct 2017.

Drawing on her quirky fellow musicians and orchestral experiences, she created the mystery series, "Musical Murders." The first is *Music is Murder* (Release date, 6-8-2021). *Ballistics at the Ballet* is the second of the series (Release date, 9-14-2022). The third is *Fireworks on the Fourth* (Release date TBA). She is a member of Sisters in Crime and lives in Colorado Springs, Colorado, with two canine friends. She has a song for any occasion.